Sense & Sensibility

A Latter-Day Tale

Praise for Rebecca H. Jamison

"I am in love with *Sense and Sensibility: A Latter-day Tale*! I love the way Rebecca updated this classic, favorite Jane Austen story. The characters feel so real, like I could know them in my daily life, and I laughed with their hilarious situations and cried with their challenges. Set aside a whole afternoon to read this because you won't be able to put it down."

—JENNIFER GRIFFITH, author of *Big in Japan*

"Jamison's writing is engaging and full of vivid, amusing lines."

—*PUBLISHER'S WEEKLY*

"Jamison's incredible storytelling champions her characters and brings them to life."

—*DESERET NEWS*

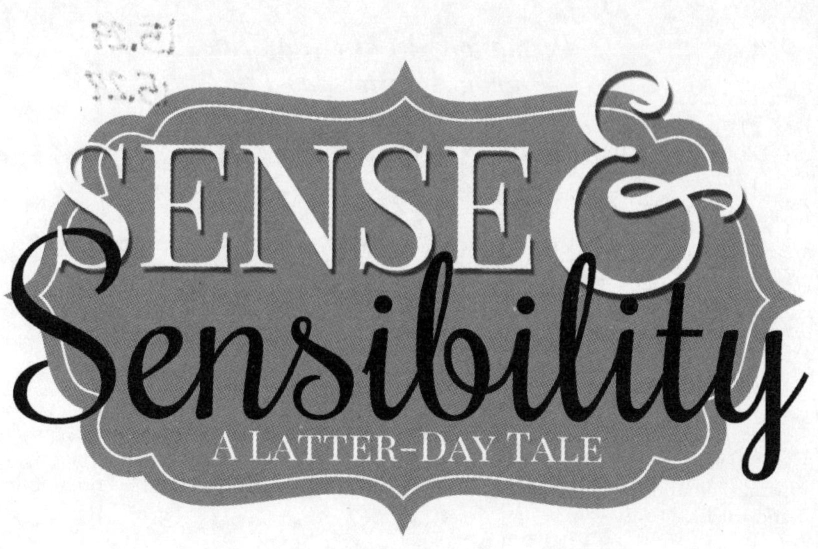

REBECCA H. JAMISON

BONNEVILLE BOOKS ™

AN IMPRINT OF CEDAR FORT, INC.
SPRINGVILLE, UTAH

Also by Rebecca H. Jamison

Persuasion: A Latter-day Tale
Emma: A Latter-day Tale

ISBN 13: 978-1-4621-1456-6

Published by Bonneville Books, an imprint of Cedar Fort, Inc.
2373 W. 700 S. Springville, UT 84663
Distributed by Cedar Fort, Inc., www.cedarfort.com

LIBRARY OF CONGRESS CATALOGING-IN-PUBLICATION DATA

Jamison, Rebecca H., 1970-
Sense and sensibility : a latter-day tale / Rebecca H. Jamison.
p. cm.
ISBN 978-1-4621-1456-6 (perfect : alk. paper)
1. Sisters--Fiction. 2. Man-woman relationships--Fiction. 3. England--Social life and customs--19th century--Fiction. I. Austen, Jane, 1775-1817. Sense and sensibility. II. Title.
PS3610.A56645S47 2014
813'.6--dc23

2014013572

Cover design by Kristen Reeves
Cover design © 2014 by Lyle Mortimer
Edited and typeset by Melissa J. Caldwell

Printed in the United States of America

10 9 8 7 6 5 4 3 2 1

To my children,
whom I love more than all the books in the world.

1

ELLY

THERE'S a skill set to being poor. So far, I'd learned to recognize the exact spot on the gas gauge that meant *empty* and how to fix just about anything with duct tape—I wore duct-taped pumps to my father's funeral, and I don't think anyone noticed. Today forced me to learn one more thing—how to get food without paying for it.

I wasn't stealing, but it still felt wrong. I'd never imagined myself as unemployed, single, and living at home when I turned twenty-seven. I'd done everything I could to prevent this. I had a degree. I'd worked ten-hour days. My résumé was a masterpiece. Still I came here, accepting charity.

Walking toward the red brick building that was the bishops' storehouse, I held onto Grace, my fifteen-year-old sister, by her hand. It was probably a mistake to bring her, considering her special needs, but leaving her at home with our sister Maren would've been like leaving her alone. As I pulled the heavy glass door open and stepped into a room that smelled like vanilla pudding mix, my salivary glands kicked into overdrive. It'd been a while since I'd had decent food, but I wasn't about to drool like one of Pavlov's dogs over vanilla pudding mix, was I?

In the center of the convenience store–sized room were five aisles filled with non-perishables. Grace pulled her hand from my grasp and rushed toward the center aisle, looking at the boxes on the shelves. "Where's the Pop-Tarts?"

I followed, reaching for her hand. "I don't think they have Pop-Tarts here," I said, feeling heat rise to my face. The clerk at the front of the store—the one that wasn't helping someone else—had probably already judged us as the type of people who ate junky breakfast products.

Grace rushed to the next aisle, scanning the canned foods. "I want chocolate Pop-Tarts."

The clerk walked to the back room, darting a glance our way, a glance that said she knew my secret—that Grace wasn't a normal fifteen-year-old girl. Grace was pretty with long, dark hair and dark eyes like mine, only she was more symmetrical. She didn't have a scar from a childhood accident above her lip, and her ears didn't stick out. She looked like she could be a cheerleader or a student body president. But as much as I wished Grace were normal, it was better that people knew the truth. Believe me, I'd heard plenty of angry comments from people who thought she was just a rude teenager, and today, of all days, I preferred empathy.

Grace stopped at the refrigerated section in the back and opened every door, one at a time, looking for Pop-Tarts while I pulled our food order from my purse. The order allowed for ten pounds of fresh produce. Maren had told me to get organic, but I was pretty sure from the looks of things that organic wasn't an option. Four bins held fruits: apples, oranges, bananas, and strawberries.

Maybe I'd save the produce for later. Grace would be more interested in breakfast foods anyway. I pointed to an aisle of boxed goods and looked at the order form in my hand. "We're getting cornflakes. You like cornflakes, don't you? Or how about pancake mix?"

"I want Pop-Tarts," Grace said, getting louder.

I scanned the list our bishop had given my mom. "How about canned peaches?"

A door opened from the back, and the clerk came out, followed by a much better-looking man than I'd ever expected to find here—or in all of northern California for that matter. He was tall and dark, the type who would've looked much more at home in Southern Italy sitting under a beach umbrella with a glass of mineral water. His good looks distracted Grace from her Pop-Tart obsession. He looked toward us, then away. He was shy. I liked shy guys. The clerk brought him over to us and introduced him. "This is Ethan Ferrero, one of our volunteers. He'll help you find what you need."

Ferrero? He couldn't be one of *those* Ferreros. I looked at the worn collar on his green T-shirt—nope, definitely not one of those Ferreros. I shook his hand. "We'd love some help. It's our first time."

As he stepped closer to look at my food order, I smelled something like sunblock. "We'll get the canned goods first," he said, bending over my paper. He read our name at the top, then looked at me. "So you're Goodwins. Are you the ones who owned the Check-It-Out software company?" He *was* one of those Ferreros.

"Yes. Our dad started the company. I'm Elly Goodwin, and this is my sister Grace." That's what I said. But what I thought was, *Kill me now.* As if it wasn't bad enough to get food from Church welfare, I had to meet one of the Ferreros, a good-looking Ferrero.

His lips turned down. "I was sorry to hear about your father."

"Thank you. It's been hard."

Hard was an understatement. There was no way to describe the trauma my family had suffered since Dad was diagnosed with terminal cancer. We lost the family business, we lost him, and now I sometimes wondered if we weren't losing my sister Maren too.

"Where's the Diet Coke?" Grace asked, loud enough for everyone inside to know that she drank caffeinated beverages.

I rubbed my hand across Grace's back. "Honey, they don't have Diet Coke here. It's not good for you anyway."

The corners of Ethan's mouth twitched.

"You'll have to excuse Grace," I said. "Her friends at school got her hooked. My mom never lets her have it at home."

Ethan crossed the store to get a cart for us. When he came back, he held his hand out. "Can I see your food order?"

I gave him the paper order form.

"See, Grace," he said, "this isn't a normal grocery store. We only carry the basics. You won't find soda, but you'll find some of the ingredients to make soda. It looks like you have sugar on your list." He handed Grace a bag of sugar from the shelf. I wasn't about to point out that Diet Coke didn't contain any sugar.

Grace put the sugar in our cart. "I like sugar. Where are the Pop-Tarts?"

"We don't have Pop-Tarts," Ethan said. "But I've made them before." He showed her where she could find flour and jam.

I folded my arms. "You don't really know how to make Pop-Tarts." I couldn't imagine a Ferrero who'd make something so ordinary from scratch. Eggs Benedict seemed more their style.

He pushed our cart to the jam. "I've made them with my nana before."

"Can you teach us?" Grace asked.

I pulled Grace toward me. "Grace, we don't need Mr. Ferrero to teach us how to cook."

Ethan pushed the cart to the tiny produce section and hefted a bag of potatoes into the cart. "I wouldn't mind."

"No, thank you," I replied.

Grace shifted her weight back and forth from one foot to the other. "You don't know how to make Pop-Tarts, Elly."

"I know how to make toast with jam."

Grace slumped down and sat on the floor. "I want Pop-Tarts."

That was her method for getting her way. She thought if she sat on the floor and refused to move, people would give her anything she wanted. The problem was, it worked.

I had to stay calm. If Grace knew I felt upset, I'd never get her to stand up. "You sit here a while. I'm going to talk to Ethan."

Ethan helped me find the canned goods while Grace stayed on the floor beside the laundry detergent.

"What's your favorite Broadway musical?" I asked Ethan, loud enough for Grace to hear.

Ethan led me to the produce section. "My favorite musical? Let me think." He handed me a plastic bag. "You can get ten pounds of fruit, so take your pick." He pointed to a scale near the bananas. I hated bananas—from the freckles on the peel to the stringy things inside. Everyone else in the family loved them, though, so I'd have to get a few.

Grace scooted out of her aisle to talk to Ethan. "My favorite musical is *Hairspray*. Elly's is *Les Mis*."

Ethan tilted his head to the side. "It's been a while since I've seen a musical."

Grace wrinkled her nose. "We saw three yesterday."

Ethan probably thought I spent all day watching TV. That's all I needed—another Ferrero who could judge me. I dropped an apple into my bag. "I watch movies while I'm applying for jobs. It keeps my spirits up. And Grace is on spring break."

Ethan handed me a flawless apple. "What kind of job are you looking for?"

"I'm a programmer." I grabbed a few more apples, wishing I could bite into one right there. It'd been so long since I'd had an apple.

"My manager's looking for a new programmer," Ethan said. "Have you applied at LibraryStar?"

I pulled the bag of apples to my chest. "Why would *I* apply at Library-Star? They drove us out of business." Ethan obviously hadn't made the connection that Jake Cannon, the founder of LibraryStar, was my ex-fiancé. Candi Ferrero was Jake's wife. After what I'd done to Candi's car, Jake would never hire me.

Ethan pulled a business card from his wallet. "We have good benefits."

Grace, still sitting on the floor, scooted up to Ethan. "Elly's good at tap dancing."

Ethan held the business card out to me. "I don't think we're hiring any tap dancers right now."

"She can't sing," Grace said. "You have to sing to be in a musical."

I took Ethan's card and shoved it in my purse. "Thanks." I stepped over Grace to grab some bananas, picking a greenish bunch that wouldn't stink up my car. "You need to stand up now."

Grace rocked back and forth. "I want Pop-Tarts and Diet Coke."

I blew my hair out of my face. "I know you do."

Ethan helped me find the meat and dairy products. Then, while I checked out with the clerk at the front, Ethan stayed with Grace. She still sat near the bananas. When I finished, I circled the cart around to the produce section. "Am I going to have to put you in the cart or are you going to walk out to the car with me?" I asked Grace.

"I want to make Pop-Tarts with Ethan," she said.

Ethan looked at his watch. "I'm done with my shift in a few minutes—"

"We'll be fine." Ethan seemed nice, but I knew better than to trust a Ferrero. "Thanks for your help." I knelt beside Grace. "Look, honey, why don't we go to another store for your Pop-Tarts? Come get in the car."

I reached for Grace's hand. She pulled away. I waited five minutes while Ethan leaned against the produce bins, watching Grace with the type of expression people wear to funerals, and believe me, I'd seen a lot of that expression lately. I reached for her hand again. She pulled away. "I'm going to have to drag her out of here," I told Ethan. Maybe I could ask him to get her legs.

Ethan sat on the floor beside Grace. "Why don't you put your groceries in the car? I'll stay with her."

Rain pelted my head as I pushed the cart outside, its wheels splashing through puddles in the pavement. It hardly ever rained in San Jose, but it meant one more thing to add to my skill set—driving on wet roads with balding tires. No big deal. It didn't take me long to load the groceries into our old Subaru station wagon. Before I finished, Grace came through the door, holding hands with Ethan, who held an umbrella with his other hand. I tried to disguise my awe.

"I hope you didn't promise her anything I won't approve." I could see him buying her a case of Pop-Tarts.

Ethan opened the passenger side door for Grace. "I didn't promise her anything." He handed her the seat belt. Then he shut the door and grabbed our cart. "Have a nice day."

I should have gotten into the car then, but I stood there, watching him as he moved across the parking lot, wearing faded Levis. He was too good to be true. There had to be something wrong with him.

I felt a tinge of disappointment as I pulled out of the parking lot. It wasn't that I'd wanted to accept Ethan's offer. It was the reminder that, even though Jake and I broke up three years ago, my past still controlled me. After the breakup, I'd let my emotions bottle up until I exploded in a disastrous tantrum. Ethan was sure to hear about it if he hadn't already.

It was a long ride back to our quiet subdivision in South San Jose, where all the houses had matching tile roofs and neat green patches of lawn. By the time I pulled into the driveway, I'd decided that a crush on Ethan Ferrero was a hopeless endeavor. I crunched his business card into a spit wad–sized ball and tossed it into the kitchen trash as I unloaded the groceries.

I gave Grace her favorite job, arranging cans and boxes by color in the kitchen closet. Our home was simple: tile floors in the kitchen, carpet in the living areas, and white paint on the walls. As I walked upstairs to Maren's room, I expected to see Dad sitting there in his favorite recliner in the living room. It'd been six months. I didn't want to forget him, but sometimes I hated the way my grief snuck up on me. Would it ever stop doing that?

Maren still lay in bed, her honey-colored hair sprawled over her pillow. "Grace and I just got home with groceries. Want to help unload?"

Maren moaned. "It's so early."

I tugged on her window shade, flooding the room with light. "It's 3:45 p.m."

She lay motionless, facedown on the bed. There was a time three years ago, after Jake broke up with me, when I'd been the one who had needed someone to drag me from bed. Maren had enticed me with movies and shopping trips until I found better reasons to wake up. Before Dad's illness, she'd always been so passionate about life.

"I hope Grace isn't eating all the strawberries," I said, heading out of her room.

Even though strawberries were Maren's favorite fruit, she didn't hurry. By the time she emerged from her bedroom, Grace and I had stocked the shelves and the refrigerator. Maren slumped into a kitchen chair, letting her tangled hair hang across her face. She wore her signature look of the past few months, a vintage nightgown trimmed with lace and ruffles.

Maren and I were opposites. She'd inherited our father's lighter coloring while I had our Portuguese mother's dark hair and eyes. But that wasn't the only difference. Maren was curvy—from her curly hair to her hourglass figure. "Where's Mom?" she asked.

"At work." Ever since Dad died, Mom had worked most mornings and afternoons at Tic-Toc-Taco, a fast food place less than a mile away. "You might feel better if you got dressed," I said.

"Did it ever occur to you that I don't want to feel better? Mom says that in Portugal, it's traditional to mourn for six months after a parent dies. Sometimes people wear black for the rest of their lives."

I was sure that Mom didn't want Maren to endure a lifetime of depression. If only we could get Maren past her denial. She needed medical help.

I dug a wide-toothed comb out of my purse and worked it through her curls. "I think Dad would say you've mourned enough. Would you like me to go to Dr. Jenner with you? We could—"

"I need to feel my grief, Elly. I need time to let it seep through me. That's what I need."

Mom had taken Maren to Dr. Jenner a few weeks after Dad passed away, but it hadn't done much good. Maren refused to fill the prescription for the antidepressant.

I heard the front door slam, and Grace came in with a stack of mail. In the ten years since Dad bought the house, we'd had the same postal worker, and she'd always come at 3:30 p.m. Everything about our upper-middle-class subdivision was quiet and orderly.

After Grace piled the bills in front of us on the kitchen table, Maren sifted through the stack. "These are sopping wet. Is it raining outside?" She pulled out an envelope marked "Important Time-Sensitive

Material." "When will people ever stop sending us these kinds of ads? It's probably for a used car dealer. I hate to think how many trees die for this sort of thing."

I reached for the envelope and tore it open to read "Notice of Sale." It looked official. "Notice of Sale?" I read the bold print at the top of the paper. It was our address. "There must be some mistake. Is there another Spring Hill Road in San Jose?" Someone was trying to auction off our house on May 10th—less than a month away.

"How could there be another Spring Hill Road in San Jose?" Maren asked.

I read through the paper until I saw the word *foreclosure,* and I shivered. Mom hadn't told me it'd gotten this bad. She hadn't told me we were behind on our house payments. We were losing the house. I needed a job. We needed money fast.

2

Elly's voice mingled with my dreams. Has that ever happened to you—when you can't tell the difference between reality and imagination? She kept saying *Jake*, her ex-fiancé's name. Was I dreaming of the past again? It was my only escape lately—to dream that the past two years had never happened. But Elly's voice remained after I opened my eyes. The photograph of Dad still sat on my desk, the one I'd placed there on the day of his funeral.

I rolled out of bed and pushed open my bedroom door. Sitting on the corner of my bed, I could see into Elly's room across the hall. Elly paced back and forth with the phone to her ear. "Yes, I can make it by ten thirty. Thank you so much, Jake. I appreciate this."

I watched her set her phone down. "Was that Jake Cannon?"

Elly ran her hands down the sides of her cobalt-blue pajama pants. "I asked him for a job."

"You what?"

Elly practiced one of the dance moves she'd learned a few years before in tap class, shuffling and stomping her feet on the carpet. She always tapped when she felt nervous. "He said he knew I was qualified, and I would always have a job at LibraryStar. All I have to do is come in for an interview. How hard can that be?"

I pursed my lips. "Jake wreaked havoc on your psyche, and now you're going to work for him?"

Elly kept tapping and hopping. "I need to start earning money, Maren." She flapped her feet. "You don't want to end up in a homeless shelter, do you?"

I rolled my eyes. "I wish you wouldn't tap-dance while we're talking."

Elly repeated her tap dance, flapping her arms along with her feet. "I'm celebrating the fact that I have an interview at ten thirty. It's better than that, though. He already promised me the job."

"You're nervous," I said.

Elly stopped. "Pray for me, okay?"

"Okay."

She looked at her watch. Her eyebrows slanted, folding the skin above her nose. "9:30! I'd better hurry if I'm going to make it." She ran toward the bathroom.

I shut my door and said a prayer for Elly before I flopped back into bed. I should have opened my laptop and applied for jobs. But what was the use? I wasn't likely to get any of them.

Have you ever felt like God has abandoned you? Like there's no way you can ever be happy? In church, they told us that joy was the purpose of life, but it didn't seem that way for me. My life was a charcoal drawing—colorless and cold.

Mom knocked on my door. Not waiting for my response, she peeked into the room. "Are you okay? I thought I heard you crying."

"I'm fine." Everyone had tiptoed around me since we got the foreclosure. So what if I'd shed a few tears? Crying was healthy.

Mom stood in the doorway. She hooked a lock of her salt-and-pepper hair behind her ear. "I'm worried about you." Her forehead creased with concern.

I rolled onto my back. "We're losing the house. Elly's going to work for Jake Cannon. Grace hasn't eaten breakfast in over a week. And you're worried about me? I'm twenty-three, Mom. I can take care of myself." Maybe I could get a job in telemarketing.

"I miss the way things used to be, *querida*," Mom said. *Querida* was her pet name for me. It meant "dear" in Portuguese. "I miss the way you used to sing while you painted watercolors. And I miss having you style my hair. Do you think you could do my hair for me today? It'd be easier to face the real estate agent if my hair looked nice."

I tried to smile. "I'll be there in a few minutes."

Mom left, and I lay in bed, thinking of all the things I needed to do. So much to do. Then I thought of Elly, and I wondered, *Would she really agree to work for Jake Cannon? If so, would he actually hire her?* Jake was a suave talker, but he wasn't a reliable friend. Unless Elly had something he needed.

3

ELLY

MY plan to apply makeup at stoplights didn't save me much time. I arrived at LibraryStar's headquarters eighteen minutes late. I'd never been to the building before, but it was exactly what I'd imagined. Its glass exterior and three-story height shouted *Silicon Valley.*

Stan, the programming manager, stood in the marble-floored foyer waiting for me. He was a paunchy, middle-aged guy with a graying beard. His friendly banter put me at ease . . . until we entered the conference room and I smelled that mix of raspberry, citrus, and flowers. That's when I knew I'd made the right decision to blow-dry my hair and press my red cotton shirtdress. Sure enough, Jake's wife—Candi Ferrero Cannon—was coming to my interview. She sat at the end of the long wooden table and wore a belted pink blazer—one that would have looked good on me if I could have afforded it.

Back when Candi and I went to high school together, the other students used to tell me that Candi was my doppelganger. I doubted anyone had the nerve to tell Candi, though. We had the same dark hair, olive skin, and brown eyes, but that was where the similarities ended. Candi was a girl who liked to compete in beauty pageants; I was a girl who didn't.

Candi Ferrero was the only one I knew who scooped her spoon away from herself while eating soup. She also refused to chew gum, never wore capris without pumps, and said "yes, ma'am" when she spoke with any woman older than she was.

Stan introduced her as the head of the Human Relations department.

The interview started out normal enough. Like my father's company,

LibraryStar created software that helped library employees and patrons keep track of books. Stan asked about the programming languages I knew and my job experience. After conducting hundreds of job interviews at Check-It-Out, I could've answered those questions in my sleep. Even the dreaded "What's your greatest weakness?" didn't faze me.

I held his gaze without a flicker of embarrassment. "I have a bad temper."

Candi drummed her fingers on the top of her closed laptop. "Tell me something I don't know."

I gripped the edges of my skirt underneath the table. "It's never a problem at work. I have prevention strategies to keep it under control."

Candi arched an eyebrow. "And those are?"

I straightened in my chair. "Umm." *Should I really share these?* "Tap dancing, journaling, disassembling machinery—that sort of thing." Maybe I should have left out that last part.

Candi smiled and folded her hands prayer-like on top of the table. "What kind of machinery?"

My chair swiveled as I squirmed. "I would never take apart any of the machinery here. Journaling is usually enough. If not, I can tap-dance in my socks in an empty conference room. It's not like I lose my temper all that often."

For the first time since the interview began, Candi opened her laptop and typed into it as if she were taking notes. "When was the last time you let your temper get out of control?"

I squinted at her. "Three years ago."

"What happened?" she asked, as if she didn't already know.

Candi had overstepped her bounds, but what else could I do but answer her question? While Stan looked on in confusion, I reminded myself why I was here—to keep my family out of the homeless shelter. "I broke something."

Candi rolled her eyes. "You broke *something*?" She was trying to get me to lose my temper right there in the interview.

I looked at the ring on her left hand. It was Jake's grandmother's ring, the same ring I'd worn. Despite his Italian suits and gold cuff links, Jake was a total cheapskate when it came to love. I was glad to be rid of him; I'd be gladder still if I could forget him entirely.

I bit the inside of my cheek until I tasted blood. "I got angry because someone took something that belonged to me. I thought it was something valuable. Turns out it wasn't such a big deal. That's why I don't have as many problems with my temper now. Because most things aren't worth it."

She glanced at her laptop, as if her screen held a list of awkward interview questions. "What was your greatest professional disappointment?"

Considering that Candi had so much to do with two of my three greatest disappointments, I chose carefully. "Losing my father."

Candi closed her laptop. "Losing your father is a *personal* disappointment. Would it be fair to say that losing your family business was the greatest disappointment in your career?"

If she expected to make me cry, it wasn't going to happen. I did three silent shuffle stomps on the carpet under the table. "Yes."

Candi slid her laptop into her attaché. "I'm going to be completely up-front with you, Elly. Having you come to work for us would constitute a conflict of interest. How can we trust someone who used to be our competitor?"

I couldn't stand to look at Candi anymore, so I smiled at Stan. "Check-It-Out has folded. It's clear I can't help them any more." It was also clear—to me, at least—that Jake had promised me this job. "I'll work as hard for LibraryStar as I did for Check-It-Out. The customers are still the same, and I wouldn't do anything to hurt our libraries."

Candi stood. "I guess that's all the questions I had. Thanks for coming in. We'll call you if you make the cut."

I walked out of that conference room certain that I'd never hear back about that job. An hour later, Stan called to offer me a *temporary* job, starting the next day. It wasn't exactly what Jake had promised, but I took it.

4

ELLY

EVERYONE who worked in the white-collar world knew there was an unspoken class system among employees. There were those who had offices and those who had cubicles. LibraryStar took this to a new low: I had to *share* a cubicle. I'd never even seen a double cubicle before. It was like two small cubicles with a half-wall between the desks, as if I'd be collaborating with the intern next to me, a guy who had yet to remove his earphones. Really, it was fine by me. I never had trouble focusing on my work.

My first assignment from Stan was to come up with a program that made book and movie recommendations for library patrons based on their check-out history. It was a more challenging assignment than I'd expected to receive, considering my status as a temporary employee.

Stan saw the shock on my face and shrugged. "Jake told me you could handle it."

I dropped my purse into my bottom desk drawer and slammed it shut. "Show me the code." If I wasn't good enough to receive full-time benefits, why had I gotten such a difficult assignment?

Stan helped me access the program, then left me to figure it out. As I scrolled through hundreds of pages of code, my emotions started to fizz. This was too much of a coincidence. Jake had to know I'd already spent months working on the exact same application for Check-It-Out. Someone must have told him about it, and now he was using me—trying to get months worth of work for the wages of a temporary worker.

I'm too good for this, I thought as the vent above me blew cold air onto my head. The programs seemed familiar, too familiar. As I paged through, I could see it wasn't that different from the software code at Dad's company. Would Jake copy that much from us? Would he take what he'd learned from Dad and use it to put us out of business? Was that how he pulled together a successful business less than a year after he stopped working for us? No. Jake wouldn't do something like that. I was overreacting.

I paged through the code, reading the names of programs. Over half of them were the same as the programs at Check-It-Out, but there were other, newer programs too. I couldn't figure out how everything worked together.

"Hey," I heard a voice say behind me. A deep voice. "I heard you were starting today, but I didn't believe it. I thought you were some other Elly Goodwin." It was Ethan Ferrero. He wore a blue button-down shirt and khaki Dockers.

"A job's a job," I said.

Stan wandered by. "You should offer her some candy," he told Ethan.

Ethan's eyebrows popped up. "Oh yeah. Be back in a second." He came back with a red bowl full of suckers. He didn't strike me as the type of guy who'd keep a candy dish at his desk.

I didn't want a sucker, but something about Ethan's smile made me take a green one. He stepped closer to look at my monitor. There it was again—the sunblock smell. I unwrapped the sucker and was about to pop it in my mouth when I noticed a grasshopper encased in the middle. Ethan watched me out of the corner of his eye, probably expecting me to be disgusted. I opened my mouth to eat the sucker. Ethan reached for my hand. "Wait! It has a bug in it."

What was it about him that made me do the exact opposite of what I wanted to do? I popped the sucker into my mouth. "So?"

He swallowed. "You're the first person who's actually eaten it."

I gagged. "Tastes like mouthwash."

He pointed to my trash can. "I won't be offended." I kept it in my mouth a few more seconds before I dropped it into the trash. He cocked his head to the side as if trying to figure me out. "I owe you one for that."

"Point me in the direction of Jake's office, and we'll call it good."

Ethan set his candy dish on my desk. "Jake's office?"

I tried not to sound angry. "I need to talk to him about this assignment."

Ethan led me up a back stairwell and through the customer support center into something that looked like a conference room with a large table and six or seven chairs. I folded my arms, wondering if Candi had told him about me tap dancing in conference rooms. "This is *not* Jake's office."

Ethan brushed past me to close the door. "Stan told me about your interview. Everyone knows you're qualified for the job, even Candi." He had a hard time maintaining eye contact, but it wasn't hard for me, considering his eyelashes. It wasn't right for a guy to have dark, thick lashes like that, nor was it right for me to be attracted to anyone related to Candi Ferrero.

I transferred my attention to the poster hanging on the wall. It pictured a celebrity reading her favorite book. "How are you related to Candi?"

"She's my sister." His words almost squelched my attraction—almost.

I folded my arms. "I wanted to ask Jake why he won't put me on as a regular, full-time employee." On the other hand, nothing good had ever come from me expressing my emotions to Jake. Nothing good ever came from expressing my emotions to anyone. I was better off being calm and logical—calm and logical.

Ethan pulled a chair out from the table and sat in it. "Jake's not your problem. Candi is."

I sat on the edge of the table with my side toward Ethan. "Jake was like a son to my father. Dad taught him everything he knew."

Ethan leaned back, resting his feet on another conference chair. "And he turned around and used it against you."

Was he trying to bait me into saying something I shouldn't? I'd known people at work who tried to act friendly but were just out to get their coworkers. Ethan didn't seem like one of those people, but he had to be on Candi's side. He was her brother. If I told Ethan I was angry at Jake, Candi was sure to find out. "How do I know you're not a spy?"

"Well, I use my real name, and I don't have a prosthetic nose." He leaned forward and pointed to his nose. "Test it out if you want."

Did I dare? Yes, I did. I touched the end of his nose with my pointer finger. "Very convincing, but I'm not fooled."

Ethan laughed, revealing his beach-worthy smile. "I think we can trust each other."

I headed for the door. "You're Candi's brother."

I didn't blame Candi for being the way she was. If our roles were reversed and I were Jake's wife, I wouldn't want to employ his ex-girlfriend either, especially not one with a temper like mine. I was sure that Candi had told Ethan what I'd done to her car. Why else would he try to keep me in line?

Ethan scrambled to get to the door before I did, holding onto the handle without opening it. "That's why I can tell you it's a bad idea to go talk to Jake. You want Candi to forget you're here." He swung the door open. "How about a tour of the building?"

I walked out the door to see four employees gathered at one cubicle. I recognized two who used to work at Check-It-Out. They turned to stare at us. "Thanks for offering," I said. "But Stan already showed me around. What I need is a tour of the software code."

Ethan didn't speak until we stood in the stairwell. "I can help you with that."

When we got back downstairs, Ethan pulled his chair to my cubicle and drew me a map of the programs, outlining which ones had to do with checking out, checking in, cataloguing, or searching. I had a hard time processing any of it while he sat so close to me. I memorized his face instead of the map. He had friendly brown eyes framed under dark hair that waved and twisted as if he'd simply let the wind blow it into place. His smile extended wide across his face, causing dimples in both his cheeks. When he explained the programs, he spoke to me as an equal. It wasn't until Candi walked by that Ethan decided he'd explained enough.

After he returned to his own desk, I studied the map he'd drawn and looked up the programs I needed. Since the current software didn't keep a check-out history, I'd have to build a new program to keep a more permanent record of items checked out. I scratched out a new code until Candi came to check on me again.

She leaned her elbows along the top of my half-wall. "Having trouble adjusting?"

I pulled my mouth into a tight smile. "Not at all."

She puckered her glossy lips. "I hope you won't need any more help from Ethan. He's working on a deadline."

Ethan hadn't told me about any deadline. "I'm sure I won't." I wanted to tell her that the code seemed remarkably similar to the code at Check-It-Out, but that would've revealed my suspicions.

I typed a few lines while Candi stared at my screen. I could've typed an Irish limerick, and she wouldn't have caught on. She didn't know an end statement from a get statement. After ten more lines, she left.

Because I'd spent my last months at Check-It-Out handling management crises, I hadn't written code in over a year, yet it came back to me as naturally as kissing—not that I ever thought about kissing. It was just me and my code, reunited after far too long. The clock, the coworkers, and even Jake Cannon held no interest for me.

The overhead lights had turned off when Ethan found me at my cubicle. "You know they put a cap on temporary workers' hours?"

I saved my file before looking at Ethan. "I lost track of time. Thanks for your help earlier. If I had any money, I'd treat you to dinner or something." My brain must've been fried to think of asking him out. After all I'd suffered lately, I wasn't ready to get involved with a man. And a relationship with Candi's brother was an even worse idea.

He looked at the bike helmet in his hands. "You're the one who's new. I should treat *you* to dinner."

Now that I thought about it, I *was* hungry. My watch said six thirty. I shut down my computer and grabbed my purse. "You don't have to do that." Mom had talked to a real estate agent about having a short sale on our home. I'd promised I'd help her clean tonight.

"I know a great Cuban place," Ethan said. "I'll treat if you'll drive."

It probably wouldn't hurt to go out to eat with him, but I'd already decided not to get involved. "Maybe another time."

We walked together out the side door and into the parking lot. Ethan followed me to my car. "See you tomorrow."

"Thanks for your help." As I opened the door to my Subaru, the smell of overripe bananas wafted out. Sure enough, in the front seat sat a large fruit basket filled with freckled bananas. The card read, *We're glad to have you at LibraryStar.* It wasn't signed, but I could guess who'd put it there.

I turned the key, planning to roll down the windows as soon as possible. Nothing happened. I turned the key again with no result. I could see Ethan pushing his bike up to my car. He opened the passenger door. "Car trouble?" he asked.

"I don't think so," I said.

He stared at the card on top of the basket of bananas. "I didn't know we gave fruit baskets to new employees."

I held my hand under my nose. "I forgot to lock my doors." I turned the key again. Nothing.

Ethan picked up a cluster of bananas, examining the bruises. "Maybe you can make banana bread."

I didn't tell Ethan, but I liked to make banana bread about as much as I liked changing litter boxes. I turned the key again. The engine didn't make a sound. "This is just my luck." I looked at the bananas and gagged for the second time that day. I couldn't help it. Bananas did that to me.

Ethan lifted the fruit basket, placing it on the pavement outside my car. He looked at the warning lights on the dashboard. "Pop the hood. I'll take a look at it."

I popped the hood, but I didn't expect much from Ethan. Looking under the hood was one of those things men did as a courteous gesture. Most men knew enough to check the fluids and wipe off the battery—that was about it.

I followed him around to the front of the car. As I suspected, he started off checking the oil, using tissue paper from my fruit basket to wipe the dipstick.

"It smells like you have a bad alternator," he said. "I'll bike to the auto parts store and get a new one." He handed me a set of keys. "There's a toolbox in the closet near the restrooms. We'll need the wrenches." He pointed to a large gold key with a square tip. "Use this one to get into the building."

"Are you sure you know what you're doing?" I asked. I couldn't imagine how anyone who grew up with a Fortune 500 parent would know how to fix an alternator on a twenty-year-old Subaru.

"I like to take things apart when I get frustrated." He winked, snapping on his bike helmet.

My breath caught. "Did Candi tell you that?"

"Stan—he was explaining how you'd fit in with the team."

"Let me give you some money." I opened my purse and reached for my wallet, knowing it contained less than ten dollars.

Ethan hopped on his bike. "We'll worry about that later. It won't be that much."

As he rode off, I headed back to the building with his keys, hoping this wasn't a trick to get me fired for stealing tools. Before I opened the door, I searched the parking lot to make sure Candi wasn't still in the office. Her parking space—marked "Reserved for Candi Cannon"—sat empty, so I opened the door, trying to act calm for the surveillance camera overhead. Probably no one ever watched the films from those cameras.

After finding the tools, I sat at my desk, jotting down notes from Internet tutorials about replacing an alternator. That's when the lights came on and Jake strolled in, wearing a tailored suit and tie. I could smell his cologne—Acqua di Gio, the same he'd worn when we dated. It used to remind me of long rides in the car on an autumn day, but today it reminded me of the five years I wasted dating him, only to be tossed aside for a woman with enough money to help him start a business.

He smoothed his blond hair. I'd always loved his hair.

"I thought I heard someone back here."

I wasn't attracted to him anymore, but I still felt the wound of his rejection. Trying to distract myself, I scribbled down a note to remind me to unplug my car battery. "I didn't plan on being here so late," I said. "I had car trouble. Eth—someone went to get a part for me."

Jake swirled his key ring around his finger. "Don't tell me Ethan's helping you. That guy loves to play the Good Samaritan."

I guessed that made me the pitiful figure left for dead on the side of the road. "He seems good with cars."

Jake leaned on the half-wall beside my cubicle. "I wish he'd come fix ours. I got Candi a brand new Mazda convertible. You would not believe how much trouble that thing has been. First it was an indicator light about the tires, and then it was the stereo."

I did two quiet shuffle stomps under my desk. "That's too bad."

Jake slid his cuff up to examine his gold watch. When I'd first met Jake, he was a poor college student who wore secondhand designer clothes. The only thing he had going for him was his ambition. That's what had attracted me to him—his confidence that we could accomplish anything we wanted. Back then, I'd felt like the two of us were a team.

"You won't be much longer, will you?" he asked.

I slung my purse over my shoulder. "I was just leaving." I grabbed the notes off my desk. "Thanks for the fruit basket, by the way."

"You're welcome." His eyebrows pulled together. "I sent you a fruit basket?"

I pushed my chair under the desk. "I figured it was from you. It was full of ripe bananas. Someone left it in my car." I watched Jake's eyebrows rise before I turned to leave. He remembered how much I hated bananas.

5

ELLY

BY the time I saw Ethan's bike coming up the street, I'd disconnected the battery and taken out the old alternator, placing all the bolts, the belt covers, and the alternator belt in a neat row along the curb. Before Ethan turned into the parking lot, I bent over for a quick check in my side-view mirror. A patch of grease smeared across the bottom of my nose. I wiped at it with the back of my hand, causing it to smear across my cheek. Rather than let him catch me primping, I straightened as he came into the parking lot, leaving the smear on my face.

Ethan parked his bike beside my lineup of car parts. He put his hands on his hips as he looked at the parts. "Good work."

I leaned against the Subaru. "It's been a frustrating day."

He maneuvered the new alternator into place. Then I handed him the bolts, the belt, and the belt covers, letting him put it all back together on his own. Only after we got a jump start and the car rumbled to life was I sure that Ethan actually knew how to fix cars.

"Thanks," I said. "I owe you one."

"Okay, then." He grinned in triumph. "How about you come to dinner with me? I don't like eating alone."

Thirty minutes later, after we'd driven around enough to recharge my battery, we sipped tropical milkshakes in a little Cuban restaurant with yellow walls and red tablecloths. The smell of roasting meat and the clamor of voices surrounded us.

Ethan drank his shake straight from the cup. I ate mine with a spoon instead of a straw. I'd avoided straws ever since I'd burped three times on a homecoming date with Jake when I was a freshman in college. Not that this was a date. The fact that Ethan had ordered the garlic chicken proved it. We were simply coworkers getting to know each other.

Ethan hadn't spoken more than a few sentences since we'd left the LibraryStar parking lot. He measured his words as if on a tight budget, saying only what would satisfy a need. I, on the other hand, already had enough economy in my life. I would say whatever I wanted, tactless or not. "You'll probably never be homeless."

Ethan gulped down his shake, leaving a rim of froth along the top of his lip. "Why do you say that?"

I examined the pictures of Cuba on the wall next to us before I decided how to answer. "Your parents are rich."

He wiped his mouth. "I don't take money from my parents."

"But your parents would rescue you if you ever became homeless."

"I'd probably go back to house-sitting instead of asking for help . . . Why are you worried about me being homeless?"

I stirred my shake. "No reason."

He pushed his glass aside and leaned back against the wrought-iron chair. "I don't like to ask my parents for money. It always comes with strings attached."

I took another sip of my shake, straight from the cup like Ethan. "What kind of strings?"

Ethan smiled, handing me my napkin for what I guessed was an enormous shake mustache across my top lip. "My parents wanted me to take over the family business," he said, "but I didn't want to sell medical products for the rest of my life. I wanted to serve in the military."

I tried not to act too shocked. "You don't seem like a military guy."

Ethan's face fell. "That's what the Army said, and the Navy, Air Force, and Marines. I have flat feet. They say I won't be able to run long distances."

"Sorry," I said. "I didn't mean to imply you weren't—you know—strong enough." Sheesh. What was I saying? "At least you won't have to cut your hair." His dark hair had just the right amount of curl.

He grinned. "You like my hair?"

I'd definitely revealed too much. "I meant you don't seem violent."

"I'm more interested in preserving peace," he said. "I went to school in Maryland, hoping I could work for the military as a civilian, but that didn't happen either."

"My grandma lives in Maryland. We visited once when I was ten."

He combed a hand through his hair. "It's a nice place, but I'm glad to be home."

"Even if you are working for family?"

Ethan gave his shake a stir. "When Jake hired me, he agreed to donate a portion of his profits to a charity I help run."

"You help run a charity?" There was a first for everything. In this case, it was the first time I'd met a single guy who'd even mentioned a charity. Once again, I had to remind myself that I would never date a Ferrero.

"It's called One-on-One USA," he said, pulling out his phone. "We help individuals in the military who don't have supportive family and friends. It's kind of like a dating website but for online friends. You tell the software your hobbies, interests, political views, and religious preference. Then it pairs you with a serviceman. I usually talk to my deployed friends first thing in the morning. That's why I come in later and work through lunch." He showed me the website on his phone, complete with an American flag and smiling soldiers. I paged through the information until I saw Ethan's name at the top of the board of directors.

It was too late for me now. Despite my best intentions and the fact that he was Candi's brother, I was already falling for Ethan Ferrero. I slid his phone back toward him. "Let me get this straight—you volunteer at the bishops' storehouse on Saturdays, and you run a charity?"

He put his phone back in his pocket. "It's not much compared to what our servicemen and women do every day. The charity mostly runs itself. I only need money to keep up the website."

Silence settled over us. It was a comfortable silence, like I used to have with my dad. While pretending to look at the black-and-white photographs on the wall, I analyzed whether I could handle this. It wasn't the best time to enter a relationship. Sure, I was over Jake. But Dad's death and the loss of our company had left me with serious responsibilities. I couldn't open my heart to Ethan. Too many other concerns occupied it.

Our entrées came, and Ethan turned his attention to the garlic chicken while I discovered that the black beans and rice weren't so bad for being the least expensive item on the menu.

I'd almost cleared my plate when Ethan spoke again. "I noticed

Annie is playing at one of the high schools. Do you think Grace would like to go?"

I gave my shake another stir. "I don't know if my mom would approve. You're a little old for her."

Ethan bent to pick up the napkin that had fallen off his lap. He barely avoided bumping his head on the edge of the table as he sat up again. "I could take both of you."

I smashed a bean with the back of my fork. "That's sweet, Ethan, but Grace has a hard time with theaters. It's an autistic thing."

Ethan rubbed the back of his neck. "I think she'd like it."

I didn't want to disappoint him, but it was a bad idea. "You saw how she was when she couldn't get Pop-Tarts. She's worse in crowds."

Ethan took his wallet out of his back pocket and extracted three tickets. "Well, do you mind going with us if she wants to go?"

I looked at the three tickets trembling in Ethan's hand. "I'd love to go," I said, knowing it could be the most embarrassing thing I'd done all year.

6

Maren

How could Elly and Mom forget? It was the six-month anniversary of Dad's death. Yet the day proceeded exactly like any other day with Elly and Mom racing off to work. They operated on autopilot, moving without thinking—working, laughing, and eating as if Dad had never existed. It was one thing for Dad to die. It was another for him to die in their memories.

Death was real to me now—the inevitable result of living. The death of my father made me crave death and fear it all at once. I believed I would live with Dad again someday after I died. Until then, he had to live in my memory.

Grace came into my room as I tried to remember Dad's voice—not the tinny version on my cell phone, the real version in all its fullness. "Can you take me to school, Maren?" Her words crowded out the sounds I'd heard in my mind. My memory was like that sometimes. It shifted as swiftly as a mirage.

"Of course I'll take you to school," I mumbled.

She stayed beside my bed. "When are you going to wake up?"

I laid an arm over my eyes, blocking out the light. "I am awake."

She dropped her backpack on my floor with a thud. "Why don't you get out of bed?"

"I'm remembering Dad. I do it every morning, so I won't forget."

"How do you remember?" Grace asked.

I opened my eyes and pushed myself up onto my elbow. "I imagine that he's talking to me," I said. Then I recalled that autistic people sometimes struggle with imagining. "But there are other ways to remember. In some cultures, people wear special clothing. Other people make shrines, where they keep pictures and other objects."

"Objects like Dad's Old Spice?"

"Yes, you might put something like that there."

Grace slept every night with Dad's container of deodorant. The smell comforted her. She was like me that way—she needed to remember. If I could only help the others remember too. Would jewelry or a painting help?

"Should I put Dad's Old Spice in a shrine?" Grace asked.

"No, sweetheart. Shrines are places where you go to worship, and we don't need to worship Dad. He doesn't need us to pray for him either, because spirits don't have any problems in the spirit world."

Golden light shone through my window on Grace, backlighting her. "Why are people so afraid of dying?"

I lay back down on my soft pillow. "They're afraid of the pain that leads up to death. After death, there's nothing to fear. All pain leaves us." I longed for that kind of peace. I longed to go home to Dad.

7

ELLY

MOM called me at work on my third day, her voice exploding with emotion. "Maren got her beads out this morning and made three necklaces. Now she's cleaning her room. She's acting like she has a purpose for living again."

"That's good," I said, typing in a little code and hoping I could end the call quickly. I couldn't slack off on the first week of my temporary job. "Sounds like she's getting back to normal."

"It's not good, Elly. It's a sign of—I can't say it—you know, the s-word." The tone of her voice rose much higher than normal at the end of her sentences.

I laughed. "Maren hasn't combed her hair in the last month. I don't think you have to worry about men right now."

"Not *that* s-word. The *outra*—other one." The fact that Mom had slipped into Portuguese, her native language, was not a good sign. "I'm afraid she's going to take her own life. That's what the experts say—a renewed sense of purpose can be a sign that she's finalized her plans." It sounded like Mom had read the phrase off a medical website. "I'm worried she's making us necklaces as a parting gift."

I wanted to tell Mom she was wrong, that Maren would never commit suicide, but I knew that Maren fit the profile. I swiveled away from the computer and moved as far into the corner of my half of the cubicle as possible. "I talked to her about going back to Dr. Jenner the other day, but—"

"Oh, she's going." My mother's voice held that tenacity I associated with the time she'd taken away my phone for texting too much.

"You got her an appointment?" I asked.

"Not exactly. I got *you* an appointment, and I told her she needs to get you to go. She's on her way to pick you up."

"What?"

"It was the only way, Elly. Just play along. I told her you're suppressing your emotions, and you need to see Dr. Jenner to help you sort them out. I already talked to the nurse over there. He's going to fill Dr. Jenner in on everything I told him."

I looked out the window to see our old, dark-green family van pulling into the LibraryStar visitor parking lot. I didn't ask how Mom would get to her fast food job without a car. "So the appointment's for *me*?"

"Maren will do anything to help someone else," Mom said. "It's the only way."

I fingered a cup of cherry tomatoes Ethan had left on my desk, presumably to make up for the basket of overripe bananas. A Post-it note on them welcomed me to LibraryStar. "I can't leave, Mom. It's my first week."

"Your sister's life is at stake."

I watched through the window as Maren emerged from our van, wearing jeans for the first time in months. Mom was probably overreacting. Still, I couldn't ignore the possibility that Maren had taken a turn for the worse. Even if she hadn't, she needed medical help. "She's here," I told Mom. "I'd better go." Stan wasn't at his desk, so I left a note, explaining that I'd had a family emergency and that I'd make up the time later.

Maren seemed almost like her usual self on the way to the clinic, except that she blared that song from The Band Perry about dying young. Before Dad died, she'd hated that song. "Thanks for coming to get me," I shouted over the music as we pulled onto the freeway.

Maren revved the engine to pull ahead of a semitruck. "You're welcome." The pointer on the speedometer passed eighty miles per hour as Maren zoomed past the semi. That's when I decided Mom might be right about her. She didn't seem to care whether she lived or died.

The idea of losing her made my hands tremble and my stomach clench. I gripped the armrest. "The speed limit is fifty-five here, isn't it?"

She stared straight ahead. "Why? Are you afraid of my driving?"

I watched the pointer on the speedometer climb still higher. "Yes." This whole situation scared me. Her driving only made it worse.

Maren darted a glance my way. "A little fear can be therapeutic. Let yourself feel it, Elly." A pair of fuzzy dice swung wildly from the rearview mirror as she wove between lanes.

I covered my eyes. "I'd rather feel peace and happiness." I wondered how Mom expected me to pull the switch at the psychiatrist's office. What if Maren wanted to wait in the car? Or stay in the waiting room?

With my eyes still covered, I heard the engine settle into a higher gear. "Okay. I'll slow down," Maren said. "I just wish you weren't so numb to the tragedies that surround you. Are you happy now?"

I peeked to see we were a safe distance from the car ahead of us. Maren had eased off the gas pedal. I swallowed the bile in my throat. "I want you to be happy too," was all I could get out.

Maren's expression remained passive. She didn't say anything else during our ten-minute drive. Inside, I prayed I could make this work. Maren needed help, but she craved acceptance for her condition. I didn't want her to think I rejected her when I only rejected the disease.

Maren pulled off the freeway near the university. That meant we were almost there. I wiped the sweat from my forehead. "I've never gone to a psychiatrist before."

Maren examined me while she stopped at a light. "There's nothing to be nervous about. All you have to do is let go and talk—let your emotions come out of hiding." Maren turned from one narrow street to another, never pausing to read a street sign.

A minute later, she pulled into a parking lot. "This is it," she said. The car faced a red brick wall splattered with white along the bottom rows of bricks.

I opened my door to the smell of urine. "Are you sure?"

"Of course I'm sure. This is my third time. Make sure you don't leave anything in the car."

I grabbed my purse and a couple bags Grace had left in the backseat. "You're going in with me, right? I don't want to talk to the doctor by myself."

Maren didn't exactly smile, but she didn't frown either. "I'm here for you, Elly."

And I'm here for you, I thought. "Don't leave me, okay?"

She tilted her head as if she wondered why I'd ask such a thing. "I won't."

I pulled open the front door to find a small, empty waiting room. When the receptionist handed me forms to fill out, I stood at the reception desk with shaking hands. Maren and I trusted each other in a way that meant she'd told me about her secret crush on a boy named Drew in junior high. She left her diaries lying out, knowing I'd never read them because I already knew everything inside. She'd never told our parents about my poor report card at the end of eighth grade, and I'd never told about the time she rode down the freeway in the back of Jordan Butler's pick-up.

Feeling like a traitor, I wrote Maren's name on the sign-in form and whispered her name to the receptionist. Since they already had Maren's records on file, I went back to my seat without the usual paperwork for a new patient. Maren had her eyes closed and didn't notice.

I gripped the edge of my seat as the nurse opened the door to call the next patient. "Maren."

"You must mean Elly," Maren said, grabbing me above the elbow and pulling me toward the nurse.

The nurse squinted at his chart and then checked the room to make sure there wasn't another patient with the correct name hiding in the corner. Then he seemed to remember something. "Sorry, I meant Elly."

The nurse escorted us to a room full of well-worn doctor's equipment. It was far removed from any psychiatrist's office I'd seen on TV. No leather couch or plush carpet graced the room. I practiced my tap dancing cramp rolls while I sat in my plastic chair. Maren tried to take a nap.

Dr. Jenner came in five minutes later, staring at the chart. She was thin with short gray hair and wore a red sweater set. "It's nice to see you, Maren."

Maren opened her eyes. "It's nice to see you too, but the appointment isn't for me this time. It's for Elly."

The doctor stared at the chart. "So you've had a hard time since your father's death?"

Maren didn't answer, so I decided to do what Mom said and play along. "That's right," I said. I hoped Dr. Jenner had gotten Mom's message.

She looked at me over the top of her reading glasses. "It's been how long?"

"Six months. Would you say it's normal to stay in bed all day still?"

The doctor slipped her glasses off, allowing them to hang from a chain around her neck. "It's normal to feel grief for months after a loved one's death, but sometimes normal grief can slip into depression. After a certain period of time, your grief shouldn't interfere with normal activities like getting up, getting dressed, and going to work."

I felt Maren's glare.

"Is it normal to go back to work the day after the funeral?" she asked.

The doctor's eyes lingered on mine, telling me she knew what was going on. She nodded to Maren. "It's a healthy coping mechanism to throw yourself into your work."

Maren folded her arms. "It's not a healthy coping mechanism if you never let yourself cry."

"Tears aren't always an accurate measure of feelings." The doctor studied Maren's knotted bush of hair. "Staying in bed all day, neglecting personal grooming, feeling overwhelming grief for an extended period—those are signs of severe depression. It's a good thing you came in today."

Maren pointed to me. "I'm not here for me. I'm here for Elly."

"Dad wouldn't want you to spend the rest of your life in bed," I said. "That's why Mom wanted you to come here with me."

Maren's eyes narrowed, becoming distant. The doctor held her hand up to stop me from saying anything else, but Maren was already headed for the door. We followed her through the office and into the parking lot, where she stood beside the van, looking through her purse for the keys. I put my arm around her.

Dr. Jenner stood a couple feet behind us. "I can see you loved your father very much, Maren. It's good to grieve for him."

A tear slid off the end of Maren's nose. "You should be telling Elly that."

"Right now I'm more concerned about you," Dr. Jenner said.

Maren shrugged my arm off from around her shoulders. "Are you coming, Elly?" She opened the driver's side door and got in.

I watched Maren put the key in the ignition. If I gave up now, it would be more of a betrayal. I had to get her help. The doctor said she needed help. "Can you at least talk to the doctor before we leave?" I called, running to the back of the van, where I stood behind the bumper.

Maren honked the horn, but I didn't budge. The doctor walked to the side of the car, her arms folded. I was so sure I'd done the right thing that I stayed there when Maren backed up a few inches, then a few more inches until the bumper touched my leg. She backed up some more, forcing me to scramble off to the side of the car. "What are you thinking?" I yelled. "You almost—" Before I could finish my sentence, pain seared the tip of my right foot. She'd run me over with her back tire. My own sister had run me over.

8

Maren

Have you ever thought things couldn't get any worse and then they did? Seeing Elly there, crumpled on the asphalt with her toes looking oddly flat, I felt a pain other than my own. My nerves flared in sympathy. The hurt burned like a fire, consuming my feet and then blazing up my leg. "I could have killed you," I cried. "I'm so sorry."

Elly couldn't say anything but, "Ow."

Dr. Jenner spoke, but her words scattered around me. She raised her voice in a second attempt. "Elly needs to go to the hospital, Maren. Help me get her in my car."

Elly stiffened as I touched her arm, as if every movement hurt her. "I can't believe I ran you over," I choked out between sobs.

Elly groaned in response, a groan of pure animal pain. Her lips narrowed to a straight line with her bottom lip pushed forward.

Dr. Jenner reached under Elly's arm. "My car's there," she told me, pointing to a silver Buick ten feet away.

I moved as though in a dream of blacks, whites, and grays. Together, we lifted Elly up and half-carried her to Dr. Jenner's car. I'd lifted Grace that way many times, but I'd never lifted my older sister. Elly wasn't the type who ever needed lifting. That day, though, as much as she wanted to keep all her weight to herself, she had to spread it across our shoulders as we walked to the car. How could I have done this to her?

Dr. Jenner arranged Elly sideways in the backseat with her leg elevated. She sat me in the front seat, handing me a box of tissues for my tears. "It was an accident, Maren. She's going to be okay." After commanding me to stay put, she went to park my van, which I'd left in the middle of the parking lot.

We drove to the hospital with Elly groaning at every bump in the road. She held her instep in both hands, trying to absorb the shock of movement. As I watched her, my chest tightened. I'd hurt Elly. But it wasn't really me that hurt her. It was the darkness inside me. I'd thought I suffered from my depression all by myself. Now it was also hurting the people I loved. I felt as if the weight of the van had also pressed down on my heart. "I'm ready to get help," I told Dr. Jenner.

She nodded, placing her hand on my forearm as she drove. "And I'm ready to help you."

Dr. Jenner drove to the emergency room entrance, helped Elly into a wheel chair, and pushed her into the emergency waiting room, where a receptionist took down our information. "This woman needs pain meds," Dr. Jenner told a medical assistant. Then we left Elly there, sitting in that wheelchair in front of the admissions desk, listening to a baby scream.

I turned my head back to look at Elly as Dr. Jenner and I walked down the hallway. "Shouldn't we stay with her?" I asked.

"I want to get you some help too. I like to bring my patients here when they first start on medication for severe depression." She waved her security pass over a sensor to open the wide hospital doors. "Elly can come visit you after she sees the doctor."

I paused before walking through the doorway. "What do you mean, visit me? *I'm* not going to be in the hospital, am I?"

Dr. Jenner faced me. "You told me you're ready to get help."

"Right," I said. "But I thought you could give me a prescription." I didn't want to be in a hospital. Hospitals were expensive, and we didn't have any money. They were the source of tragic news. How could anyone recover from depression in a hospital? My stomach ached at the thought of having to stay there.

Dr. Jenner put her hands on my shoulders. "I want you to be in the hospital so I can monitor you while we determine the best treatment plan. The professionals here will help me decide on the best medication, and they'll help you learn coping mechanisms."

I reached my hand to the wall, trying to steady myself. Her words had taken away my strength. I trembled as if I'd had the flu for a month.

"It's up to you, of course. I talked to your mother about it this morning before you came. She said she could bring you your things."

Should I do what Dr. Jenner said? I didn't want to hurt anyone else in my family again. But it sounded like it would take more than a few hours. "How long will I be here?"

Dr. Jenner led me through the doorway. "It shouldn't be longer than a week or two. You can have visitors during daylight hours." Her expression remained calm with her mouth slightly open.

I watched the doors shut behind us. A week or two? I couldn't stay in a hospital for a week. I knew what it had cost to have Dad in the hospital for a week. We'd have benefited more from a weeklong vacation to Disneyland, creating happy memories and buying overpriced souvenirs. I turned back to that security doorway. As I pushed against the doors, I felt Dr. Jenner's hand on my shoulder. "Maren, no one's forcing you to stay here. I can open the door for you if you want."

"Open the door please," I said. She swiped her card across the sensor, and the doors swung open. I hadn't expected her to open them. The decision was too hard to make for myself. I couldn't stay in the hospital when we didn't have any money. I wanted Dr. Jenner to force me, to sit me down in a wheelchair like she'd done with Elly, and have someone give me medicine for the pain.

I stood in front of the open doors and thought of how Elly had stood behind the van, trying to keep me from driving away. Elly. I hadn't been there for her since Dad died. I hadn't been there for anyone.

"Would it help to talk to your mother about it?" Dr. Jenner asked.

My mother was at Tic-Toc-Taco, the fast-food place where she worked. She could maybe take a phone call, but she wouldn't be able to come get Elly. It was Elly's right foot that I'd run over. "Elly needs me to drive her home," I said.

"Tell you what," Dr. Jenner said. "We'll go upstairs and look around while we wait for your sister. You can make up your mind later. You don't have to check in today. You can come tomorrow or next week if that works better for you."

I followed Dr. Jenner down the hallway to wait for the elevator. The whole time, I thought of Elly's foot. What if she could never tap-dance again? What if she couldn't work? What if she limped for the rest of her life?

The elevator doors opened, and Dr. Jenner stepped inside. "There aren't any padded cells. I promise."

I stepped in after her, wondering how I'd gotten to this place in my life. I'd always felt so normal. My parents hadn't abused me. I had friends. As far as I knew, I was healthy. How did I get here in this dark place?

We got out on the third floor, where she led me to a large, wallpapered room. Two women dressed in fluffy bathrobes sat together on a sofa reading fashion magazines. One was blonde and looked ten years older than me. The other was younger with shiny black hair and Asian features. Dr. Jenner introduced me to them. Then she told me my first assignment—to let them give me a makeover.

I didn't normally allow strangers to take care of me. No one in my family did. We paid for service. The blonde must have sensed my hesitancy because she explained that Dr. Jenner had done the same thing to them when they first arrived. Then the other woman told me how she'd like to curl my hair.

"This is our therapy too," she said. "It makes us happy."

Happy—it'd been so long since I'd been happy. Like a size I'd long ago outgrown, happiness was something for other people.

They took me to a bathroom, bent my head over a sink, and washed my hair with coconut-scented shampoo. Tears coursed down my face, dripping off my nose into the sink, as I explained to them how Elly had taken me to the doctor and I'd run over her foot.

"She'll be glad you're here," the blonde said, working conditioner into the ends of my hair. She was right. Despite the expense, Elly would be glad if I stayed.

While the women gave me a deep conditioning treatment and painted my toenails a rich burgundy, they took turns telling their own stories. Like me, they both came from good families. The only abuse had come from bad luck and their own tortured consciences. While they rinsed and combed my hair, I told them about Dad and the family business. I told them how I'd applied for over three hundred jobs without a single offer. They joked about the monotony of ramen noodles, and I wished I could've laughed with them. It took a good half hour of combing to undo all the tangles in my hair, but they told me I couldn't apologize.

We talked over the sound of the blow dryer. Then they curled my hair with such precision that I felt like I was going to the prom. We'd just started on the makeup when Elly hobbled in with a big black boot on her right foot. The foot I ran over. Seeing her like that, I felt the pain throb through my leg. "That's my sister," I told the women. "The one I ran over." Their eyes held no judgment.

Elly stepped into the room. "I'll be okay. I broke a couple of toes and a small bone in my foot—that's all." Her lips pressed together.

I stood up, pushing away any thoughts of BB cream and lip liner. "I'm not going to stay here. You need me to drive you home."

Elly shook her head. "No, Maren, I want you to stay. I'll get a ride."

I raised an eyebrow. "But there's no one to give you a ride. Mom doesn't have a car."

Elly glanced down toward the left. "A guy from work said he'd drive me back."

She'd worked for all of three days, and now she'd asked someone to come all the way downtown to get her—that didn't sound like Elly. "You're lying."

"I'm serious," she said. "After I told my boss why I'd be late coming back, my coworker called to offer me a ride."

Elly must have been desperate for me to stay if she would take a ride from a guy at work. She never associated with male coworkers outside the office. That was the equivalent of a cat taking a bubble bath.

9

ELLY

A SILVER Mazda convertible turned into the hospital parking lot twenty minutes after Ethan called me. I raked my teeth across my bottom lip, trying to reassure myself that Ethan wouldn't have borrowed Candi's car. As the car skidded to a stop, I saw it was worse than I'd feared. Candi sat in the driver's seat.

Ethan popped out of the passenger side of Candi's Mazda, looking like Spring Break personified with his wavy hair and broad smile. "Hi, Elly." He eyed my black boot. "Do you need to keep your foot elevated?"

"I'll be okay for the drive home. Thanks."

He held the passenger side door open. "Candi's going to drive us to get your car, then you and I can drive it back."

I slid into the passenger seat, being careful not to chip Candi's paint job with my boot. Candi stared straight ahead. "Thanks so much for coming to get me," I said.

She smacked her lips. "My pleasure." Funny how the word *pleasure* came out sounding more like pain when she said it. Maybe she'd fire me for this.

I held onto my armrest as she sped from the parking lot. "I hope it wasn't too much trouble," I said.

"Oh, I don't mind helping Ethan with his little service projects."

Was that what I was? Ethan's service project?

"Just don't let it happen again."

Except for a few directions from me to Candi, it was a silent drive back to the clinic to get the van. I consoled myself that if I lost my job, at least I'd helped Maren.

Ethan helped me out of the car, and then held onto my elbow as Candi drove away. I hobbled to the van. "You brought a different car today?" he asked.

I gave the easy answer, "Yep," as I made my way to the driver's side. I couldn't let him distract me from the fact that he'd brought Candi here to see me at my worst.

Ethan pulled me toward the passenger side. "Oh no, you don't. I'm driving."

I stepped away from him, folding my arms across my chest. "Remember how you said I need to make Candi forget that I work at LibraryStar?"

Ethan combed his fingers through the waves in his hair. "I thought if she saw you in a vulnerable moment, she'd ease up on you."

Surely by now he'd heard what I'd done to Candi's car. "If anyone deserves to be resentful, it's me. She stole my fiancé, and then she helped him put my father out of business. All I did to her was—"

"Wait." Ethan held his hand up to stop me. "You're the ex-fiancée?"

"You didn't know that already?"

He held his hand over his mouth, trying to stifle his laughter. It didn't work. "No." He stopped to laugh some more. "I didn't know *that* Elly and Elly Goodwin were the same person."

Why did I ever think I could be friends with Ethan Ferrero? I hobbled to the passenger side. "Sorry to disappoint you. I'm *that* Elly."

Ethan followed, now silent, as I unlocked the door and got into the car all by myself. When he didn't come around to the driver's side, I looked behind the car to see him talking to a woman with long gray hair. I guessed she was a beggar, asking for money to buy a bus pass. That's the type of person that hung out in this part of town. Everyone knew she'd probably use the money for drugs. It was best to politely refuse her and send her on her way. Ethan did the exact opposite; he brought her around to my side of the car. As she approached, I saw she carried a mess of crocheted flowers. I guessed they were supposed to be roses, floppy roses. Ethan picked a blue one and handed it to me. "Would you like a rose, Elly?"

I reached for the rose and, out of habit, tried to smell it. "Thank you." It smelled of mothballs. Ethan paid the woman five dollars before he came back around to the driver's seat. I handed him the keys. "In the language of flowers, you just told me you're sorry I broke up with you."

He placed his hand behind my headrest as he backed the van out of the parking space. "What do you mean, the language of flowers?"

I rolled the yarn-covered plastic stem of the rose between my hands. "The colors each have a meaning. Red means passion, pink stands for love, yellow is for friendship, and blue is for regrets."

"So the flower means that I regret you got hurt." Ethan turned from the parking lot into heavy lunch-hour traffic. "I wish I'd known about this flower language sooner. It would've been a lot easier to send a few yellow roses than to have the 'I just want to be friends' talk."

I jammed the stem of the flower into my purse. "Maybe you chose the color blue because you're sorry to find out I'm the monster Jake once dated."

Ethan laughed again. "I don't think you're a monster."

"Then you probably don't know the whole story." I reached for the bottle of hand sanitizer Mom kept in her cup holder. As much as I loved getting flowers, I couldn't trust this one to be germ-free.

We stopped at a traffic light, and Ethan turned to face me. "What's the whole story?" The light changed and the car behind us honked, but Ethan still looked at me.

I pointed to the light, and Ethan drove forward. *Okay*, I thought, *I might as well get this over with.* "Jake and I were engaged for two years—that was after we'd dated for three years in college. He kept putting off the wedding because he wanted to establish himself in business. Not that he had to worry about anything. My dad planned for him to be the next CEO of Check-It-Out. So two years and three weeks into our engagement, Jake took me on a picnic in Sonoma Valley. He had this fancy spread of artisan bread and European cheese laid out on a tablecloth with music playing. I thought he was going to tell me he finally wanted to set a date, but that wasn't it at all. After all that time, he broke off the engagement."

"So far, you're not the one that sounds like a monster," Ethan said. We stopped at another light, and Ethan tried to remove Maren's fuzzy dice from the rearview mirror. "Sorry, I can't drive with these things. They block my view."

When the light changed, I unwound the dice and removed them from the mirror. "It was such a shock that I didn't think to return his engagement ring. So the next day, after I'd had a chance to think, I packed a box of all the stuff he'd given me. I put his ring in it, plus a few other things like books about how to succeed in business, some love notes, a chunk of petrified wood, and this huge bottle of Jennifer Lopez perfume. I stuck the box in the backseat of my car and drove to Jake's house. In the back of my mind, I still hoped we could get back together. I turned onto his street behind a red Volkswagen Beetle."

"Don't tell me," Ethan said. "It was Candi."

Three years later, I still clenched my fists thinking of that day. Trying to relax, I stuffed the fuzzy dice into my purse beside my mothball-scented rose. "What kind of man dates someone else while he's engaged?"

Ethan shook his head. "I couldn't say."

"Of course not," I said. "Nice guys like you don't act that way. Anyway, Candi parked in my usual spot in front of Jake's house, so I parked across the street. Before I had time to get out of my car, I watched Jake come and kiss her in the driveway—less than twenty-four hours after he'd broken off our engagement and two hours after he gave my dad his notice."

I wondered, after I said it, if maybe I'd said too much. Ethan pressed his lips together as if he might not believe what I'd said. And why would he? He hardly knew me. After contemplating for a moment, he spoke. "Candi probably didn't know he was engaged when she started dating him."

My clenched fists loosened. He believed me. "She probably didn't," I said.

"So how are you a monster?" he asked.

"Because of what came next." I bit my bottom lip, telling myself it was better he heard this from me. "I watched them drive off in Jake's car before I got the box out. I figured I'd leave it on Jake's front step. If someone stole his grandma's engagement ring, what did I care? But as I passed Candi's car, I saw she'd left her windows open a few inches. I couldn't resist. I shoved every single love note into her window—all five years' worth, starting from when we met in college. Jake dated all his letters, and I hoped Candi would read every single one."

"You still don't sound like a monster," Ethan said, laughing. "Jake deserved to have her find out."

I pulled in a jagged breath. "It gets worse. After I threw in the engagement ring, the books, and the bottle of perfume, I chucked in the petrified wood. It broke the perfume bottle. Perfume spilled all over the front seat."

Ethan pulled onto the interstate. He didn't seem at all shocked. "I think I remember when that happened."

"I should have offered to pay for the clean-up," I said. "I guess I still could . . . after I get paid."

"It wasn't that big of a deal. She got new upholstery."

"New upholstery?" She'd spent more money than I'd thought.

"It would've been worse if you hadn't returned the engagement ring," he said. "Candi told me that thing is worth a fortune."

He had a point. I could've sold the ring. No one would've blamed me for that. Instead, I did the honest thing and returned it. If I hadn't been so noble, I would've never seen Jake and Candi together. "I should have controlled my emotions better. Then things wouldn't be so awkward between Candi and me."

Ethan shook his head. "It's not about the perfume. It's about Jake."

We drove in silence for a while. I liked the way Ethan drove—not too fast, not too slow. He kept his eyes on the road and signaled well ahead of any lane changes. "Now," he said as we approached the turn-off to get to LibraryStar. "Tell me how to get to your house."

I sat up straighter. "I'm okay to go back to work." I couldn't afford not to go back to work.

He glanced sideways at me. "Are you sure?"

I nodded. "I need the money."

Based on the fact that we'd met at the Church welfare place, he believed me. Maybe it was because we'd met there that I felt safe with him. After he pulled off the interstate, I opened up to him about the foreclosure notice and how Mom had put the house on the market, trying to sell it before the bank auctioned it off. "That's why I can't afford to slow down for a broken toe," I explained. "I have to make money, or we could end up homeless."

Arriving at LibraryStar, Ethan parked the van beside my Subaru. "Are you going to explain this too?" he asked, obviously wondering how both my cars ended up at LibraryStar.

That's when I lost it. Having to explain about Maren on top of everything else turned me into a crying mess. Though I could barely get the words out, I told him how Mom thought Maren was suicidal and how I'd taken her to the doctor.

"I have a friend like that too," Ethan said, handing me a crumpled-up napkin from his pocket. "You can never be too careful."

I wiped my face as I hobbled into LibraryStar. Ethan helped me prop up my foot on a stack of books under my desk and brought me a Ziploc bag of ice from the break room. Then I overheard him talking to Stan. "I think it'd be a good idea if I traded places with Josh." Josh was the intern who shared my cubicle.

Stan chuckled. "Maybe it's a good idea for your social life, but not for office productivity."

Ethan responded in such a quiet voice that I strained to hear him. "Elly needs help finding her way around the software if she's going to get that project done for Jake. How about you let us try it for a week? Either it increases productivity, or I go back to my regular desk."

Next thing I knew, the intern toted his meager office equipment to his extra-large private cubicle, and Ethan sat three feet away from me. I didn't say anything to Stan, but I was pretty sure sitting by Ethan would be like sitting beside the office candy bowl. He would be a constant temptation, which wasn't what I wanted at all.

10

Maren

How did other people feel on antidepressants? I hoped they felt more than I did. The medicine pinched the edges off my emotions, the way Mom pinched the dead flowers off her rose bush. It may have looked neat and tidy, but there were no flowers.

I felt numb, existing in thought only. The doctors said that would change. I would feel happiness again. Meanwhile, I got up and dressed every morning. I did my hair and makeup. I watched television, went to group therapy, exercised, and talked to those medical people who cycled through my room. I lived in grays. Everything felt smooth and cold. Nothing muddy or sticky. Nothing soft. The mattress pretended to be soft, but inside it was a plastic box of air.

My long sleep of the past months faded away. I couldn't blame myself for it. I'd only wanted to stop the downward slide that had become my life. First, it was the company. Revenues went down. We lost contracts. Then Dad got sick. We lost more contracts amid trips to the hospital, layoffs, and chemotherapy sessions. We tried to solve problems with fewer employees, but somehow more problems surfaced. We plugged holes in a dam that was about to burst. And it did burst. We lost the company the same week we lost Dad. Elly and Mom clung to the wreckage, but I knew we were sunk. My bed had been my refuge. Now it was time to wake up.

Did I believe I could be happy? No. I'd lost that hope. I did believe in some things, though. I believed in prayer, not that it'd worked for me lately. So I prayed like that man in the Bible who wanted Jesus to heal his son. "'Help thou mine unbelief.' Help me believe I can be happy." Then I pushed through the exercises Dr. Jenner gave me to do.

My first assignment was to write down my aspirations. I didn't have any, so I thought back to the goals I'd had as a teenager. Number one: Become a designer for Check-It-Out. That dream died along with the company, but I told myself I could get a job elsewhere. I'd applied for dozens of jobs after graduation, but nothing had come of it. So many San Franciscans wanted to be designers. I couldn't compete with hundreds of people for one job.

My number two goal had always been to sing. When you grow up hearing people compliment you on your perfect pitch, you expect that somehow, someday, your voice will take you places. I took ten years of voice lessons before I realized no one pays you for having perfect pitch. Not usually, at least.

After staring at the blank paper for a half hour, I wrote: *Find a job.* Now that I had the medicine in my system, I could see it didn't matter anymore whether it was a job in art.

More than wanting a job, I wanted to help people. I would help my family, but I also wanted to paint pictures for cancer patients. I wanted to travel, but not to see the world. I wanted to build schools in South America, dig wells in Africa. I wanted to adopt the kind of children no one wanted. These all seemed impossible dreams. I couldn't accomplish any of them without money. My dream of adopting children seemed doubly doomed. It also hinged on my being married.

I wrote my next goal with reluctance: *Find love.* I'd wanted a relationship like my parents'. Mom said she knew the moment she heard Dad's voice that she loved him. They met in a roller-skating rink while they were in college. Mom worked at the snack bar. Dad was the deejay who never left his little booth. He studied for his classes while the songs played, and ate peanut butter sandwiches instead of coming to the snack bar. But Mom always had a way of getting what she wanted.

One day she brought real ingredients to the snack bar—garlic, olive oil, tomatoes, and steak. She cooked a whole Portuguese meal on a hotplate, and for the first time, Dad left his booth. Dad always said they had the kind of love where you know from the start that you want to be with that person forever.

Love—was it a goal? Or a dream? I'd always wanted someone full of surprises—the kind of man who could dive off cliffs but still appreciate the beauty of a wildflower; someone who loved to read and write but couldn't bear to sit through a class. Men like that existed outside my dreams. I felt sure of it.

Elly was in love. I could tell by the way she said his name—*Ethan*. The E at the beginning stayed in her throat far too long. She had a little bit more excitement to her voice now. Highs and lows replaced her usual monotone. How I wanted to be happy for her.

"It sounds like Ethan's falling for you," I told her while we talked on the phone.

"No," she said. "He just feels sorry for me because I can't drive. And Mom invites him for dinner every night."

Elly was too oblivious about men. Since she'd dated Jake Cannon, she felt sure every man would reject her. Expecting rejection was the worst way to prevent it.

"It's a good thing Mom's doing her best to reel him in," I said, "since you aren't."

"What am I supposed to do?" she asked. "We're coworkers."

I lowered my voice to a throaty whisper. "Forbidden love is the best kind."

Elly laughed. "You sound like a soap opera."

"I feel like a soap opera," I said, "lying here at the mental hospital with a security bracelet on my wrist."

Elly sighed. "As long as you're getting better. I want that more than I want any guy in the world."

That was the sad thing about Elly. She wanted a lot of things more than she wanted a man. Like a rope-climber who'd spent so long on the cliff that she'd lost her grip, Elly couldn't hang onto love. Worse than that, I worried she didn't want to.

11

ELLY

SINCE I couldn't drive, I usually stayed home with Grace while Mom visited Maren in the hospital. I used the time to help Grace prepare to go to the play with Ethan.

It was like we were rehearsing, only we didn't rehearse to be *in* the play—we rehearsed to be in the audience. First we practiced sitting still. I'd gotten her a squishy ball to feel whenever she felt like rocking back and forth. Next we tried some earplugs, in case the sound grew too loud for her. I also told her about intermissions and coached her on when to clap.

When the night came, Grace wore her dark purple, velvet dress, the same one she'd worn to Dad's funeral, along with Mom's string of pearls. I wore a simple black dress, not only because it matched the boot I had to wear for my broken toes, but also because it would help me blend into the crowd.

It was an event, that was for sure, and if Ethan didn't know how big of a deal it was, he caught on when Mom made us pose for pictures in the front room, on the front steps, and beside the For Sale sign in the front yard. She continued to snap shots of us as Ethan helped us into his rusty Ford Escort. It was the only thing that had made Mom smile since Maren went to the hospital.

For once, Ethan wore something that looked new—a pair of charcoal gray chinos with a white oxford and black v-neck sweater. Seeing him all dressed up made me wish it was just him and me. At least I got to sit beside him in the front seat.

I leaned toward him as we drove to the high school. "Thanks for taking us. I hope it isn't a disaster."

Ethan smiled at Grace through the rearview mirror. "No matter what happens," he said, "we're going to have a fun time."

Though Ethan had already seen Grace at her worst, I wasn't sure he knew what he'd gotten himself into.

When we got to the high school auditorium, Grace sat between Ethan and me, plugging her ears with her fingers. Being there with Grace helped me notice things I usually wouldn't have—the scent of Pine Sol, the way the seats tilted when I lifted my knees up, and the purple stripe of hair on the woman sitting in front of us. All these things shouted to Grace, vying for her attention.

I took Grace's finger out of her ear to remind her of the rules about sitting still during the play. There would be no rocking back and forth, no standing, and no dancing. Ethan helped her read the playbill. By the time the lights dimmed for the opening scene, Grace had memorized the names of all the principal actors.

I sat back, feeling confident I'd thought of everything. Grace sat still, transfixed by the actors. I could hear her whispering their names as they appeared on stage. "Annie, played by Tiffany Tsu, Miss Hannigan, played by Janessa Brown."

Then the music started, and I realized I hadn't thought of one little thing as Grace sang along to "It's a Hard-Knock Life." Her voice rose loud enough that the purple-haired woman turned around to look.

I leaned across my armrest to whisper in her ear. "I forgot to remind you, you're not supposed to sing at the theater."

Grace pointed to the stage. "*They're* all singing."

"The actors sing. The audience doesn't," I explained while Ethan bit back a smile.

Grace pinched her lips shut between her thumb and forefinger.

Everything went fine for the next fifteen minutes. Grace sat perfectly still, sometimes humming, sometimes mouthing the words to the songs. Then we got to the part where the dogcatcher comes for Annie's dog, Sandy. It didn't matter that it was a kid dressed up as a dog, or that Grace had already seen this part in the movie. She stood up from her chair and shouted. "You can't take Sandy!" I pulled on her hand, trying to get her to sit back down. "Don't let him take her!" she cried.

While the dogcatcher chased Annie and the dog off the stage, Ethan escorted Grace to the aisle. "Let's make sure the dog's okay," he whispered. "Come on." I felt around in the dark for Grace's purse and coat.

That was one good thing about the theater—it was too dark for people to recognize us. After I found Grace's things, I hobbled along behind Ethan, watching the heads turn as Grace passed. She was still yelling about the dog.

Once in the lobby, she looked for a way to get backstage. "Where is he? I want to see him."

Ethan and I exchanged a look, in which I communicated that I was done with the musical. He laughed a little before growing serious. "I forgot to tell you how beautiful you look in that dress."

If this was his way of trying to get me to go back into that auditorium with Grace, it wouldn't work. "Thanks," I said, staring at the hem of his pants. That was exactly what Jake would have done. Jake would have pushed on with the musical, no matter what.

He stepped closer, forcing me to bring my gaze up to the space at the base of his neck where he'd left his collar unbuttoned. "I think I know where we can find Sandy. Are you up for walking a dog?"

That moment marked the end of my seeing Ethan as just a friend. He understood Grace and me in a way Jake never had. I brought my eyes to his. "That sounds perfect, except for my foot."

He offered me his arm. "We'll find a slow dog."

"You sound like that's going to be easy."

As we walked to the high school parking lot, Ethan explained that he'd spent the summer house-sitting. Since his house-sitting often involved pet-sitting, Ethan knew the perfect dog, an older yellow Lab named Peanut. The elderly man who owned her lived a short drive away in an upscale neighborhood.

Luckily, the man was home. Ethan spent a few minutes talking to him while Grace and I got acquainted with the dog. Grace called him "Sandy" and told him she was glad the dogcatcher hadn't gotten him. It was late enough that the tulips in the garden had folded their petals into the shape of little pink ballet shoes. Getting tulips like that in April meant putting the bulbs in the freezer during the winter. We didn't have a change of seasons in San Jose—fall melded with spring, skipping winter altogether.

When the elderly man went back in his house, freeing us to begin our walk, Grace kept the leash so tight that Peanut couldn't venture past the confines of his front yard. "We can't walk on the sidewalk in the dark," Grace told him.

I hobbled along beside Ethan, holding onto his arm for support that

I didn't really need. "We can walk outside tonight because we're with Ethan," I said, turning around to wait for Grace.

Grace allowed Peanut onto the sidewalk. "We can walk in the dark because Ethan's a man?"

"Because we're in a group, and we're in a good neighborhood," I explained.

Ethan was right about Peanut. With all his sniffing, we'd be lucky to make it up and down the tiny cul-de-sac where he lived. As Peanut marked a neighbor's mailbox, Grace looked at Ethan. "Elly wants to marry a returned missionary. Are you a returned missionary?"

I pulled back from Ethan's arm. "Grace! You're not supposed to talk about people getting married when they're not even dating." Beside me, Ethan shook with silent laughter.

"Why not?" she asked. "Isn't he good enough to marry you?"

I groaned. "It would've been less embarrassing to stay at *Annie*."

Ethan's voice betrayed his amusement. "I'm definitely not good enough for Elly."

Grace kept walking, forcing Peanut to trot behind her instead of marking another tree. "You should serve a mission."

I stopped, letting Grace get a little farther ahead. "Grace! Ethan was kidding. Now can we change the subject?"

Ethan stood still beside me. "I served a mission in Washington, DC."

"I'll bet you were a good missionary." He might as well know I admired him.

Ethan breathed out a laugh. "It'd be more accurate to say I learned a lot. I broke my leg in my first area, got appendicitis in my second, had a dog bite me in my third, got lice in my fourth."

"Let me guess. You got a Dear John in your fifth area."

"Nope. My nana passed away." Though it had been several years, a hint of grief sounded in his voice.

"Not the one who taught you to make Pop-Tarts?"

"That's the one. I lived with her for a year when I was eighteen." He stepped forward, resuming our walk behind Grace.

"So you served a mission, lived with your grandma, volunteer at the bishops' storehouse, gave me a ride home from the hospital, and fixed my car. You definitely aren't good enough for me. I don't even think I should be hanging onto your arm."

I hadn't meant for Grace to hear. She didn't understand sarcasm. She turned around, twisting the dog's leash around her legs. "Promise Elly you won't marry her, and it'll be okay."

Ethan winked. "I don't make promises to women I've just met." For a shy guy, Ethan was a great flirt. "My apartment's on the way home. We should stop by for a snack."

His apartment was by the university, a little two-bedroom place with cinder block walls. His roommate, Dave, a recently divorced man, had his two little boys for the weekend. They built forts with the couch cushions while Dave played a video game. Ethan introduced us.

When he took the blueberry pie from its box on top of the fridge, Dave and his boys gathered to the table. It seemed a given that Ethan would share.

Dave took a stack of mismatched plates from the cabinet. "I'll bet you the last piece of pie that you haven't told Elly anything of importance about yourself."

Ethan looked at me as he sliced through the pie with a table knife. "Bring it on."

Dave handed me a plate. "If you miss three out of five, the last slice is mine. First question: what kind of music does Ethan like?"

I took an educated guess, based on my knowledge of twenty-something men from the Bay area. "Alternative?"

Ethan punched his hand in the air. "Score one for me."

Dave rocked back in his chair. "Lucky guess. How about his favorite TV show?"

"Anything on the Discovery channel?" It was another guess.

Dave shrugged. "I would have said the History channel, but I'll give it to you."

"If I get five out of five, do I get to keep the pie?" I asked.

"Sure," Dave said. "Here's a hard one. How long have Ethan and I been friends?"

I looked around the apartment for clues, maybe a photograph or two. I found nothing. "A year?"

Dave threw his arms up. "We met in preschool. Been best friends ever since. Okay, next question: What sport did Ethan play in high school?"

Behind Dave, Ethan pantomimed something that looked like golf or maybe, "Baseball?"

"Lacrosse," Ethan said.

Dave smiled. "And this one for the game: how many women has Ethan brought home to meet me?"

I bit my lip. "Can I ask how long you guys have been roommates?"

Dave counted on his fingers. "Seven months."

I could see a blush rising up Ethan's neck. Whatever the number, he felt embarrassed about it. "Fourteen?" I guessed.

Dave reached across the table for the pie plate. "The number is two. You and Grace are it."

12

ELLY

TWO good things happened the next week. First, Maren was doing well on her new medications, so the doctor said she could come home from the hospital. And second, someone made an offer on our house. We'd have to sell it at a loss, but it was better than the alternative—having the bank sell it at an even greater loss. This way, at least the bank wouldn't come after our other possessions.

What was another $10,000 on top of the $500,000 of business debt we already had? It could have been worse. If Dad hadn't carried life insurance, we'd have owed much more. I'd always felt my parents budgeted well. We'd scrimped all through my life to invest in Dad's business. Yet we had nothing to show for it.

Mom danced around in the garage as if she'd solved all her problems. She packed box after box, seeming not to consider that we had no place to take the boxes and that Maren would still need a lot of help. "I've decided to throw a welcome-home party for Maren Friday night. Why don't you invite your boyfriend?"

I taped across the box she'd filled with extension cords, doubting we'd have room for twenty extension cords at our new home. "He's not my boyfriend," I said. "And how can we have a welcome-home party for Maren when we're the only ones who know she's gone?"

Mom put her hands on her hips. "He'd be your boyfriend if you were more expressive about your feelings toward him. He's stayed for dinner how many times now? I'd say five or six times."

Every day since I broke my foot, Mom had driven me to work, and Ethan had driven me home. That meant Ethan drove his Escort, requiring him to pay for gas. The least I could do to thank him was invite him for dinner. "I think he likes your cooking more than he likes me."

Mom patted her temples with the tips of her fingers. "No. I can tell he likes you. It's all in his eyes. Your father used to look at me that way."

I shook my head. "I don't know." Considering how much time Ethan and I had spent together, he ought to at least have attempted a hug. The most he'd done was let me lean on his arm.

All the uncertainty in my life weighed me down—not knowing where we would live, how I'd find my next job, how long I'd be working at LibraryStar, or what would happen to Maren. The only thing that made it better was work, partly the work itself, but also knowing Ethan would be there, sitting next to me.

Monday mornings felt different now—a relief from too much time without seeing Ethan. Instead of doing my hair and makeup while Mom drove me in the car, I woke early enough for the whole works—shampoo, style, lips, eyes, and cheeks. I felt like a teenager again.

This Monday morning seemed different, though. When I arrived at the office, the intern sat in the desk across from mine, and Candi sat in my chair, talking on my phone. I waited with my arms folded until she hung up the phone and swiveled around.

"I've moved Ethan back to his old cubicle. It's better for his productivity," she said, still sitting in my chair.

"So is this still my desk?" I asked.

Candi snorted a laugh. "Yes, this'll be your desk for as long as you work here." She emphasized the words *for as long as you work here.*

I dropped my purse into my bottom drawer and slammed it shut. "You can tell Jake I'm a quarter of the way through the project he gave me. I hope I can stay long enough to finish."

Candi stood up from my chair, brushing off a spot on her skirt as if it came from me. "There's no telling. The résumés are pouring in right now."

The last thing I wanted to do was apologize to Candi, but I needed this job. "I still feel bad about the damage I did to your car. When I get the money, I'd like to pay you back."

Candi snorted again—this time without laughing. "You should have thought of that three years ago."

"Better late than never." I should have left it at that, but my mouth kept on going. "Three years ago, I thought you got the better deal. Now I'm pretty sure I did." I sat in my chair and swiveled to face my computer.

"You are so fired, Elly Goodwin," I heard Candi say before she swished past me to her own department.

The door clicked shut behind her as my brain caught up with my emotions. Did Candi have the authority to fire me? Whether or not she did, I would have to apologize *again*. I leaped from my desk chair and ran to catch up with her, my boot thumping as I walked. I stood behind her as she chatted with some employees, and then I followed her to her office—her extra-large, corner office with windows that framed a view of palm trees.

I stood in the doorway while Candi rearranged a bouquet of lilies with her back to me. "Can I help you, Ms. Goodwin?"

If I thought it would help to fall down at her feet, I would have. Instead I clasped my hands. "I need this job, Candi."

Candi kept her back to me while she flipped through the mail on her desk. From what I could tell, everything in that pile of mail could've gone straight to the recycling bin without much consequence.

I stepped forward. "I'm sorry."

Candi dropped the papers on top of her desk and pivoted toward me. "The only reason you're here is because Mr. Cannon needs you for the Book and Movie Picks project. If you want to stay, you'll have to agree to my terms." She turned again, picking up the papers from her desk.

I waited. When she didn't elaborate, I asked, "And your terms are?"

Candi placed her hands at her waist. "You're here to work, only to work."

I walked back to my desk, wondering what she could mean. It wasn't like I surfed the Internet or played games. I took breaks to go to the restroom, which only happened every couple of hours, and I always went to the restroom farthest from Candi's department. If it was that big of a deal, I could probably cut back to once or twice a day. Dehydration was a small price to pay for a job.

As I arrived back at my desk and saw the intern sitting across from me, I finally figured out what Candi meant by "you're here to work." This was about Ethan. Candi thought we were more than coworkers, more than friends. I stood, giggling beside my desk, causing the intern to remove his earphones.

"What's so funny?" he asked.

I slapped a hand over my mouth. "Nothing."

If Ethan's own sister thought we were more than friends, maybe we were. I'd gotten used to the idea of dating a Ferrero, and the fact that Candi disapproved made it all the more appealing.

I was still laughing when Ethan came in a minute later. "Where's my stuff?"

I swiveled my chair around to face him. "Candi moved it back to your old cubicle."

He furrowed his brows. "You look like you're happy about that."

I tried to pull my lips straight, but it only made me smile more. "I'm not happy you've moved. I'm just happy." *What could I say now? I'm happy your sister thinks we're more than friends?* "Our house is under contract."

Ethan sat on the edge of my desk. "That's great."

I walked my fingers toward his hand. "We're having a Friday party. You're invited if you want to come."

His smile came back. "I'll be there."

13

Do you know what it's like to feel numb? To prepare for a party without feeling excited? To hear your house has sold and not feel a little sad or nervous? Thanks to the medication, my feelings seemed more intellectual than real. I knew I should be worried that we didn't know where we were moving, but I sat there like a vegetable, watching people lug in Crock-Pots for the party, and feeling nothing.

Mom never did anything small. I didn't notice that about her until after Dad died. The party she'd called a simple dinner had grown into a potluck extravaganza. Mom had invited neighbors, friends, and coworkers from all over, even people she'd served at Tic-Toc-Taco.

With that many guests scattered through the rooms of our home, Elly took on the role of security guard. After running upstairs to lock the bedrooms, she stationed herself in the kitchen, frying up potatoes and codfish with Ethan at her side while Mom mingled among the guests.

"I don't know where we're moving yet," Mom told our neighbor. "I'll let you know when we decide." Her voice remained calm, and I read confidence in her posture.

It'd only been a week and a half since the day I'd driven Elly to the doctor in my worn-out jeans. Now I wore a bright-colored peasant blouse with narrow leggings. Dressing well was part of my prescription for recovery, and it did make me feel better. Slightly better.

I held my hand out to Ethan. "You must be the famous Mr. Ferrero that Grace has told me about. Do you really know how to make Pop-Tarts?"

"Sure," Ethan said. "I'll show you sometime." His lips turned up slightly even when he wasn't smiling.

Elly served fish and potatoes to a growing line of people with her foot propped on a stool. Her married friends had brought their toddlers and babies. While Elly chatted with them about potty training and sleepless nights, I asked Ethan about his volunteer work. I hoped his passion for helping people would rub off on me, but Ethan kept trying to change the subject back to food. Just when I wanted to ask about the latest military crisis, Elly interrupted. "Where's Grace?"

I slapped the side of my face. "Oh, I'm supposed to be watching her." That's when I felt that tiny bit of emotion, like a subtle wash of pink over my charcoal painting. It felt so small—a pinch of concern.

Elly stood on her tiptoes, trying to see past the crowd to the back window. "Don't worry about it, Maren. She's probably in the backyard."

Ethan headed for the back door. "I'll find her."

With Ethan out of the kitchen, Elly gave me one of her crusty looks. "You don't like him."

"I don't know if he's right for you," I whispered. "He has no passion." Right then, I craved passion more than I craved food. I wanted to paint my life with bold strokes and bright hues. I needed to feel.

Elly's eyes flashed anger. "He's a nice guy, Maren. That's what I'm looking for."

Elly thought with her head instead of her heart—kind of like me on medication. She had only left her brain behind once—when she met Jake Cannon. The first day she brought Jake home, my friend Sandra took his picture so she could put it in her locker. But it wasn't just his looks. He was smart too. His words came out like frosting on a cake—sweet, smooth, and oh so luscious.

While Elly and I stood at the counter, a teenage boy came up behind us and grabbed a bag of chips. Elly nodded toward him as he ran from the room. "Do you know that kid?"

I shook my head. *If Dad were here*, I wanted to say, *that would've never happened,* but I couldn't feel the anger. I couldn't feel.

"As much as I miss Dad," Elly said, "I'm happy things are getting back to normal. You're home, Grace is hiding, and you don't like my date—that's definitely normal."

The smell of frying potatoes tempted me toward the stove. "Did you hear about Grandma Joan?" I asked. Grandma Joan was our dad's mom, who lived in Maryland.

"What about her?" Elly asked.

I plucked out a fried potato with a fork and stuck it in my mouth. It sizzled on my tongue. I blew a little, trying to cool it off, before I answered. "She still hasn't recovered from that knee surgery she had two months ago. Mom and I are going to fly out to help her after the house sells."

Ethan came back into the kitchen with Grace. "She was behind the shed, eating chocolate cake," he explained. At least he liked Grace.

"Maren, why don't you show Ethan your pictures?" Elly asked. I'd painted all the pictures hanging in the living room during my college years. Back when I felt like painting.

I motioned for Ethan to follow me. "You can guess the artist who inspired each picture."

Elly raced to ladle the Bacalhau à Brás onto a serving platter. "Wait! I'll help him."

Since all the guests had gathered on the patio, the living room remained as quiet as a gallery. I led Ethan to the picture above the mantel, an oil painting of autumn trees in the mountains. In my mind, I could still smell the mix of paint, turpentine, and linseed oil in the classroom where I'd painted it. "Look at how the edges blur," I said. "Does that remind you of any painters?"

Ethan squinted at the painting, pretending interest. "It doesn't look anything like the paintings by that guy on PBS—the one who used to paint with a squirrel on his shoulder."

I took his forearm and pulled him back two steps, giving him a broader view. "Think water lilies. This artist is famous for painting water lilies." I pointed out how I'd used bold strokes of clear colors—viridian green, cobalt blue, alizarin crimson, and cadmium yellow. He looked at me as if I spoke a foreign language. "Can you see the wind moving the leaves in the strokes?" I asked.

"I think so." By his studied expression, I could tell he couldn't see any movement at all.

After a few more hints, he finally guessed Monet. I led him to the painting of sunflowers, my most obvious copy. "This one's easier to guess."

Ethan examined the art for a minute, his hands in his back pockets. Elly came in from the kitchen to stand behind him. "It's probably on the tip of your ear."

"Oh." Ethan rubbed the side of his head, laughing. "You mean the one who cut off his ear."

"Van Gogh," I said, wishing I could laugh along with him.

He walked to the watercolor above the piano, the one of Elly dancing in toe shoes and a leotard. "This one's nice," he said, turning to Elly. "Is this you?"

"Yeah," she said, a little blush spreading across her cheeks. How would it feel to blush?

Ethan stepped closer to look at it. "These are beautiful, Maren. I can see why your parents hung them in the front room. You have a lot of talent."

Anxious to move on, Elly pointed to the painting by the front door. "The other one is some Anasazi cliff dwellings we visited on vacation."

"The colors are nice," he said. "I like the way the blues and greens contrast with the orange and tan." I suspected he was being polite—talking around the fact that it wasn't realistic enough for him. But I liked that he could at least pretend to appreciate art. Maybe he wouldn't be a terrible boyfriend for Elly.

"That's Mesa Verde, right?" he asked.

"Right," I said, remembering the days I'd spent layering the paints from thinnest to thickest—waiting days in between for the oils to dry. I'd painted the picture after our visit, working from a photograph and trying my best to capture the natural light peeking into the cliff.

Elly settled on the couch, resting her boot on the ottoman. "That one's my favorite. It's supposed to be like Cézanne."

Ethan found a place next to her on the sofa and propped his feet on the ottoman. The sides of their legs touched from hip to ankle. Ethan's arm rested behind Elly on the sofa. And I had suddenly become as invisible as a breeze. "I have a phone call to make," I said, but I didn't really need to say anything. They'd already forgotten me.

I drifted back into the kitchen, where I set to work putting plates in the sink. I'd barely cleared a square foot of counter space when the doorbell rang. "Maren, can you get that?" Elly called from the living room. She didn't want to move. Not with Ethan sitting that close to her on the couch.

I put a few plates in the sink. "Okay." The doorbell rang again. "I wouldn't dare make you move," I said, rushing through the living room. I swung the door open. "Welcome to the party. Come on . . . in." It couldn't be. Not now.

"It's nice to see you again, Maren," Jake said. He stood in our entryway, overdressed in a suit. His wife, wearing a vermilion wrap dress and stretching her mouth into a fake smile, followed him inside. Who invited them?

14

ELLY

CANDI'S mouth hung open as she saw Ethan and me on the sofa. The look she gave me stole away all the comfort I'd felt.

I hopped up. "Jake and Candi, how nice of you to come." I hobbled toward the entryway in my boot. Ethan followed me.

Jake extended his hand. "Hi, Elly. You know I can't pass up an invitation from your mom. When she said she'd make that codfish stuff, I had to come." He shook my hand as if we'd never been anything more than business colleagues. Then he reached for Ethan's. "Ethan. How's it going?"

Maren folded her arms. "How dare you—"

"Come on back to the kitchen," I interrupted. "I'll get you something to eat." With all the stress about Maren, I hadn't bothered to fill Mom in on my situation at work. She had no idea that Candi disapproved of me dating Ethan.

I led Jake and Candi to the square kitchen table, where Grace sat eating yet another piece of chocolate cake. I hated for Candi to see Grace that way. Hunched over the cake with frosting on her chin, she hardly lived up to her name.

"This is my little sister Grace," I told Candi. "You remember Jake, right, Grace? This is his wife, Candi." Thankfully, Maren had stayed in the living room, where she was probably giving Ethan a detailed history of Jake's faults.

Grace looked at Jake for a few seconds before recognition showed in her face. "You're the one who wanted to marry Elly."

I faked a chuckle as I wiped chocolate frosting off Grace's chin. "You'll have to excuse Grace. She's fixated on the idea of marriage now."

Jake took a seat across from Grace. "Like she used to be about musicals?"

"Right." I grabbed two plates, trying to hold them steady as my hands shook. "Can I get you some codfish, Candi?"

Candi wrinkled her nose as she sat down next to Jake. "A little."

I scooped out a child-size portion for Candi and a restaurant-size portion for Jake as Mom came into the kitchen carrying a bag of ice. "Jake, I'm so glad you could come." She laid the ice on the counter and kissed Jake Portuguese-style, first on one cheek, then on the other. "And you must be Candi." Mom extended her hand.

Candi forced a smile. "Nice to meet you."

I set the two plates in front of Jake and Candi as Grace said, "Elly's going to marry Ethan now."

Candi dropped her fork with a clank and stared at Grace. Jake laughed. "Is that so?"

Grace stuffed another bite of cake into her mouth. "Mm-hmm."

I picked up Grace's napkin off the floor and put it back in her lap. "You shouldn't say things that aren't true, Grace. Ethan and I are just friends." It wasn't a lie. Sitting close together on the couch wasn't the same as holding hands or kissing. "Candi is Ethan's sister, so she'd know if Ethan planned to get married."

Mom looked at Candi with her mouth open wide. "Oh, you're Ethan's sister. Ethan's such a sweetheart. He's driven Elly home from work every day since she broke her toe."

Candi glared at me. "Ethan doesn't have time to drive out here every day."

Mom laughed in that dramatic way of hers. "You know what they say: 'Love will find a way.'"

I could've kicked myself for not telling Mom a little more about what went on at work.

Candi held her fork in a tight grip, poised over her plate. She still hadn't taken a bite of her food. I remained silent. What could I say to get out of this mess?

Jake paused between bites of codfish. "This is as good as I remembered, Paula. You didn't happen to make your famous rice pudding, did you?"

The inner corners of Mom's eyebrows pulled up. "I haven't had the heart to make it since Henry died. It was always his favorite."

Candi laid her fork beside her plate and scooted her chair out. "I'll be waiting in the car . . . with Ethan." She walked toward the front door, calling Ethan's name.

Mom picked up her plate. "Here, I'll get some plastic wrap. You can take your plate with you."

Candi paused before exiting the room. "Oh no. I couldn't."

Mom opened a cabinet, in search of plastic wrap. "You can return the plate to Elly at work."

Candi looked straight at me with a razor-sharp glare. "I'm afraid I won't be seeing Elly anymore at work."

Jake stuffed another forkful into his mouth and stood up. "I hate to eat and run, but I guess I'd better be going too. Thank you for having us. And good luck with the move."

"I appreciate all you've done for Elly," Mom said. "Lately."

"No problem." Jake tugged on his collar as he exited the room. "See you later."

"What was that all about?" Mom whispered.

I rubbed my sweaty palms down the sides of my pants. "Candi thinks there's something going on between Ethan and me. She told me the other day that if I spent any more time with him, I'd be fired."

"There *is* something going on between you and Ethan."

"No, there isn't. We're friends, Mom." I looked around the corner to make sure Ethan stood out of hearing range. "He's never taken me on a real date or held my hand or kissed me."

"What does that matter? He's falling in love with you all the same."

I shushed Mom as I walked to the living room to see if Ethan really had left.

Maren sat on the sofa by herself. "Ethan and I were in the middle of a conversation when Jake's wife came and dragged him out to her car."

"She's his sister," I explained. "And now I'm going to get fired because she caught us together."

"I'm dying to know," Maren whispered. "Did he kiss you when you were sitting together on the couch? I could feel it coming."

I didn't want to worry Maren when she'd just gotten home from the hospital, but I had to tell someone. "Jake's wife said if I spent any more time with Ethan, I'd lose my job."

"Lose your job?" Maren rolled her eyes. "Because a man fell in love with you?"

I pressed my hands against the nervous ache in my stomach. "We're just friends."

"Friends who curl up on the couch together," Maren said.

That's when I noticed that Mom no longer stood next to us. She'd gone out the front door. I pulled back the window drapes to see the four of them standing beside Jake's car—Candi with her arms folded, Jake looking as if he might explode into laughter at any second, Ethan scuffing his shoe against the curb, and Mom giving them all a dose of Latina fire. I could hear every word she said from inside.

"Elly will date whomever she pleases. Employers aren't supposed to concern themselves with the personal lives of their employees."

I didn't know what to do, but I couldn't let Mom keep talking. As I opened the door and walked down the front steps, Jake put his hand on Mom's shoulder and tilted his head with that fake sympathy I knew so well. "Look, Paula, the last thing I want is for Elly to get her heart broken."

I froze in the middle of the yard, stunned by Jake's words. He still had a pull on my emotions. He said he didn't want to break my heart, but he had—over and over again. And he was doing it again. So much for the five years I wasted on Jake. So much for the hundreds of cookies I baked, the tutoring I gave him for free, and all the hours I spent listening to his goals. I was nothing to him, nothing but an employee, nothing but a threat to his new family standing.

Mom slapped Jake's hand off her shoulder. "When you hired Elly, I thought you'd begun to regret your past actions. I thought you wanted to make things up to our family. But it's clear to me that you don't feel the least bit of remorse for what you've done. You won't even allow her to date your wife's brother."

That's when Ethan looked up. "Elly and I aren't dating. We're friends. That's all. Even if I were free to date her, I don't think she'd want me." He looked straight into my eyes when he said it.

I wanted to declare right there in front of Candi that I did want him, that I'd sacrifice my job for him, but there was something in the way he looked at me. He didn't want me to fight it.

Candi opened the passenger side door of her convertible. "There seems to be a misunderstanding. You're all talking as if Ms. Goodwin were an employee. She's a temporary worker. We hired her on a temporary basis to fill a temporary need, and we no longer need her."

Mom, Ethan, and I stood watching as Jake got in the car and drove away from our home. Mom folded her arms. "I think this is God's way of telling us it's time to move on." She patted my shoulder. "You two go for a walk. I'm going to clean up."

I didn't know how to say what I needed to say to Ethan, so I walked toward the park where I used to walk with Dad. Ethan followed me. We walked all the way down our street without saying a word to each other. A block later, I still hadn't figured out how to say it, so I just opened my mouth and let it all come out.

"You didn't have to say all that about how you're not good enough for me. I appreciate you helping me hide things from Candi, but, at this point, it's not going to help."

"I wasn't trying to hide anything," he said, his voice low. "I told them the truth. I'm sorry our friendship cost you your job."

As we passed the house with the metal frog sculptures, Ethan maintained his distance, leaving no chance for our hands to brush. Mom and Maren were right. Ethan had spent way too much time with me for this to be simply a friendship.

I stopped and turned to face him. "Don't feel bad about me losing my job. It was bound to happen. Candi didn't want me there." I waited for Ethan to respond. He didn't. "At least I got to meet you."

He should have looked into my eyes. Instead, he looked straight ahead at the pavement. Maybe I'd read too much into our relationship. I wished he would say something, confirming that my assumptions were either right or wrong. We walked on, crossing the street and sitting on a park bench at the playground. I could smell the eucalyptus trees. Their smell usually energized me. Today it reminded me of cold medicine. "This whole thing with Candi is too much pressure. I'm happy to be friends if that's all you want."

Ethan kept his hands in his pockets. "It's not what I want, Elly, but all I can be is your friend . . . for now." He looked at the sky and groaned. "If I'd known you were going to come along, I wouldn't have—" He let his words hang between us as we watched a child swing back and forth on the swing set.

I let a minute of silence pass before I prodded. "You wouldn't have what?"

He rubbed his hand across his forehead. "I've gotten in over my head with my volunteer work. It's going to take a while to get it all resolved."

I remembered the financial agreement Ethan had made with Candi and Jake. As long as he worked for LibraryStar, they would send money to One-on-One USA. It made sense that Ethan couldn't risk offending his largest supporter, especially if his charity had run into financial troubles. I knew all about financial troubles.

Even so, alarms sounded in my brain—here was another guy making me his second priority. My instincts told me to run for the nearest exit. Ethan frowned, waiting for bad news. That's when I fell right over to the side of commitment. I couldn't give up on him because he needed money. I placed my hand on his. "I think I understand."

His fingers closed around mine. "I'm sorry, Elly."

I rested my head on his shoulder. "All I needed to know is that you'd rather be more than friends."

He pressed his cheek against the top of my head. "It would be easier if you didn't smell so good."

"We could keep it a secret."

He stiffened, releasing my hand and lifting his head. "That wouldn't be fair."

I lifted my head off his shoulder. "It's not fair to let Candi control our lives. You and I deserve to be happy."

Ethan stood up from the bench and combed his hand through his hair. "I'm sorry, Elly." There it was again, the familiar sting of rejection. He kicked a dirt clod as he walked off. It scuttled over the pavement, leaving a dust cloud in its wake.

We walked in silence back to the house. This time, though, it wasn't a comfortable silence. Anger brewed inside me as I wondered how Candi could justify messing up my life again. Just when I'd started to rebuild myself, she had to knock it all down. I didn't have a job anymore. I didn't have a boyfriend. And I didn't have a place to stay. Thanks to Candi, all I had was my family, a twenty-year-old Subaru, and $510,000 in debt.

With each step of my black boot, my temper threatened to boil over. But I knew better. This time, I'd do things the grown-up way. I'd call our lawyer first thing Monday morning and tell him my plans for an intellectual property lawsuit against LibraryStar. Candi was right. I did have a conflict of interest.

Ethan stopped when we got to his rusty Ford. "I wish things could be different."

"Me too." Things would be even more different when Ethan heard about the lawsuit. I couldn't let Jake keep destroying my family.

By the time I walked back inside the house, all the guests had left. I found Mom in the kitchen. She'd cleaned up the dishes from the party and knelt to scrub the grout on the floor. That's what she did when she had to think.

I walked to the other side of the kitchen and went to work on our broken garbage disposal. Like Mom, I had plenty of things to think about, none of which I could mention. I knew she wouldn't like the idea of a lawsuit. If I wanted to talk to the lawyer, I'd have to go on my own.

I wouldn't tell her about my conversation with Ethan either. Knowing Mom, that would worry her more than the lawsuit. Replaying what Ethan had said in my mind, I tried to convince myself that our relationship was nothing like the one I'd had with Jake. But here I was again, getting pushed aside because the guy I loved had a higher priority.

After every bit of grout on the kitchen floor shone lighter and the garbage disposal ran smoothly, Mom called Maren into the kitchen. "Grandma Joan has offered to let us stay with them while we get back on our feet. The more I think about it, the more it makes sense. She needs our help, and we need hers."

Though I'd spent the last half hour analyzing my options, moving across the country hadn't been one of them. I'd thought about moving across the city maybe, but never across the state, much less across the country. We hardly even knew my grandmother.

"You think we should move to Maryland?" Maren asked.

Mom removed her apron. "There are better jobs in Maryland. Today, when I looked, I saw hundreds of openings for designers and programmers. A lot of people there work for the government, and you know how the government never runs out of money."

Mom's decision seemed so out of character that I suspected she might change her mind by the morning, especially considering Maren's depression. Surely Maren's doctor wouldn't want her moving across the country.

Maren sank into one of the kitchen chairs. "We can't leave San Jose. This is our home. Dad is buried here. I couldn't stand to leave his grave. And what about all our friends?"

Mom straightened herself to her full five foot two inches. She puffed out her chest. "You and Elly can decide for yourselves. Grace and I will miss you if you decide not to go, but this is what I'm supposed to do. I've prayed about it all week and talked to Dr. Jenner about it a couple times. She says a change will do us all good."

There was strength in Mom's voice, the kind of strength that came when she bore her testimony in church. Maybe this wouldn't blow over after all.

I went to bed, but I didn't sleep. I thought and prayed. As much as I hated to agree with Mom about moving to Maryland, she was right. If we could live someplace for free, and if I could get a decent job, we might make progress on the $510,000. Of course, if Maren decided to stay in California, I'd stay with her. We couldn't leave her alone after all she'd been through. But I hoped she'd decide to go. I needed a change. I needed to get away from the Cannons, the Ferreros, library software, and men who smelled like sunblock. I needed to move across the country.

15

ELLY

I FELT like I was sneaking around. But I had every right to sneak around. At least that's what I told myself on Monday morning when I walked into LibraryStar. Hoping no one would notice me at my cubicle, I plugged in a flash drive to download the LibraryStar software code. I turned off my screen while it downloaded and then found a box for my things. There wasn't much to pack—three family photographs, two motivational posters, some breath mints, and my orange water bottle. I unpacked and repacked each item over and over again while I waited for the download to finish. To buy more time, I wrote a thank-you note to Stan and put it on his keyboard.

Ethan walked in as I ejected the flash drive. I'd hoped to avoid him. "I'm glad I caught you," he said, dropping his bike helmet on my desk to fumble with his backpack. Why did he have to be so cute when he fumbled? "Remember my roommate, Dave? He's looking for a head programmer at his work. I got his number for you." The way he said this so casually made me suspect he'd agonized over my job loss.

I started to think moving was a bad idea. Until I reminded myself that Ethan, like Jake, had other commitments. "That's sweet of you, Ethan, but I'm not applying for any more jobs in San Jose."

He stopped fumbling. "Why not?"

I slipped the flash drive into my purse. "We're moving to Maryland."

His shoulders dropped. "Oh."

I picked up my box of stuff. "We're going to stay with my grandma for a while."

He reached for the box. "Here, I'll help you with that."

I kept my grip. "It weighs, like, two pounds." I limped toward the parking lot as quickly as my black boot would allow. The longer I stayed around him, the harder this would be.

He hustled along beside me. "I'll, umm . . . get the door for you."

When we reached the door, I pushed it open with my back. " 'Bye, Ethan." Maren was waiting in the Subaru.

Ethan followed me out to the parking lot. "I'll be in DC this summer. Maybe I can drop by and see you at your grandma's."

I opened the back door of my Subaru. "I'm sure Grace would love to see you."

"Just Grace?"

I shoved the box into the car. "As much as I like you, Ethan, I don't think I can handle being friends." I thought of my plan for a lawsuit. "When you find out what I'm going to do, you won't want to see me anyway."

Ethan reached for the handle on the passenger side door. "I'll always want to see you."

This was not what I'd expected after our last conversation. I leaned against the car. "What are we, Ethan?"

"What do you mean?" he asked.

I wouldn't back down. "You know what I mean." This would've been a great time for him to sweep me up in his arms. If he did something like that, I'd stay in San Jose.

He stepped back. "Friends with potential?" If he wanted me to stay, he'd have to fight harder than that. I reached past him, opened the door, and got in the car.

He bent to talk to me. "I'll stop by later to see if you need any help with the move." He waited for my response. When I didn't say anything, he closed the door. So much for clarifying the relationship. He obviously didn't feel as much for me as I did for him. I should have told him not to drop by later. I could handle the move much better if I didn't also have to wonder how he felt.

Maren widened her eyes. "Why didn't you kiss him good-bye?"

I blew out my breath, reminding myself that Maren was in too delicate a state to worry about my problems. "We can go now."

As Maren pulled from the parking lot, I wondered why Ethan felt so reluctant to make a commitment. Was there a bad breakup in his past? If that was the case, our relationship phobias weren't meshing well. I needed more commitment, more clarity. I needed to know he wouldn't leave me.

A "friend with potential" wasn't enough to keep me from talking to the lawyer. "Can you take me to Market Street?" I asked.

Maren flicked the blinker on. "What are you going to do there?"

"Talk to Dad's lawyer."

She turned her eyes from the road to look at me. "You're not going to declare bankruptcy, are you? Dad always said he'd never—"

"No," I interrupted. "It's something else."

Maren sighed. "Everything about our lives is changing."

I forced myself to say something positive—for Maren's benefit. "Change can be a good thing." It felt like a hollow pronouncement. I didn't want anything to change. I would've loved to keep living in our house, working at LibraryStar, and ignoring the fact that Jake had stolen from us. But like it or not, change would come.

Maren waited in the car when we got to the lawyer's office. Located near the freeway in a run-down complex, the office didn't inspire confidence, but I trusted my dad's opinion that Mr. Douglas would take care of us.

I opened the door and greeted the elderly receptionist. "Mr. Douglas got your email," she said. "He's expecting you." She escorted me past the front desk to where Mr. Douglas sat, perusing law books at his desk.

He pushed his reading glasses up on top of his head. "I have thirty minutes. Show me what you've got."

With trembling hands, I laid out all the evidence before him. I'd brought along the software code from Check-It-Out, along with the code I'd downloaded from LibraryStar. I showed him a few programs from LibraryStar that resembled ours.

"If you can come up with some more solid evidence, you might have a case," he said when my half hour ended. "But I have to tell you it'll be a doozy to win. We'll need to hire consultants. It'll be time consuming. And even if we win, LibraryStar likely has ways to protect their assets."

I left his office feeling more nervous than I'd felt when I came. I hadn't considered that Jake might have already protected himself from this kind of lawsuit. Besides that, Dad wouldn't have wanted it. And I could sabotage any future relationship I might have with Ethan. Still, I had to do it.

16

Maren

What was the feeling in the room? Even my medication couldn't disguise it. Tension seeped through us like a poison gas, barely detectable but present all the same. At first, I thought it came from my resentment. I didn't want to leave and, therefore, didn't want to pack. But it wasn't all me. It was also Elly. She wore the expression of a burned-out third-grade teacher. Dark shadows sunk beneath her eyes. When she spoke, she spoke in monotones.

Ethan showed up at dinnertime carrying empty boxes—an obvious excuse to see her. Elly set him to work posting pictures of the living room furniture to sell online. While he did that, she packed boxes in other parts of the house. She acted like she'd decided about the move. She told Mom she'd already started applying for jobs in Maryland, and I knew she had. Yet I'd also caught her looking for apartments in the Bay area. She was more like me than she wanted to admit. I'd felt peace about the move when I prayed last night. This morning, when I woke, the peace had disappeared.

I told Mom and Elly that I hadn't decided about Maryland. But I knew if Elly didn't go, I would. It was an unspoken agreement between Elly and me that one of us would always be there to help with Grace. Mom couldn't handle Grace on her own, especially not if she had to help Grandma too. Grace hated transitions, and this would be the biggest transition of her life. Even now, I could hear her crying in her room, tormented by the thought of selling our furniture.

Crying—I hadn't cried since I'd been in the hospital.

How do you decide what to take and what to leave? I'd pictured us driving across the country with one of those big U-Haul trucks—the biggest one available with a trailer towing a car behind. I thought Mom would take everything important to her—everything we hadn't thrown away. Elly had a different idea—we'd ship the necessities and sell the rest. That was the most economical way. It also happened to be the most heartless way.

After Ethan took a picture of Dad's favorite chair, I marched into the hall, where Elly sorted through our linens. "I hope you're not going to sell Dad's recliner." I didn't care that Ethan stood close enough to witness our discussion.

Elly dropped the towels. "I hadn't thought about the recliner. Maybe we can ship it . . . if we make enough money from selling everything else."

I sunk onto the floor. "Every time I think of selling our things, a little part of me dies."

Elly's brow twisted with sympathy. "I know. I'm sorry."

"If one of us decides not to go to Maryland," I said. "We can keep the recliner for Mom."

Elly swallowed. "Okay."

"I could keep it for you," Ethan offered. It was a sweet gesture, but Elly didn't acknowledge it.

I rolled a towel to put in Elly's box. "How are we supposed to decide what to take and what to leave?"

"We'll take what we can't replace." She pointed to my paintings on the walls. "Like your pictures. And Dad's recliner."

I pointed to Ethan downloading pictures on his laptop. "And what about him? I'm pretty sure he's not replaceable." I meant for Ethan to hear it, and he did. He reminded me of a stray dog, the way he looked at Elly.

Elly kept her eyes on the box of towels she packed. "We'll have to see." She didn't smile when she said it, but Ethan did—after the flash of hurt passed over his face.

The last thing I wanted was for her to feel sorry for me because of the depression. I could handle myself, even if I hadn't done so well in the past. "Do you remember in *The Sound of Music* when Maria finally discovers she's in love with the captain?"

Elly looked up from the box she packed. "Yeah."

"What does the mother superior tell her?"

She rolled her eyes. "She can't use the convent to hide from her problems."

"I'm beginning to think Maryland might be your convent," I said. "You'll move into Grandma's basement, take up needlework, and never touch a man's lips again. I have the feeling you're better off staying here. I'll go to Maryland with Mom and Grace."

Elly laughed. "Thanks for thinking of me, Maren."

I didn't want to go either, but I didn't want to mess up Elly's life by staying here. She already broke her foot because of me. I couldn't make her sacrifice Ethan too.

17

ELLY

MY moving was as much Ethan's decision as it was mine. He was the one who wanted to be friends with potential. He was the one avoiding commitment. Yet, despite his hang-ups, he proved himself irreplaceable during the next three weeks. He helped with our garage sale, lifted furniture, and drove way too many carloads of stuff to the Goodwill store.

"I'm afraid Elly takes you for granted," Maren teased him as we packed the last carload of boxes to ship. We would leave the next day for our cross-country move, and I was finally free from my big black boot.

Ethan shrugged. "She can take me for granted anytime."

Maren raised an eyebrow. "You play the henpecked boyfriend so well. You should make it official." It hadn't done any good to tell Maren what Ethan had said about us being friends. She was still convinced he was in love with me.

I slammed the trunk door down. "You're officially fired from giving us advice, Maren."

Maren lifted her face toward the sky. "Oh, how I'll miss you, California. I'll miss your breezy weather and your open sky." She walked toward the house, talking to the plants as she went. "I'll miss your fig bushes and your peace lilies." For the last few days, she'd seemed like the old Maren, but I wondered how long it would last.

"I don't think you've taken a break in the last three weeks," Ethan said.

I folded my arms. "You haven't either."

He held me by the shoulders. "And you've been avoiding me. Now that your toes are better, we should take a walk on the beach."

A walk on the beach? I didn't have two hours to drive to the beach and back. He must have seen my hesitation because he added, "I'll treat you to dinner while we're at it."

I stepped back so he couldn't touch my shoulders anymore. I already felt vulnerable because of the move. The last thing I needed was to add an ambiguous dinner to the mix. Still, I couldn't say no after he'd spent so much time helping us pack.

After dropping off our stuff at the Goodwill store, we drove to Highway One.

My stomach growled. I felt hungry enough to eat one of those stalks of fennel that grew beside the road. Ethan hadn't said where we would eat. He hadn't said much at all since we'd gotten in the car. It took us an hour to get past all the city traffic and make our way to the coast.

Ethan took the slow, scenic route. Once we got to Highway One, I let the sights soak in—the tall grasses and white sands I wouldn't see again for who knew how long. Everything appeared calm and clear, a direct contrast to what went on inside me.

We chatted off and on about neutral topics—the Sunday School class he had to substitute that week, job applications, the weather.

We drove for another half hour, mostly in silence, before arriving at a restaurant that overlooked San Francisco Bay. It was a white building with stark modern lines. While Ethan tried to find a parking spot, I noticed a line of people snaking from the entrance. "Looks crowded."

"That's okay," Ethan said. "We have a reservation."

A reservation? That meant he'd pre-planned this. Guys don't pre-plan dinners with friends. As my hopes rose, I remembered I'd be leaving the next day, and my hopes crashed back down. Ethan could've taken me on a date weeks ago, but he'd waited until now.

Ethan parked the car. "I wanted to do something special for our last night together."

I stayed in my seat as he walked around to my side. Right before he reached my door, I opened it myself. No way would I fall victim to a last-minute attempt at romance.

As we approached the crowd at the front of the restaurant, he grabbed my hand so we wouldn't get separated. We wove around groups of people, all of whom were dressed better than I was. Even Ethan, wearing an oxford shirt, had outdressed me. That should have made me nervous, but his touch calmed me. So much for keeping my distance.

I expected him to let go of my hand when we got to the front of the line. He didn't. He kept hold while the hostess led us to our table at the farthest corner of the back porch.

I looked across our view of the bay to see the Golden Gate Bridge. Below us, sea lions lay on the rocks in the middle of the surf. "There aren't any sea lions on the East Coast, are there?"

Ethan opened his menu. "No. They have crabs mostly. I'll have to take you to my favorite crab place when I visit."

"What do you do at a crab place? Run around and catch them in Dixie cups?"

He laughed. "It's a restaurant, but we could try the Dixie cup thing too if you want."

I opened my menu. The food wasn't what I'd expect from a guy who drove an old Ford Escort. There were no hamburgers or ribs. I ordered something called scallops with hazelnuts in browned butter. Ethan ordered a seared tuna steak with mango salsa.

"You'll like Maryland," Ethan said as the server walked away with our menus.

I fingered the stem of my water goblet. "I'm more worried about Grace and Maren liking it. You know how Grace is. And Maren's so . . ."

Ethan leaned toward me. "I can put you in touch with some depression support groups there."

I straightened in my chair. "Don't tell me you volunteered at a depression support group."

Ethan gazed out across the bay. "They helped one of my friends from One-on-One USA. Mental illness is a big problem in the military, bigger than most people realize."

"So is your friend better now?" I asked.

He frowned. "I'm more worried about you right now."

My nose tingled, signaling tears were on their way. I took a breath, trying to steady my voice. "I never got this way before Dad died."

Back then, if I had any stress in my life, I'd sit at the kitchen table with him and pour out my problems. How I wished I could still talk to him. I had at least an hour's worth of worries saved up.

Thinking of Dad made the tears spill over. With the tears came words I couldn't hold in any longer. I told Ethan how I'd never driven outside the state of California before, how all our stuff probably wouldn't fit in our cars, and how Grace screamed during long car rides. I told him my worries about finding a job, keeping Maren on her medications, enrolling Grace in a new school, and living with a grandmother I barely knew. Then I told him about the $510,000 debt that hung over our heads.

When our food arrived, Ethan replaced my wet napkin with his own and asked the server to bring him a new one. My tears had stopped by then. The tightness in my chest had loosened. It was almost as if I'd talked to Dad. Ethan had hardly said anything, yet I knew he was on my side. "Thanks for listening."

"Anytime," he said.

I took a bite of my buttery, tender scallops. "This is delicious."

The side of his lip tipped up. "I'll miss the way you tap your feet and hum while you chew your food."

I put down my fork. "I don't hum and tap my feet while I chew my food." He grinned back while I tried not to hum and tap my feet. "Stop watching me."

Only then did Ethan look at his food. While we ate, he told me about his favorite places around Maryland. He described how he'd biked along the C & O Canal, gone sightseeing in Washington, DC, sailed a boat on Chesapeake Bay, and visited Baltimore Harbor. He said he'd like to take me to the Kennedy Center and see a Broadway musical sometime. I listed a few popular musicals, but Ethan didn't seem familiar with any of them. I summarized the stories while we ate the last of our food. Dinner ended far too quickly.

"You don't like musicals, do you?" I asked as he helped me back into his car.

"I like that you like them," he said before shutting the door. I could have asked how many musicals he'd seen in the past, but I left it at that. It was enough that he wanted me to be happy. Jake had never sacrificed his own tastes like that.

We drove back along the coast, stopping to take a walk on the beach. Ethan parked at the top of a cliff edged with yellow wildflowers. As we started our walk, the trail descended so sharply that my feet slipped, and I slid down at least five feet on the seat of my pants. Ethan, who wore sneakers instead of flip-flops, ran to catch up. "Sorry. I should have held onto you."

I got up without grabbing onto the hand he offered. "I didn't do that on purpose."

Ethan reached for my elbow. "I didn't think you did."

I figured it wouldn't hurt to let him hold onto me until we got to the beach. The sand stretched out in wide, rolling hills, littered here and there with charred chunks of driftwood. It felt good to be free of my big, black boot, letting my feet sink into the sand. "Candi's pregnant," Ethan said.

"Oh." I should have expected something like that. After all, she and Jake had been married for two years.

"That explains a lot about the way she treated you," Ethan said. "Don't you think?"

I shrugged. "Maybe." Ethan probably thought telling me this would help me empathize with Candi, but I couldn't help thinking of the injustice of it all. She was married; I wasn't. She had a job; I didn't. And now she would be a mother too.

"It's weird to think of them having children," I said. "If things had been different, it could've been me."

Ethan shook his head. "I can't see you with Jake. He's so . . ."

Cold waves licked at my ankles. Wanting to keep my jeans dry, I headed higher up on the shore, away from the water. "Career driven?"

He chuckled. "That's a tactful way to put it."

I drew arcs in the wet sand with my toe as I walked. "Jake was my biggest mistake. I was so used to being with him that I thought I was in love. I wanted to be in love. Does that make sense?"

Ethan stepped over a strand of seaweed. "You wouldn't believe how much sense that makes to me." I waited while he looked at the ocean, hoping he would open up about his own failed relationships.

After a minute of silence, I prodded. "It's not fair you know so much about my past when I hardly know anything about yours."

Ethan picked up a piece of driftwood and threw it into the waves. The scars from his past must have been more painful than I'd thought. On top of that, he had a control freak for a sister. "Do you think Candi will ease up on you now that she has the baby to distract her?" I asked.

Ethan furrowed his brow. "What do you mean?"

I kept to the edge of the wet sand. "Is she still worried that you're spending time with me? I wouldn't want you to lose your job or the money for your charity."

Ethan walked beside me, his hand occasionally brushing mine. "When you took a job at LibraryStar, Candi thought you wanted to copy our programs or find reasons to sue. She thought you were using me. I told her she's wrong. You're not that kind of person."

He'd barely finished when a big wave swooshed up the beach. Ethan grabbed my hand, and we ran toward drier sand, but not before the wave soaked us to our calves. All I could think, though, was how Ethan said I wasn't the type of person to sue LibraryStar.

He let go of my hand. "I'll be in DC sometime in July," he said. "I have some meetings for One-on-One USA when one of our board members gets back from deployment. That'll take a couple of days. I'll have the rest of the week free. If it's okay, I'd like to take you to some of those places we talked about."

I still thought about the lawsuit, wondering what Ethan would say if I told him about it. "Can I ask you a question?"

Ethan kept his eyes on the sand in front of us. "Sure."

"What if you *were* dating the kind of person who would sue LibraryStar?" The conversation distracted me so much that I didn't notice another big wave coming. This one soaked me in icy water to my knees.

I walked up the shore and sat on the dry sand to roll up my jeans. Ethan sat beside me. "I'm *not* dating the type of person who would sue LibraryStar. I don't care what Candi thinks anyway."

Wind chilled my wet skin. I hugged my knees to my chest to keep from shivering. "If you don't care what Candi thinks, then why did you wait until the day before I left to take me to a nice restaurant?"

Ethan leaned back on his arms, extending his legs in front of him. "I just wanted to do something special before you left."

His answer seemed too safe, considering how much time we'd spent together. I stood up. "Would you have taken me to that restaurant if I was going to stay?"

He squinted at me in that way guys do when they don't quite understand.

I elaborated. "You told me we couldn't get involved because you were in over your head with your volunteer commitments. But now you say you don't care what Candi thinks."

He rose to his feet. "I *am* in over my head with my volunteer commitments."

"Why should that make any difference to us?" I put my hands on my hips. "You know what this whole volunteer thing is about? Guilt. It's you feeling guilty that you can't serve your country. It's not helping anyone, Ethan."

I turned to walk back the way we'd come. I liked Ethan. Who was I kidding? I loved him. And I'd destroyed a nice evening.

I didn't hear Ethan coming up behind me. That's the way it was with sand. He appeared at my left side without any warning. We walked together without either one of us saying anything until we headed toward the cliffs. "Can you listen to me for a minute?" he asked.

I stopped.

He stood with his hands in his pockets. "The volunteer work isn't a hobby for me. It's life and death. Those soldiers need someone to care about them. It gives them a reason to live. I can't quit on them."

I looked to the waves rolling beside us. "I don't see how that has anything to do with us." All this talk about his volunteer work was an excuse.

He came closer, close enough that we almost touched. His face was inches from mine. His chest. His lips. His breath warmed the tip of my nose. If I'd wobbled a bit, I could've closed the gap, but I stood still, looking up into his eyes.

"Will you let me take you to the Kennedy Center in July?" he asked.

Stepping back, I folded my arms. "Only if we bring Grace." What I'd really said was: *Go ahead and reject me.* He wouldn't want to take Grace to the Kennedy Center.

He didn't skip a beat. "Then it's a date."

18

What was it about moving that made our house seem like a tomb, sterile and rigid around us? The blank walls mocked me, letting sounds echo metallically through the empty rooms. Everything seemed too plain, too white, and too clean. The air even smelled different—something like cardboard and window cleaner.

Mom bought chocolate Pop-Tarts in honor of our last breakfast at home. She'd forgotten, though, that we'd already sold the toaster. I ran a finger across my Pop-Tart's smooth glaze while Grace choked hers down, breaking off pieces in chunks. While we ate, Elly told me about her date with Ethan. I didn't say anything until she got to the end.

"He took you out for a romantic dinner and a walk on the beach. Why didn't you kiss him?"

Elly chipped the frosting off her Pop-Tart with a knife. "He's not ready. It's like I told you."

I leaned across the table toward her. "Are you going to kiss him this morning?"

She shook her head. "I don't think he'll be here. He calls his military friends every morning."

"Then why is he outside, waiting in his car?" I leaned back and bit into my Pop-Tart. Its hard, frosted exterior reminded me of linoleum.

Elly peeked around the kitchen corner to peer out the front window. "I can't believe he skipped his morning calls." She bit her lip. "I know he cares about me, but after all he's told me, it wouldn't make sense to kiss him."

"Does everything have to make sense?"

Elly gave me that look of hers. The one that reminded me I was the younger sister, the one who'd recently spent a week in the psychiatric ward. "Why do you care so much about it?"

Was it so wrong to care about my sister's love life? "Because I can see you have a chance at love, and you're refusing to take it."

Elly held her Pop-Tart halfway between her mouth and the table, probably thinking.

"If you kiss him, you'll know how he feels. That makes sense, doesn't it?" I prodded.

She wobbled her head from side to side. "I *would* like to know how he feels."

Ethan hung around like a store security agent while we jammed the last few things into the van and the Subaru. When Mom and Grace got in the van, he stood with his hands in his pockets, looking at Elly.

" 'Bye, Ethan," I said, sitting in the driver's seat of the Subaru with the door open. Elly was going to drive with me in the Subaru for the first leg of the journey.

"I'm glad you came this morning," Elly told him, staring at his lips. "It means a lot." She clasped his forearms, pulling him toward her.

Ethan held onto her arms, moving closer to her. "You've got my number, right?"

"You might regret that I have it," Elly said. "I'll call you too much." Then she did it. She threw her arms around his neck and aimed for his lips.

I felt like a peeping Tom, watching a love scene gone wrong. He kept his eyes open, struggling to act out his part. His arms moved around her tentatively. Then he closed his eyes and pulled her closer, finally proving his passion. At the same moment, Elly pushed away. It was done.

Elly's face burned crimson. So did Ethan's. I entered our destination into the GPS navigator to avoid looking at them. Maybe I'd been wrong about Elly needing to kiss him. And wrong about Ethan's feelings.

When Mom started her engine, they kept on talking. Ethan waited until Mom pulled the van out of the driveway before he opened the passenger door for Elly. He bent to wave good-bye to me. "Stay safe."

Elly must have told him something about my driving style. "I've never been in an accident," I said, hitting my fuzzy dice so they swung from the rearview mirror.

Ethan shut the door and then watched as we drove off.

Elly turned down the volume on the stereo. "He didn't want to kiss me."

What could I say to that? She was right. I saw it myself. "Of course he wanted to kiss you. If he didn't, he would have stepped back."

Elly touched the side of her face. "He didn't have any trouble once we got started." She sighed. "It was the hesitation at the beginning that bugs me."

Driving down our street for the last time, I sensed the weight of Elly's disappointment. I wished I could have felt our losses more fully—to really mourn that we had to leave—but Elly needed me to stay positive. "Take some advice from Dr. Jenner," I said, "and focus on what went right. Don't tell me you didn't enjoy any of it."

Elly stayed quiet for a while before she spoke again. "This is exactly why I need to leave. I can't keep loving him this much when he hasn't made up his mind."

I shook my head. "Stop being so logical. We all know he loves you." I turned up the music as we drove through our subdivision for the last time. It was music Dr. Jenner would approve of—fast and furious, meant to keep us awake through the long drive and rev up our spirits. My spirits needed plenty of revving. With every rotation of the tires, I wanted to turn back. The problem was there was nothing to turn back to. We no longer owned our beautiful house with the terracotta tile roof.

Dr. Jenner said I should view this as a new adventure. One part of me knew she was right. Months of depression had done nothing for my social life in San Jose. Though my friends had forgiven me for ignoring their calls and for the careless things I'd said, I could never get back the trust we'd had before. I'd still have my friends in San Jose, but moving gave me the possibility to meet new friends who couldn't judge me by my past.

I'd also given up hope of finding a design job in California. The Washington, DC, area would at least have different opportunities for art majors. In a way, it was like traveling. I wouldn't be building a school in South America or digging a well in Africa, but I hoped I could find an opportunity for service. Most of all, I hoped the change in scenery would motivate me to paint again. I could almost feel the paintbrush in my hands as I imagined the scenes ahead of us—the Eastern mountains, soft and worn, the swollen rivers, and the plants growing outside their bounds. As much as I wanted to stay in my home, I longed to paint what I'd yet to discover. I longed for something new.

19

ELLY

THERE was only so much bonding I could do with my sisters. Sure, it was fun the first day to sit and talk. We'd been so busy packing that to do nothing was a relief. But I wasn't like Maren, who could look out the window and imagine painting the scene. I missed my to-do list. Sitting for hours seemed like such a waste of time when I could've been applying for jobs.

Driving with Grace was the hardest. She'd taken to sleeping in the car and staying awake at the hotel. As long as the stereo played music from *Joseph and the Amazing Technicolor Dreamcoat*, she slept peacefully on Dad's old pillow. She'd brought a little collection of Dad's things in the car—a blue silk tie, a bathrobe, and Old Spice deodorant that warranted front seat status.

As we drove through the flat plains of Kansas, I couldn't stand it any longer. I plugged my iPod into the stereo and let the local bands of San Jose take over the airwaves. Grace woke up right away. Before she had a chance to complain, I pointed out a red splotch on the windshield. "I think that's a mosquito."

"No," she said. "It's a mayfly."

I pointed to a green splotch. "How about that one? What's that?"

Grace leaned closer to the windshield. "Maybe a stink bug. Dad would know what it was, wouldn't he?"

I laughed. "We'd need a bug expert to tell what that was."

She hugged Dad's pillow to her chest. "You could marry a bug expert."

"Or *you* could marry a bug expert," I said. "Better yet, you could go to school and become one yourself."

Grace ran her finger from one bug to another, as if doing a dot-to-dot. She connected about twenty bugs before she spoke again. "Do people like me get married?"

Even at fifteen, Grace was so much like a child. I doubted she'd ever be mature enough to marry, but I couldn't tell her that. I squeezed her hand. "Sure, people like you get married. The tricky part is finding someone who's good enough for you."

I'd once thought Jake was good enough. My life had revolved around him. My goals, my career, my friends, the clothes I wore, and the places I went to all centered on Jake. Talk about stupid! After our break-up, I had to build myself a whole new reality. For years afterward, marriage wasn't part of my plan. Partly because I didn't trust myself to love anyone else, and partly because I didn't trust anyone else to love me.

"What do you mean, good enough?" Grace asked.

I had to think carefully to put it into words Grace would understand. "I mean, he should treat you the way Dad treated you. If he tries to hurt you or hurt your feelings, that means he's not good enough."

Grace got out her notebook and wrote what I'd said, asking me how to spell *treat* and *feelings*.

Together we listed the requirements for Grace's future husband. I couldn't help thinking of Ethan while we made the list. After our discussion about lawsuits and our disastrous good-bye kiss, I'd wanted to move to the other side of the country and forget about him. But he called me that first night and the second night and the third night. He couldn't forget me any more than I could forget him.

After I'd broken up with Jake, I wrote a software application—a sort of questionnaire—to make sure the guys I dated met my requirements. I saw the program every time I opened my laptop. At the time I wrote it, Maren had called me *stringent*. "You'll never meet someone that perfect." That was the point. I didn't want to date again.

I knew the questions by heart because I'd used them to eliminate every guy who attended our singles ward in San Jose. In my head, I ticked off the requirements—Ethan had a job, a degree, a temple recommend, and a calling at church (ward clerk). He also knew how to fix things and got along with every member of my family. He never answered his phone in my presence (unless his mother called). So far, he'd understood most of the words that came out of my mouth. And, last but not least, he knew how to sew. (He'd mended a hole in our sofa before he put it up for sale.)

I considered adding a few new qualifications—maybe something about playing a musical instrument or owning real estate property—but it was no use. Ethan had already qualified.

Still, I heard his words in my head: *I'm not dating the type of person who would sue LibraryStar.*

"There's one more thing you should avoid," I told Grace. "Long distance relationships."

For now, I liked talking to Ethan every night. We laughed about Grace's antics and compared notes on our cross-country road trips. But I could see how our lives could become so separate that there would be nothing to talk about. That's what had happened with every other long-distance relationship I'd had—I hadn't kept in touch with my friends from high school any more than I'd kept in touch with my Grandma Goodwin.

I wondered how it would be to see Grandma again. Would I feel the same bond we'd shared when I visited as a little girl? Or would our relationship feel just as distant as it'd felt when we lived 2,500 miles away?

20

Maren

Was this what we came all the way across the country for? As a child, I'd thought Grandma's house seemed like a forest castle. Now, I saw a house overgrown and run-down. Ivy and moss crept up the brick walls. Any artist knew the importance of blank space—a place for the eye to rest. Here there was no blank space. Overgrown plants and discarded objects cluttered the yard and front porch. Instead of grass, Grandma's yard sprouted dandelions, moss, clover, and little star-shaped white flowers.

Four dogs ran to us as we opened the gate, jumping up to rest their scratchy claws on our legs. They were all black—a poodle, two Labrador mixes, and something that looked like a miniature Doberman. Grandma hobbled out with her walker to greet us.

I could have painted her petite form there, standing on the front porch with her auburn hair. She wore a purple tunic over white pants. A multicolored string of beads—lime green, lemon yellow, and tangerine orange—hung around her neck.

"You don't know how happy I am to have you," she called from the porch. "This is a dream come true to have family under my roof again."

After we all hugged Grandma, the dogs followed us inside, where it became obvious that Grandma hadn't moved around much for the past several months, or maybe even years. In order to sit on the couch, we had to move a pile of laundry. Stacks of mail, magazines, and newspapers toppled from every flat surface. Chaos assaulted my senses from every direction.

"I have jobs lined up for Maren and Elly," she said. "A little something to earn money while you're looking for more suitable work."

I watched a green parakeet fly in from the other room and land on

Grandma's head. I tried not to wonder where the bird might have left its droppings.

"What kind of jobs?" I asked.

"You'll be working at my friend Colton Bradshaw's dairy store. He needs someone to man the counter and serve ice cream cones—that sort of thing. It's best if there are two of you there during the afternoons and evenings. He doesn't mind if you bring your laptops to apply for jobs during the slow times."

An ice cream shop? That didn't sound bad.

"That sounds great," Elly said.

Grandma patted Elly's knee. "I think you'll like Colton. I've been hoping to find the right woman for him."

Elly's feet tapped and shuffled as she sat on the couch.

"Elly already has a boyfriend," Mom said, sitting as straight and tall as a queen on Grandma's flowered sofa.

Grace held her stomach. "I'm hungry."

Grandma looked at her watch. "Darned if it isn't lunchtime. Will one of you girls do me a favor and put some frozen pizzas in the oven?"

I volunteered. It wasn't hard to find my way to the kitchen—that was the only room in the house that seemed the same as I remembered it. Stepping into it was like stepping back in time to my father's childhood. The shuttered windows, chrome accents, and rich autumn colors would have made a great background for a period piece.

Opening the freezer at the top of Grandma's harvest-gold refrigerator, I found three gluten-free, dairy-free frozen pizzas. My hopes plummeted. I walked back into the living room with the boxes. "Are these the pizzas you want me to cook?"

Grandma's lips stretched to an open-mouthed smile. "Those are the ones: gluten-free and dairy-free for Grace's benefit."

Five years earlier, my parents had put Grace on a special diet in the hopes that it'd cure her autism. All it did was make Grace ten pounds thinner. I could still feel the gritty texture of rice flour at the back of my throat and picture the pasty white color of the bread in my mind.

Mom's nostrils flared. "That's sweet of you, Joan, but Grace isn't on any special diet."

Grandma picked up her littlest dog, the one that looked like a dwarf Doberman. "Well, it can't hurt."

I wanted to tell her that yes, it could, but Elly spoke first. "We appreciate you taking us in, Grandma, and getting food for us."

"Oh, you're so welcome, dear. What are families for?" Grandma grabbed her walker and stood up. "You ought to go down and look at your rooms before you bring in your things. I'm sorry I haven't done as much rearranging down there as I'd hoped." We followed her through the kitchen to the staircase. "You go on down while I call my friend Colton to help you bring everything in. He's the one I told you about that owns the dairy farm."

I turned on the oven and unwrapped the pizzas. Then I followed the others down to our rooms. The maple wood stairs creaked as we descended with Elly in the lead. I heard her gasp as she opened the door and peered into the basement. The door wouldn't open all the way, so we had to crowd together to see what made her gasp.

Stuff crammed the room in front of us from floor to ceiling. There was a trunk here, a birdcage there, and boxes stacked on every side. To our right stood a bookshelf full of old magazines. To our left sat an old bathtub packed with empty canning jars. A stack of flowerpots rested behind the door. I was grateful, for once, that I couldn't feel the emotions Mom and Elly felt at that moment. I needed the blank space, even if it was only inside my head.

Mom stepped over a rolled-up rug on the floor. "The bedrooms are this way."

We followed her sideways through a narrow hallway lined on both sides with Rubbermaid totes. She opened a door and switched on a light to reveal the first bedroom. Inside, a queen-sized water bed crowded the room. The closet held an assortment of vintage clothing while cardboard boxes covered the floor.

"I'm sure Grandma won't mind if we make space for our things," Mom said.

Grace bounced up and down on the edge of the water bed. "I want to sleep with Mom on this bed."

Since Grace had made up her mind, Elly and I went to look at the other room, which had two twin beds with white metal frames, a marble-topped bed stand, and twin blue-glass lamps.

Even with the medication watering down my emotions, it was love at first sight for me—the only hopeful thing I'd felt since catching my first glimpse of Grandma's house. I grasped onto the emotion as if it were a rescue line. "This furniture is perfect for shabby chic style."

Grandma's friend Colton stood ready to meet us when we climbed back upstairs. Colton was a man who hid sadness behind his smile. He had wavy light-brown hair and looked to be at least thirty years old. A sprinkle of gray at his temples reminded me that he would be our new employer.

How could Grandma think it was a good idea to have our new employer help unload the cars? Everyone knew employers judged employees by their cars. A messy car meant a sloppy, unorganized worker; a clean car meant dependability. In this case, Colton would discover more about our lives than I ever wanted to reveal—things like my depression self-help books, my penchant for wearing red underwear, a bag of medicines for my sensitive stomach, and the ashes of our cat Butch.

On top of all of that lay my stack of canvases. I found Colton looking at my Cézanne imitation. "Who's the artist?" he asked when I approached.

"Me."

"This is good." He looked from me to the painting. "It reminds me of Cézanne."

How would he know that? Did men in the East know more about art than the men out West did? I didn't want to encourage him, but Elly couldn't help it. "I can't believe you figured that out. Most people have never heard of Cézanne."

I stood beside Colton, picking up my paints that had fallen out of their box.

Grandma sat watching in a kitchen chair on the front porch. "Elly is going to be disappointed in love again. See there. Colton's already chosen Maren instead."

Why did old people always say things loud enough for you to hear when they talked behind your back?

Colton's neck seemed unusually rosy as he bent to grab the tube of cerulean blue paint that had fallen into a crevice between the van's seats. "These are almost used up," he said.

Grandma went on talking to Mom. "I knew he would fall in love with my granddaughter. My only error was which one."

I turned to glare at Grandma. She smiled and waved. "She is a beautiful girl, but she's a bit of a shrinking violet, isn't she? She takes after Henry that way. He never talked much."

Living here would cost more than I'd realized, at least in terms of my dignity.

21

ELLY

I THOUGHT the distance would help me forget Ethan. It didn't. Everything reminded me of him—the way Grace called Grandma's black Lab "Sandy," the broken clock in the hallway that called out for a repair, and a can of crabmeat in the kitchen. Even Colton, in his own way, reminded me of Ethan. I couldn't help comparing the two. Like Ethan, Colton was quiet.

I'd never seen a man eat so little as Colton did at that meal. He served himself one-sixteenth slice of gluten-free pizza, which he chewed slowly. Then he downed a quarter glass of soy milk in one swallow.

After we'd all finished, he placed his plate and cup in the sink. "Dinner was wonderful. Thank you for having me." Like Ethan, he was polite.

"Don't leave so soon," Grandma said, eyeing the uneaten pizza on Grace's plate. "The girls are expecting a tour of your farm and store."

Grace hopped out of her seat. I glanced at my watch, automatically subtracting three hours. Ethan still had another few hours of work. I had time to go out before he called.

"Now, Colton," Grandma said, "make sure you get Grace some dairy-free ice cream. You have that, don't you?"

"Uh," Colton stammered.

"I'll make sure she gets something she can eat," Maren said, following Grace toward the front door.

"On second thought, why don't we all go?" Grandma said. "Paula and I'll go in my Cadillac. The girls can go with Colton."

Grandma didn't have room in her garage for her Cadillac. She kept it covered with a blue tarp at the end of her long, asphalt driveway. After we helped take the tarp off, Grandma made sure Maren and I got in Colton's Toyota truck.

Normally, Maren would've carried the conversation as we drove down the lane, but, thanks to Grandma's attempt at matchmaking, I was on my own. I struggled through a conversation about gas mileage as the woods passed by on either side. How I missed driving in silence with Ethan.

It was a good thing the dairy was only five minutes away. Soon the woods opened to fields. Maren drew in her breath at the sight of them. "It's as green as Ireland."

Colton grinned. "Welcome to Honey Hills."

Here and there, brown cows wandered. "Is this your dairy?" I asked. It was different from the crowded pens of cows I'd imagined.

We rolled over a few more hills before the dairy store appeared in the middle of the fields. It was a new building with overhanging eaves and shuttered windows. A painted sign on the roof read, "Honey Hills Organic Dairy." I looked at Maren when I saw the word *organic*, but she didn't seem to have noticed.

From Grandma's description, I expected an ice cream parlor, but this was more of a country store with displays of local crafts and a refrigerated case full of milk products. On the left-hand side of the store stood a curved glass case with tubs of ice cream for scooping. A blackboard on the wall listed the available flavors.

Colton introduced us to the teenage girl behind the counter, explaining that she would be leaving the next week. "I'm looking for a couple of new employees if you're interested. We get pretty busy here in the summer."

"We're definitely interested," I said. Maren didn't say anything, but I knew she'd like working there. Selling organic ice cream while operating a craft boutique—how could she not like that?

There weren't any tables. Instead, Colton kept a stack of tied quilts for customers to spread on the lawn outside. And there wasn't any nondairy ice cream. Relieved, Grace only took a second to decide what she'd have. She always picked pink—the pinker the better. I chose mango. Mom and Maren tasted samples and asked the clerk about her favorite while Grace and I wandered outside to the lawn with Colton.

A patch of medium-height soft grass divided the pasture from the store and its parking lot. Beside us, a small, brown cow grazed beside the fence. Around her neck hung a copper bell that rang softly as she moved. Grace walked to her.

"This is Guinevere," Colton explained. "She's my pet, follows me all over the place. I raised her from the time she was a few days old."

I reached to touch the bell around her neck. "I don't remember ever seeing a cow with a bell, except in cartoons."

Colton grabbed a handful of long grass and held it for Guinevere to eat. "The bells help me keep track of them."

I listened to the bells as Maren came outside with a dark chocolate ice cream cone. There was something soothing about the sounds traveling over the pasture, something almost musical. Maren paused beside us. "Those bells are tuned to the key of F, aren't they?"

Colton opened his mouth to speak, but nothing came out.

"Is she right?" I asked.

When Colton spoke, his words came out carefully measured. "In all the years I've made these bells, you're only the second to recognize that they're tuned to the key of F."

Maren stroked the cow's nose. "She's beautiful. She's the color of rich caramel. Look at her long eyelashes and her big, glassy eyes."

Behind us, Grandma spoke to Mom in one of her stage whispers. "Colton's wife left him a little after he opened the store. It's been—let's see—two or three years now. I think Maren can help him get over it."

Colton stared at the cow's face in a distant way, his lips tight.

"When would you like us to start work?" I asked.

He took a while to reply, as if he had to first exit a room in his memory. "Whenever you're ready. I'm flexible." The way his eyes traveled along Maren's face, I could tell Grandma was right. He liked Maren. And he was bound to be disappointed.

Maren sighed. "I hate it when old people decide to play matchmaker. How could it possibly make anyone feel better to have their grandma arrange their social life?"

Her words startled me, and I worried, once again, that she couldn't handle this new situation. Maybe Mom was wrong about the change being good for her depression.

Colton gave a half smile. "She means well."

My phone rang. I walked a few steps away from the others to answer it. “Other than yellow roses,” Ethan said, “how do you let a woman know you only want to be friends?”

I couldn’t tell whether he was teasing. “Stop calling her while you’re supposed to be working. That makes it seem like you can’t stop thinking about her.”

He paused. “I’m not talking about you.”

I licked a drip off the side of my cone. “Who are you talking about then?”

He didn’t answer.

“Don’t tell me it’s that Brenda from Human Resources.” I could see her hanging over his desk in one of her low-cut blouses. “You could burp a lot or grow a mustache.”

He laughed. “A mustache?”

“A long, shaggy one.”

“I could do that.”

I took a few bites of ice cream before I decided to come out and say it. “Why can’t you tell her the same thing you told me about your volunteer work?”

“That was different.”

“How?”

He took so long to answer that I wondered if we’d been disconnected. “I’m not a player, Elly. I only have room in my heart for one woman.”

“Then tell her about me.” After I said it, I wondered how I was so bold to assume I was the *one woman* in his heart.

He responded immediately. “I don’t know, Elly.”

I walked along the gravel drive that circled around to the back of the dairy store. “Why not? It’s not like I work there anymore.”

“It’s not Brenda.” He paused again. “This woman is much more insecure.”

I licked another drip off my cone before it got to my hand. “It sounds like you need to be more direct. Tell her you’re not interested.”

He sighed. “I was afraid you’d say that.” I wondered, once again, why it was so hard for Ethan to express his emotions. It seemed to cause problems not just in his relationship with me, but also in his relationships with other women. It seemed about time for him to fix that problem in himself.

22

Maren

Have you ever gone on a pioneer trek? Grace wanted to go, and she needed a chaperone. I knew Elly couldn't go four days without Ethan's phone calls, so I became the sacrificial maiden in pioneer garb. I told myself it would be good for me to learn about the pioneers. It would teach me gratitude, and I could feed my soul on the beauties of nature.

The trek started three days after we arrived at Grandma's house, and, as usual, we had no money. Grace and I had to dress in whatever clothes we could find. She wore a black-and-white striped maxi skirt with a long-sleeved T-shirt. I wore Mom's white button-up oxford over a color-infused maxi dress that went from midnight blue to indigo. Most of the other girls had labored on their outfits for months. Grace and I drifted in a sea of sweeping skirts and subtle hues. I'm afraid we ruined the whole aesthetic with our 1970s-inspired fashion.

We met at an orchard owned by a member of Grandma's stake. Even I could see that the place was run-down—everything wore the gnarled look of old age. Weeds grew thick and tall around overgrown apple trees.

As we pulled the handcart, weeds clung to my skirt, snagging the fabric. Grace walked on my right side, clinging to my arm and forcing me to pull her along with the handcart. She shrieked as the weeds brushed against her legs.

Five people shared each handcart. Our group was all girls. Two of us pulled while three pushed from behind. I looked around for a man I could convince to join our cart. There weren't any single men my age.

Colton was the youngest male leader—and the only single one, from what I could tell. The girl beside me explained that he was in charge of repairing the handcarts. As we crossed through the pasture, he worked his way back to ours, which trailed behind all the others.

As he sprayed lubricant on our axle, I asked, "Aren't you worried leaving Elly alone on her first day at the store?"

"Should I be?"

With the handcart stopped, I looked at my palms, already scarlet from pulling on the handle. "No. Elly's very responsible."

Colton took a pair of work gloves from his backpack and handed them to me. "I brought an extra pair."

I slipped my hands into the loose leather gloves. "Thank you."

"Let's see if the wheels turn better now." He pushed against the back of the handcart. Our cart rolled more easily over the rough ground now, but I didn't know whether that was because of the lubricant or because Colton helped push. "My manager's there to help Elly," he said. "But I'll call her if it makes you more comfortable."

I turned to look back at him. "I thought we weren't allowed to bring phones on the trek."

He stifled a smile. "The youth can't."

I tipped my head toward the sky. "You mean the leaders can bring phones? I wish I'd known that. Elly could've come instead of me. She's better at camping."

He chuckled. "But not better at giving up her phone."

I pushed against the handle, tugging the handcart and Grace up a hill. "Elly has a boyfriend in California. They call each other constantly . . . It shouldn't affect her work, though."

Grace held up four fingers. "Ethan is coming to visit in four weeks. Elly has to clean the house."

Colton's eyes widened. "That's a lot of cleaning." He was right. Cleaning Grandma's house was more work than one person could accomplish in a year. But Elly's clean-up effort was more of a countdown—her way to cope with missing Ethan more than she wanted to admit.

I drew in my breath as we pushed up the hill. "She has a whole lifetime of possessions." I had to take another breath. "And she's attached to all of them." It was embarrassing how out of shape I felt. "I can understand how she feels," I huffed. "I had to sell most of my treasures before we moved here."

"Her house wasn't always that way," Colton said. "It's gone downhill since she started having knee problems." He wasn't out of breath at all. "I can help with the yard and hauling away trash if she'll let me."

The way he said "if she'll let me" made me think Grandma had refused his help in the past. "Thank you," I said.

Before we crested the hill, Grace sat down in the weeds. The other girls stood around her, taking sips from their water bottles. They assumed Grace had taken a little break. They didn't know what I knew: that she'd finished her hike. I thought out a prayer of desperation as Grace rocked back and forth.

Colton searched my face. "She can ride if that works better," he whispered. "I'll help pull." He went to work rearranging items in the handcart.

"Thank you." It was a good idea, but how would I get her in the cart? I couldn't pick her up. She had to get in willingly or she wouldn't stay in.

That's when a miracle occurred. The girls started singing. As the words of "On My Own" from *Les Mis* filled the air, I joined in. So did Grace. When we finished that song, the girls started on "Popular" from *Wicked*. I stepped toward Colton. "Can you help me lift her into the cart?"

He didn't wait for my assistance. He gathered Grace in a cradle hold and placed her in the cart. Grace smiled as Colton stepped behind the handle. I took my place beside him. "I hope the singing isn't driving you crazy."

"I don't mind," he said. To prove it, he suggested the next song—"Seize the Day" from *Newsies*—and sang along in a soft baritone. It wasn't the type of song an average man would know by heart, but he sang every word.

I looked at him, the unspoken question hanging between us. "My ex-wife," he explained. "She loved musicals."

He returned to singing. What had happened between Colton and his ex-wife? It seemed to me that divorce was most often the husband's fault, yet the fact that he'd learned those songs suggested he might have been a decent husband.

I felt the edge of pity for him—as much as I could feel with the medicine in my system. I pitied him the way I'd pity an amputee. A man could fall in love in that head-over-heels way only once. Every other relationship would be tainted by its memory. Dating a divorced man was not for me. Colton seemed too old anyway. I didn't want to become his midlife crisis.

We went along all morning, singing, pushing, and pulling. As the sun rose, the air grew heavier and hotter. My sweat stuck to my skin like grease on a grilled burger. Increased sweating was a side effect of my antidepressant, as was lethargy, and I definitely felt lethargic. My hands swelled and blistered inside the gloves Colton had given me. The skin on my legs grew raw. By lunchtime, I felt as if I'd run a marathon through a briar patch.

I craved a sandwich and a cool piece of fruit. Instead, I got hot beans and biscuits. The woman slopping out beans from the Dutch oven told me that, to preserve the authenticity of the experience, beans were on the menu for every single day of the trek. That meant four more days of beans to look forward to. We'd eaten beans for months after Dad died—beans and rice, bean soup, baked beans. I didn't want to eat beans ever again. Instead, I would feast on the beauties of nature.

I grabbed a few biscuits and sat by the creek, sketching the bugs that skimmed along the water's surface. If I'd brought my watercolors, I'd have pulled out burnt umber and burnt sienna for the colors of the creek with highlights of cerulean blue. The woods blended contradictions—new life sprouting from dead logs, fuzzy moss growing on smooth rock, and slippery mud oozing next to rough bark. I studied the trees, imagining how I'd paint them. Trees weren't easy. Like water, they twisted in unpredictable directions.

Colton stood a few feet upstream, casting with a fly-fishing rod. "If you ever want to sell your artwork, Maren, there's space in my store."

I put down my pencil. "I don't sell my work."

Colton took his eyes from the creek to look at me. "You should. You're talented."

"I could never use my art for profit."

I thought that was the end of the conversation. Colton cast out his line again, and I returned to sketching the water bug. "What do you want to do with your art?" he asked.

I considered changing the subject, but he seemed like the type of person who could understand. "I'd like to paint for cancer patients . . . as a service, not for money." I didn't tell him I hadn't painted since Dad died.

A group of teens jumped into the water upstream, and Colton stepped closer to me. "I remember wishing there was better art in the hospital when I stayed there with my mom."

"Is your mom . . ." There was no right way to ask the question.

Colton let his fishing line rest on the water. "She passed away two years ago."

"I'm sorry," I said.

"Have you tried donating your art to a hospital?" he asked.

I nodded. "Because of the fire codes, my paintings could never be a permanent part of a hospital room. I can only donate to individual patients."

"Is there anything I can do to help you get started?" he asked. "I could donate supplies."

Not wanting to give Colton the wrong idea about our relationship, I closed my sketchbook. "That's sweet of you to offer, but I'd rather do it on my own." I got up from the rock I sat on. "I need to find Grace."

Grace sat by herself next to our handcart, eating the last of her baked beans. Luckily, beans ranked among her favorite foods. One of the leaders came along, passing out water bottles. I took one for Grace and one for myself. I felt thirsty enough to drink the whole thing in one sitting, but I remembered the bathroom situation—Port-A-Potties. I made sure Grace drank, but it was my goal to drink as little as possible. I'd take a few sips every hour. For me, the trek was about feeding my soul, not my body.

23

ELLY

I'D always thought I could write an app for anything. Well, apparently not for Grandma's clutter. Old newspapers filled half of the boxes in our bedroom. Not that I don't like to read the newspaper, but stacks of them from 2003, 1998, and 1986? Grandma said she couldn't discard them without going through each newspaper, page by page, to make sure she didn't want to keep any of the articles. So much for reading online. Meanwhile, more newspapers came every day—she subscribed to three—and I slept beside my clothes every night. Sweaters, jeans, T-shirts, dresses, and underwear all fought for space on my twin mattress.

I could deal with the clutter if it weren't for other things. There was the matter of Mom's allergies. Ever since we'd arrived, she'd been sneezing. She was allergic to cats, and Grandma had at least four.

"It's not a problem, Elly," Mom said when I pointed to her bloodshot eyes one morning. "I've started some medicine. It takes a few days to kick in." Her new catering job started that afternoon.

We sat on the front porch, not on Grandma's wooden benches, but on a couple of Rubbermaid totes. A collection of vinyl records occupied the benches.

"What about Grace?" I whispered. "We can't keep her on that diet." All our groceries sat in bags and coolers in Mom's bedroom because there wasn't room in the kitchen.

Mom stood. "Be grateful we have a place to stay and that we have jobs." She walked back through the front door. I had ten minutes before I had to leave for work, but what I needed was to dance.

If I could've only remembered where I'd left my tap shoes. I searched through the piles and boxes in my bedroom with no luck. It was only after I'd left for work that I remembered—I'd crammed them under the passenger seat of the car. After I pulled into the dairy store parking lot, I pulled them out and brought them into the store with me. Not that I planned on tapping at work.

As I stocked the shelves, I couldn't help thinking it was a great place for tap dancing. No one could hear me. Customers were sparse on weekday mornings, and I was the only employee.

Trying to distract myself from the temptation, I texted Ethan, asking him to call. It was 7:30 a.m. in California, and he would've been finishing his daily calls to servicemen. Five minutes later, my phone rang. "What's up?" Ethan asked.

I told him about the problems with Grandma's clutter and Mom's allergies. Then I confessed that every night for the past month, even while we packed to move, I'd applied for jobs in Maryland and DC. I'd applied for over fifty jobs, yet I hadn't received any response. My mom had gotten two job offers before we even arrived. I began to wonder if the only reason I'd ever had a job was because I'd worked for my father.

The fact that Ethan would be late for work didn't stop me from talking. I vented for a full ten minutes while Ethan reassured me that I was qualified to work anywhere. After I started to feel better, I asked how he was doing.

He groaned. "I'm having trouble with one of my soldier friends. I wish I could tell you about it."

"Why can't you tell me?"

"I promised to keep it confidential."

Knowing it'd help him to talk, I prodded a little. "You can tell me about the problems without telling me about the people."

"I'll just say this," he said. "Sometimes when people get depressed, they make so many demands that I can never do enough."

I didn't know much about military life, but I could imagine the struggles of a soldier. A deployed soldier would have to cope with the constant threat of death. He might struggle to conform to all the military rules. He might feel homesick, lonely, scared, or guilty. As bad as it was to live with Grandma, it would be worse to be a soldier—probably.

"Would it help if I sent your friend a care package? I make some pretty mean peanut brittle." Ethan didn't answer. "What?" I asked. "Are you worried about my cooking skills?"

His reply was long in coming. "I think it'd be better if you sent me the package."

So that was it. He felt jealous. "I'll send you a package . . . as long as you reciprocate."

"Okay," he said. "Are you going to be at the store all day?"

"Yes. Why?"

"So I can reciprocate."

He would reciprocate within the day? That could only mean one thing: flowers.

I didn't have to wait all day to see whether the flowers were yellow. They arrived at 1:30 p.m.: five orange Gerbera daisies in a clear glass vase. According to Google, they meant growth, energy, hope, and happiness. I could live with that.

After I got all my work done, I turned up the music on my laptop and slipped the tap shoes on my feet. I tapped on the hard smooth floor behind the ice cream counter as I watched out the window for customers to arrive. It'd been a slow day, and the hours between one and three p.m. were usually the slowest of all.

I pulled up a video of Miss New York's tap dance routine for the Miss America pageant. It was a dance I'd copied before. I gave it my all. Stomping, shuffling, and jumping to James Brown, I danced from one end of the store to the other. I shimmied my shoulders and swiveled my hips. Then, on a pivot turn, I saw someone standing in the door that led to the storage room. Terrified, I jumped back.

It was Colton. "I didn't know you danced."

I held a hand over my heart, trying to catch my breath enough to speak. "I thought you were on the trek."

"I came back to check on things." He looked at my tap shoes and then at the bouquet on the counter. "It looks like you're doing okay."

How could I explain this? I slipped off the tap shoes and headed back behind the counter to turn off James Brown. "I don't usually tap-dance at work. I mean, I've never danced at work. I was dancing for . . . stress relief."

Colton glanced at the refrigerated cases that lined the back wall. I'd kept them all stocked. "It's been that bad?"

I stomped to get my sneaker on. "I'm living in my grandma's house.

The man I love is three thousand miles away. We have $510,000 in debt to pay off from my father's business. I've applied for hundreds of jobs in the last year, and I've only managed to get one temporary job in my field." I paused, realizing that I'd shared way too much information with my new boss. "Not that I don't like this job."

"So everything at the store's been okay?" he asked.

I swallowed. "The store's been great."

He walked behind the counter. "Are you running out of anything?"

I bent to tie my shoelaces. "I don't think so." I still shook a little from the shock of seeing him.

He scanned the ice cream in the display. "I'll make more mint chocolate chip when I get back."

I'd seen the kitchen in the back with the three huge ice cream makers. "You make it all yourself?"

He nodded. "You can help sometime if you want." He opened the cabinets, checking our stock of paper products. "Maren said to tell you Grace is having fun."

"Great," I said, but Grace wasn't the one that worried me. "How's Maren?" Mom and I had been praying that she'd enjoy her time on the trek.

He scratched his head. "Is she always . . ."

"A little sad?" I finished.

He nodded. "I wish I knew how to cheer her up."

I headed to the sink to wash my hands. "You could tell her you caught me tap dancing in the store." I hoped he'd laugh, and he did. "Tell her it was the James Brown routine from the Miss America pageant. She'll know the one."

"Is there something she likes to eat?" he asked.

"Don't tell me she's not eating." It was one of those moments when it seemed that nothing could get any worse. Our problems had spiraled out of my control, just as they had when we lived in California.

24

Have you ever had dysentery? Though I couldn't look in a mirror, I could tell my face wore a greenish cast. It was the last day of our trek, and I felt sure that if I'd been a pioneer, I'd probably be one that ended up buried alongside the trail. I scratched at a ring of scarlet bumps near the edge of my sock while I held my stomach. Colton told me the bumps were chiggers and that tiny bugs had laid their eggs under my skin. Just thinking about it, I almost vomited.

"I've got ointment you can put on them," Colton said.

I held my stomach. "I feel nauseated." It had been sweet of Colton to bring me food the day before, but I'd felt sick ever since I'd eaten that slice of chicken alfredo pizza.

Colton handed me a tube of ointment from a pocket in his backpack. "Your face is red. You probably have heat exhaustion."

"But I feel cold."

"You shouldn't. It's over a hundred degrees today." He took a water bottle from another pocket. "Drink as much of this as you can. Pour the rest over your head. I'll see if someone has Pepto Bismol."

"Can you do me a favor?" I called before he could walk off. "Can you please watch Grace for me?"

His lips turned down with concern. "Sure."

I took the opportunity to escape into the woods. These people hardly knew me, and vomiting made a bad first impression. If I became sick, I'd prefer to be in the woods.

As I pushed through the undergrowth, I heard leaves rustle above me. Rain. It started slow—a soft patter caught by the leaves. Then it became a shower, pelting through the canopy and drenching my hair. I might have heard Colton calling my name. But I felt too tired to turn back, too in need of my father.

Dad seemed closer as I stood in the woods. I sat on a fallen tree and listened, letting the rain drip off the tip of my nose and down the sides of my cheeks. When I was little, Dad and I would take walks in the rain. He'd hold his big, black umbrella over my head and tell me about the way the creek flooded at his parents' home, rising brown and bubbling over the edge of its banks.

I could hear running water somewhere close by. It was probably the sound of a creek flooding. I walked deeper into the woods, looking for the creek. We'd crossed a creek the day before. I didn't think it'd take long to find it. I'd turn back and take care of Grace again as soon as I saw it. I felt better now. Something about the rain had made the shivers go away.

The weight of the rainwater made my dress too long, and it tripped me as I walked. I held it up around my knees, allowing my legs to take the damage from the undergrowth. Even so, branches and bushes caught on my clothes. When I reached a giant mud puddle, I considered turning back. Then I saw it, a bare patch of mud that ran in a line the color of burnt umber—a trail. I slogged through the puddle and headed down the line of bare earth. I don't know how long I walked along that path. A few minutes, probably. But I didn't find a creek. I found myself instead on a gravel road that seemed to lead farther away from civilization.

Disappointed, I backtracked along the path. Now that the rain had stopped, the sun shone through the leaves, making patchy shadows across my skin. I could hear animals scurry through the leaves as I came closer to them. But I didn't stop to look. I had to get back to the group.

The path divided. I couldn't remember seeing a fork in the path before, but I felt confident in my choice to turn left. I walked on and on, hoping to hear some sign of the trekkers. All I could hear was the twitter of birds and the soft sound of dripping leaves.

The air smelled of mud and life and seeds sprouting. The woods seemed endless. I told myself to give it a little more time. I walked five hundred steps further. Then I turned back, searching for that mud puddle I'd stepped through earlier.

Heading the other direction, I was sure I'd recognize something and remember where to turn off the path. But before I knew it, I arrived back at the gravel road I'd reached before.

Because of the nausea, I hadn't taken my pill that morning. Dr. Jenner had told me to call her if I ever missed more than one dose—that there could be serious problems. So far, everything seemed the same. The medicine still coursed through my bloodstream, quenching my emotions. I should have felt fear, maybe panic. But it was like watching a documentary of a life far removed from my own.

I remembered the advice Dad gave me as a child: when you're lost, stay where you are. If I stayed on the road, I'd have a better chance of finding someone. They'd probably have a phone, and I could call Colton to let him know I was okay. I lay in the wet grass at the side of the road and waited. I was too tired to keep walking around in the woods anyway.

I waited for hours, napping on and off as the sun sank behind the trees. It was about dinnertime. Time for the trek to be over. By now, people would be looking for me—Mom would know I was missing. I still felt nauseated, and my head ached, so it wasn't that big of a deal that I didn't have anything to eat.

The gravel road beside me was badly worn and muddy. Water had collected in the tire ruts. In the time I'd sat there, no vehicles had driven past. Deciding it might be days before someone found me there, I picked myself up, said a little prayer, and walked down the center of the road. It was bound to lead to something—a bigger road or someone's house.

That's when I heard it, the sound of a motor. I turned toward the sound, struggling uphill and crying out, "Help!"

I ran as fast as I could, straight through the puddles. Before long, a motorcycle hummed toward me. The driver wore a helmet. Mud splatters covered his arms and legs.

He stopped beside me. As he pulled off his helmet, I expected to see some redneck with a greasy ponytail. Instead, I could've sworn he was England's Prince Harry himself right there in the middle of rural Maryland—complete with strawberry blond hair, light blue eyes, and a boyish grin.

The minute I saw him, it was like I'd dialed the last number on a combination lock. Click. My life opened up. Thanks to the medicine, it was more a thought than an emotion.

"I don't suppose you've seen a lost pioneer by the name of Maren?" he asked.

I gulped. "That's me. I . . . um, felt sick, so I took a walk in the woods." I probably looked terrible with my hair all wet and matted.

He pulled off his glove and felt my forehead. "You have heat stroke. I've had it before. You don't feel like drinking, but that's the only cure." He handed me a bottle of water. "They should have given you some electrolyte solution."

I took a sip because his smile persuaded me, not because I felt thirsty. I was too nauseated to drink much. "Did they send you to look for me?" I asked.

"My great-aunt told me to keep an eye out for you. She's the one who owns the orchard." He pulled out his phone and punched in a message. "I'll tell her to call off the search." He nodded toward the bottle of water. "Drink up."

I took another sip. "You rescued me, and yet I don't even know your name."

"Wyatt." He patted the seat behind him. "Hop on, and I'll take you home."

"Thank you, Wyatt." I pulled my dress close around my legs. "I don't suppose I can ride sidesaddle."

He looked me up and down. "No," he said, laughing. "That wouldn't work at all."

He dismounted and reached for the drawstring on the nylon pants he wore. I averted my eyes, thinking I'd been wrong about the whole situation. My rescuer was a streaker . . . or worse. My heart beat faster. Where could I run? Could I run?

His lips pulled back in amusement. "Don't go all prude on me. I've got jeans on under these." I let out my breath. Then I watched him pull the nylon pants off one leg at a time. He handed them to me. "You can wear these."

I dragged his pants behind a bushy area and slipped them on under my maxi-dress. I pulled the drawstring tight around my waist and rolled the legs up at my ankles. They made a swishing noise as I walked back.

"There're two requirements for riding with me," he said, holding out his helmet. "You're going to have to wear this, and you have to hold me tight." That didn't sound too bad. I placed the helmet over my head, strapping it on beneath my chin. I approached the bike. "One more thing," he said. "Always get on from the left side."

I walked around to the left side. There was no way to get on without touching him, so I grabbed onto his shoulder as I swung my leg over his bike. The seat slanted, causing me to slide toward him. I couldn't keep my distance. He reached down to put my foot on a peg. "Let me guess. This is your first motorcycle ride."

"Yes," I said, finding the place for my other foot. "Thank you."

He pulled on my wrists until I hugged him around the rib cage. "Hold on tight." Pressing myself against his back, I wondered if this was why people liked to ride motorcycles so much. I would've liked to experience the mix of emotions I should have felt being so close to him. As it was, I could only feel the edge of attraction. "Now," he said. "Where do you live?"

"We moved in with my grandma a few days ago. I can't remember the address. She lives in Thurmont."

"And her name is?"

"Joan Goodwin."

"I know where she lives. It's not that far. Hang on."

"Wait!" I called. "My sister is still on the trek. I need to go back to the group."

"My aunt said she's already home."

The motor rumbled to life beneath us. Wyatt eased the cycle forward, trying his best to avoid the puddles and bumps that pocked the road. All the weaving around should have made me sick. But something about holding onto a handsome man settled my stomach. Around us everything shone—the grass, the leaves drooping on the trees, the puddles reflecting a blue sky, and the little pebbles on the road. The colors glowed as if auditioning for a Monet painting.

He glanced over his shoulder at me. "It's pretty boring driving along here. You might as well tell me about yourself."

I spoke loud enough for him to hear me over the hum of the engine. "How do you know I'm not boring?"

"Any girl who wears leopard skin boots to a pioneer trek is definitely not boring. Where are you from?"

"San Jose, California."

He shook his head. "I should have known. California girls hardly ever wear practical shoes, though I'll admit they're good for riding a motorcycle—no laces."

"My boots are comfortable, thank you very much. Where did you come up with that stereotype?"

He laughed. "I'm from San Francisco."

This was getting better and better. "Really? How did you end up in rural Maryland?"

"My aunt needed my help. I run her orchard during the week and go road-tripping on the weekends. There's a lot to explore out here."

"I know what you mean. I already have five landscapes I want to paint, and I've only been here a week."

"You're an artist?" he asked.

"That's what I studied in school, but I'm not employed at the moment."

We turned onto a paved road, where Wyatt sped along at thirty miles per hour. He spoke again as we waited for a stoplight. "You'll love the museums in DC. I should take you there sometime."

"I'd like that," I said, forcing enthusiasm into my voice. The medicine still weighed down my emotions.

"I'm into glassblowing now, but I've got to stop," Wyatt said. "I have more goblets and vases than I could use in a year."

"You should sell them at the dairy store."

I felt his muscles tense. "You mean Colton Bradshaw's store?"

"That's the one."

"He and I don't get along."

I wanted to ask why he and Colton didn't get along, but the light turned green. It was probably just a personality clash. Colton seemed like a stick-in-the-mud type of guy compared to Wyatt. At the next light, I said, "Maybe I could convince Colton to sell your goblets and vases. You should come by the store tomorrow. I'll be there all day."

"Maybe I will."

I'd never been so unhappy to see so many green lights. We must have passed three of them before we finally hit another red where we could talk. I asked him what he did at the orchard. He explained that he reproduced vintage apple trees.

"I've got more buyers lined up than I have product to sell. People are sick of all the genetic engineering. They want a good old-fashioned apple that tastes good."

I studied the facts in my mind as we drove the rest of the way home:

his aunt trusted him to run her orchard, he cared about the environment, he liked art, and he looked like Prince Harry. The only bad thing was that he didn't get along with Colton. But for all I knew, lots of people didn't get along with Colton.

As we drove up to the house, I could see Mom waiting on the front porch. She ran toward us as we pulled into Grandma's driveway. I'd no sooner taken off my helmet than she grabbed me by the shoulders and kissed both my cheeks Portuguese style.

"Thank goodness you're home. We've been so worried." Then—I couldn't believe it—she grabbed hold of Wyatt, still sitting on the motorcycle, and kissed his cheeks too. "Thank you, Mr.—"

Wyatt smiled and acted like it was a normal thing to be kissed by a middle-aged woman he didn't know. "Wyatt."

"Won't you come in and have a bite to eat?" she asked. I hoped he would come in. That would give me a chance to fix my hair and face a little.

He looked at his watch. "Sorry. I've got to run."

I handed him his helmet. "I hope you'll stop by the store tomorrow. I at least owe you an ice cream for rescuing me."

He winked. "I'll do that." Then he slid the helmet on. "See you later."

I waved as he drove off. "I'll look forward to it."

I walked into the house with Mom, glad I still wore Wyatt's pants so I'd have an excuse to find him again. Inside the entryway, I examined myself in the mirror that hung beside the coat closet. There I stood, with my hair matted down, greasy, and wet against my head, with bits of nature in it. My nose glowed bright red from sunburn. My eyes looked bloodshot. My chapped lips had turned white. It was no wonder Wyatt drove away so fast.

I went straight downstairs to our little bedroom with the painted metal beds and flopped facedown on the feather pillow. The next thing I remember, I stood with Wyatt again. This time he held me, instead of me holding him. With his arms around me, I painted in bright, sorbet colors—light green, pink, and peach—on a never-ending canvas. I knew it was a dream. So I didn't wake up—not for a full twelve hours.

25

ELLY

I FELT responsible for the whole pioneer trek fiasco. After Maren finally came home, I called Ethan to talk it through. "What was I thinking, letting her go on a trek? It's only been a month since she got out of the hospital."

"For all you knew, it could've been good for her. Don't blame yourself, Elly." His voice soothed away my guilt. "We all make mistakes."

I lay on the grass in Grandma's backyard with the phone to my ear. "I just make more of them than most people."

"When I was eight, my mom asked me to watch Candi while she played in our neighbor's pool," Ethan said. "Candi was five and learning to swim. All I had to do was make sure she kept her head above water. Like a normal kid, I sat by the pool with my video game and my headphones."

"Don't tell me she almost drowned." That would certainly explain Ethan's overdeveloped sense of responsibility for others.

"Our neighbor came out of the house to find Candi floating facedown in the pool while I played my game. I just sat there, watching Mrs. Campbell force water out of Candi's lungs. I didn't even call 911. I left my earphones in while my neighbor did everything."

"You were probably in shock," I said. "It doesn't seem like Candi had any lasting damage."

"I promised Heavenly Father I'd be the best brother I could if He would let Candi live."

"So your prayer worked."

"But I haven't always been the best brother," he admitted.

We talked as the sky grew dark and the fireflies came out. He yawned. Even in California, it was late. I told him good-bye and walked inside to get ready for bed.

Maren was the type who woke no matter how quietly I snuck into the room. Not tonight, though. Tonight she snored. I lay in my bed listening to her, but I couldn't sleep. I thought of Ethan's experience with Candi almost drowning. It explained so much about him.

Then I thought of the lawsuit and how once again I'd let my emotions get in the way. First, my anger at Candi and Jake pushed me to sue them. Then my feelings for Ethan held me back. I had to look at it logically. I had to decide whether Jake had stolen something from us or whether I'd imagined it. If he'd profited from our programs, he owed my mom at least a portion of his profits.

From three a.m. until eight, I sat at the kitchen table with my laptop, paging through both the LibraryStar and the Check-It-Out codes. Looking through all that code took me back to my high school days. My first job at Check-It-Out was to make a flow chart of all the major programs. It confused me so much that I spent at least half the time waiting to talk to Dad in his office. Over the course of a few months, Dad explained how the programs worked together. Then, over the next few years, he helped me add my own programs to the mix. When Jake came along, Dad did the same for him.

I borrowed a red pen from Grandma's overflowing junk drawer and replicated my old flow chart for the Check-It-Out code, placing it alongside the map Ethan drew of the LibraryStar code. Paging through both sets of code, I started a list of programs that LibraryStar seemed to have copied from Check-It-Out. In many cases, it looked as though Jake had simply ported Dad's code into a newer programming language. At least half of the programs had only minor changes. Jake had stolen our ideas all right, and with them, he'd stolen our customers.

By the time Maren came up for breakfast, my list took up ten pages. Maren had already styled her hair in loose curls for work, and she wore a turquoise chiffon shirt with her pink capris. She sang as she filled a glass with tap water.

I opened the refrigerator to show her some expensive sports drinks. "Colton brought you these last night. You totally stressed him out."

"That's awesome," she said, making it obvious she hadn't listened at all to what I'd said.

"And Grandma got you a whole ton of organic cereals." I opened a cabinet to show her the selection.

She picked the unhealthiest-looking organic cereal of the bunch—it looked like miniature chocolate chip cookies.

"How was the trek?" I asked. "Other than the part where you got lost?"

Maren twirled around, hugging the cereal box to her chest. "Getting lost on that trek was the best thing I ever did."

I handed her a cereal bowl. "That bad, huh?"

She set down the box and bowl. "Didn't Mom tell you about Wyatt?" Her eyes opened wide. "I get to tell you, then."

She told me how a man who looked like Prince Harry had rescued her. I tried hard to be happy for her as she launched into a word-for-word description of their conversation. The problem with Maren was that she always dove in headfirst. It didn't seem to matter that she hardly knew this guy.

This type of thing had happened enough times during Maren's high school years that I already knew the drill. Maren would be in ecstasy for a few days, maybe a few weeks. Then she'd come crashing down, devastated by what I'd seen all along—that the guy wasn't who she'd thought he was. I hoped this time would be different.

There was no stopping her that morning. She already had my clothes picked out and my curling iron heated. She wanted to be early, and she helped me with my hair in order to accomplish that. "We have to wear hairnets at the store," I told her.

Maren wielded the curling iron. "I'm not taking any chances with my appearance. Wyatt might be there before we open."

I couldn't remember the last time she'd helped with my hair—probably way back before Dad got sick. Though she'd never gone to beauty school, Maren was one of those people anyone could trust with their hair. She had the knack. When we walked out of the house, I looked like I'd been to the salon.

She grabbed the keys from my hand. "I'll drive."

I followed her to the car. "Okay."

She hopped into the driver's side. "I can't believe something this good is happening to me. I was beginning to wonder if God had abandoned us." She turned the key and accelerated out of the driveway before I'd had time to shut my door. "I know what you're going to say—that I should have read the Bible and the Book of Mormon and that poem about footprints in the sand."

I strapped on my seat belt. "I wasn't going to say that."

"But you thought it."

I sighed. "Did you ever consider that since I've also lost my dad, my job, and my home, I might understand the way you feel?"

Maren looked at me in that slightly amused way she looked at Grace sometimes. "I don't think you feel things the same way I do, Elly."

I grabbed onto my armrest, bracing myself for a curve in the road ahead. "Does it count that I feel happy for you today?"

She smiled. "You look more terrified than happy. Have you talked to Ethan this morning?"

"It's five a.m. in California. He's asleep."

"Has he told you he loves you yet?"

"No." I didn't care that he hadn't said it. The distance had made us closer in a way I hadn't expected. Back in California, Ethan and I could sit in silence together. Now, if we wanted to be together, we had to communicate. I'd learned more about him in the week and a half since I'd moved than I'd learned in the two months we'd shared in California. I'd learned that he'd always dreamed of traveling to Sicily and that he thought cuff links were pretentious. Every day, he wore either a blue shirt or a green shirt. He alternated days. In high school, he'd had a boy band. He played the drums. Like me, he'd also been the president of the math club. Unlike me, he'd once dreamed of becoming a professional skateboarder.

One night he told me about his parents' divorce and how he felt guilty that he sometimes preferred spending time with his stepfather over spending time with his real father. Another time, he confessed he'd wanted to go home from his mission when he found out his favorite grandma was terminally ill.

"How many times did he call you yesterday?" Maren asked.

I didn't have to think about it. I kept a running tally in my head. "Three."

"That's the same as saying he loves you."

"It is not," I said, smiling because she'd confirmed my hope.

"I predict that he'll call as soon as he wakes up. You'll be the first one on his mind."

After spending all night thinking about a lawsuit, I didn't know what I'd say to Ethan. I was so used to telling him everything. "I think I have a case against LibraryStar."

Maren looked at me much longer than she should have, considering she was driving. "You don't mean a lawsuit?"

I swallowed. "I can prove that Jake stole intellectual property from Check-It-Out."

She looked back in time to avoid running off the road. "You want to send Jake to prison? That doesn't sound like you, Elly."

"I wouldn't want him to go to prison," I said, thinking of how he and Candi were expecting their first child. "I want him to pay some of our debts. Do you think it's wrong to sue?"

"Dad would think it was wrong. So would Mom." She glanced my way. "What does Ethan think?"

"I haven't told him."

Maren sighed. "You're in love, Elly. You should be able to talk about anything. That's the way I feel about Wyatt, like I could talk to him about anything."

I wanted to say that she couldn't possibly feel that much for someone she'd just met. But I knew Maren could. As we drove, I planned how I'd console her when Wyatt didn't show up at the dairy store. In the morning, I'd say, "Maybe he'll come later." In the afternoon, I'd say, "Maybe he had something come up." And, at closing time, I'd tell her, "He doesn't know what he's missing."

But, as we drove into the parking lot and I saw a man in leather with a flash of strawberry-blond hair, I realized I wouldn't have to say any of those things. This time, Maren's dream had come true. He stood near a gleaming red motorcycle, thumbs hooked into the loops at the side of his pants. He and Maren waved to each other as we drove into the parking lot. Maren parked crooked in the farthest spot and then ran to throw her arms around him. It seemed their half hour together on the back of a bike had meant something to him too.

I unlocked the front door of the store while Maren introduced us. Although we weren't supposed to open for another forty-five minutes, he followed us inside, looking around at the displays. "Do you still sell that homemade granola?"

I found a couple of clean aprons in a drawer behind the counter. "Over near the jam."

He bent and picked up a bag from a wooden box below the jams. "Here it is: Grandma Mitzi's Apple Butter Granola. You guys have got to taste this." He grabbed a bottle of milk from the refrigerated case, walked behind the ice cream counter, opened a cabinet, and took out three bowls and spoons.

"Oh, wait." He reached in his back pocket for his wallet. "I'd better pay first."

I took his ten. "Have you worked here before?"

He popped his eyebrows. "I used to be a regular."

By the time I punched his purchase into the cash register and got his change, he'd poured three bowls of granola and milk. Maren couldn't have been happier if he'd brought her the Crown Jewels.

"This is the best granola I've ever tasted."

I handed her an apron. "Put this on." Then I handed her a hairnet. "And this."

She stretched the hairnet between her fingers. "Do I have to?"

"Unless you want to get hair in the ice cream."

Wyatt reached for a piece of her hair. "Not that your hair doesn't look good enough to eat."

I almost gagged on my bite of granola, which incidentally wasn't all that great. While I put on my hairnet, Wyatt stuck his face into Maren's hair, pretending to eat it. Whether or not they knew each other well enough to be doing this, it wasn't appropriate behavior for Maren's first day on the job.

"Come on, Maren. I've got to show you how to open the store. Put on your hairnet."

"Let me do it," Wyatt said. Maren handed him the net. He stretched it over her head and then tucked her curls in around the edges.

That was when Colton opened the door that led to the storeroom. "I thought I'd let you know," he said, but his words stopped when he saw Wyatt behind the counter stuffing Maren's hair into the net. There was something in the way Colton clenched his jaw that I couldn't pin down—pain, anger, jealousy? He disguised his expression before I could decide which and turned to me. "I forgot to get you that skim milk you phoned me about. I'll go down the road and get more."

With that, he disappeared back into the storeroom. A few seconds later, we heard him drive his truck out from in back of the store. I couldn't help suspecting that Maren's getting lost was what made him forget about the milk.

Maren looked at Wyatt, her hand over her mouth. "Is that what you meant when you said Colton doesn't like you?"

Wyatt leaned against the counter. "That's what I meant."

I thought Wyatt would leave after that. He didn't. He stayed behind the counter, eating his granola, while I showed Maren what to do every morning. As we counted the cash in the register, I whispered, "Don't go and lose your job on the first day."

Maren rolled her eyes. "I'm not going to lose my job."

I tilted my head toward Wyatt. "Then be professional."

Wyatt hung around while I took Maren into the back to show her how to fill the refrigerated cases with milk and ice cream.

"What do you think of Wyatt?" Maren asked as soon as the door closed behind us.

"I like him." I pulled open the door to the refrigerated room. "But not at work."

She followed me inside. "Wyatt is a paying customer."

I picked up a bottle of whole milk and slid it onto the shelf. "Then he shouldn't stand behind the counter with us."

Maren huffed. "If Ethan were here, you'd let him stand behind the counter."

So much for Maren taking my advice. We stocked the rest of the shelves in silence. Maybe I was overreacting. Since Colton had mentioned skim milk, I counted how much we had left—fourteen bottles.

As we walked back to the front of the store, I could see five people already waiting for us to open the doors. Colton had said Saturdays were busy, but I hadn't expected this. Wyatt looked at his watch. "You've got one more minute."

While I unlocked the door, two more cars pulled into the parking lot. The customers filed in, all heading for the case of milk. Every one of them bought skim. Within five minutes, we'd sold all fourteen bottles.

I called Colton on his cell. "We're out of skim." I tapped out a shuffle stomp step behind the counter.

"It'll be a few more minutes," he said. "I'm loading the truck now."

A woman carrying a baby in a car seat came in. When I told her there wasn't any skim, she looked like she might cry. "I came ten miles to get skim milk."

"We have one percent," I offered, trying to keep my feet from tapping. "Or you could wait a few minutes. They're bringing more."

She looked at her watch. "I have a doctor's appointment."

"One percent isn't all that different from skim," Maren muttered, standing beside me. Later I'd have to remind her that the customer is always right.

Wyatt walked out from behind the counter. "Tell you what, ma'am, I can bring a couple bottles of skim to your house."

The woman stepped back. "You would do that?"

"Sure." He found a pad of paper in a drawer behind the counter. "If you'd trust me with your address." He pushed the pad across the counter to her. Without any hesitation, she wrote down her address and paid for two gallons of skim milk.

While I helped the other customers, Wyatt and Maren discussed how they'd run the store differently if they were in charge. They decided Colton ought to hold a festival, and they planned activities that would draw crowds to the store. In between customers, I pointed out that as much as I loved their ideas, Colton probably didn't have time to implement them.

Maren put her hands on her hips. "Well, someone has to convince him to grow his business. Maybe Colton will consider doing the events for charity. He seems like the type who likes to help people. He could donate some proceeds to a worthy cause—like microloans for Africa."

As more customers arrived, Wyatt volunteered to deliver skim milk to anyone else who complained. Most of the people shrugged and bought one percent instead. One thin man smiled and bought whole milk. "My wife's going to be disappointed I couldn't get skim."

Glancing out the window, I saw Colton's truck pulling into the parking lot. "The skim milk's arriving right now. I could get you a gallon if—"

"That's okay." He thrust a twenty-dollar bill toward me.

After I gave him his change, I turned to Maren. "Do you want to go help Colton unload?"

She looked at Wyatt. "I'll stay here." I stepped aside, letting her take my place at the cash register.

Wyatt handed me the pad of paper, where he'd written down everyone's orders. "Tell Colton I'll be delivering fifteen gallons of milk for him."

I hoped Wyatt didn't expect Colton to pay him for all this. "How are you going to deliver fifteen gallons of milk when all you have is a motorcycle?"

"We'll take them in our car," Maren answered as she rang up a customer. "Wyatt and I can go together."

"You'd better drive the car around near Colton's truck then," I said. Neither one of them moved. "Or I can do it after I stock the shelves."

Wyatt handed me the pad of paper. "Show him this."

As I walked to the back of the store, I wondered about the look that had passed between Wyatt and Colton earlier. When I met Colton at his truck, I said, "I guess you know Wyatt."

Colton loaded boxes of milk onto a hand truck without looking at me. "I notice he's still here." He finished stacking boxes in silence and then pushed the hand truck toward the store.

I opened the back door for him. "I think I overstepped my bounds just now. I let Wyatt volunteer to deliver a few gallons of skim milk. Some of the customers were upset, so we took down their addresses. They've already paid."

Colton didn't speak until we stood inside the refrigerated room. "Anything to keep people happy."

I pulled a couple of gallons from a box and slid them onto the shelf where customers waited to grab them. "They liked the idea of home deliveries."

Colton pulled out gallon after gallon, sliding them onto the shelf. "I'm sorry I put you in this situation. I should have restocked last night. Tell Wyatt to stop by my house later. I'll pay him for the deliveries."

Every time one of the customers opened the glass door to get milk, Maren and Wyatt's laughter burst upon us. "I'll tell Maren to be more professional," I whispered.

"No," Colton said. "Let her be happy. I like hearing her laugh."

I'd thought having Wyatt around would discourage Colton. Instead, it seemed that seeing Maren with another man made Colton like her even more. He lived by higher principles than I did.

"Can I ask you a question, Colton?" He looked at me with fear in his eyes, as if my question might have something to do with Maren. "It's a business question," I clarified.

He stacked the empty boxes back on the hand truck. "Sure."

"Someone stole intellectual property from my father's business."

Colton's face softened. "And it cost you money?"

"It put us out of business," I said, wondering if I'd said too much. I barely knew Colton. "I've never considered a lawsuit before. My mom won't like it, and this person is an old . . . friend."

"A friend, huh? That's tricky." He rested his arms on the back of the hand truck. "Have you talked to him about it?"

"I thought it'd be better to go through the lawyer."

"You can contact him through your lawyer before you decide to sue."

So much for calming my nerves. Talking with Jake was something I could do right away. As soon as we talked, it would change my relationship with Ethan.

26

Maren

What do you wear when your date picks you up on a motorcycle? I would've liked some advice, but Elly was at the dairy, and Mom might not have liked the idea of me riding Wyatt's motorcycle again.

While Mom cleaned up after dinner, I slipped into slim-fitting dark wash jeans, a freesia yellow top that wouldn't fly around in the wind, and my leopard skin boots. Then I sat outside on the front porch with my heart pounding. I heard the bike humming up Grandma's wooded lane before I saw him, wearing black leather on his red Ducati. He looked like he'd just driven from the set of an action-adventure movie. When he stopped at the end of the driveway, I ran to meet him.

He'd brought an extra helmet for me. I popped it on, fastened the strap, and mounted the bike from the left. It was easier to get on this time, almost as if I'd been doing it my whole life. He started slowly, but as we drove farther away, he accelerated more and more. We took back roads, narrow black pavement twisting in sharp angles around trees, hills, and boulders.

With every turn of the road, I learned to anticipate his movements in response to the curves—leaning the bike slightly away from the bend and his body slightly into it. Everything seemed so green, I wondered if the visor on the helmet had a tint to it.

"Go faster," I begged. I wanted to feel more—to push past the limits of my depression medication. I'd forgotten to take my pill again that morning, which made two days I'd skipped, and I had a headache to prove it.

Sure enough, as he sped up, my emotions surfaced—fear and attraction raced through me. The medicine was wearing off.

He accelerated until the tree trunks blurred together alongside us. The air rushed over the exposed skin on my arms, cooling me despite the humidity. I held tighter to Wyatt, resting the side of my helmet against his shoulders. I closed my eyes, feeling the tightness of his muscles through the leather jacket. This was not a dream.

I opened my eyes again as we came to a stop. There, at the bottom of a hill, a lake spread before us. It mirrored the blue sky and trees. I took off my helmet to see if it looked as good without the visor. It did.

Wyatt took my hand and walked me over to sit with him on a boulder. It seemed normal to sit close to him after the motorcycle ride. He studied my face for a long time—so long it would've been awkward with anyone other than him. With him, it felt right.

"Sorry," he said, looking away. "I shouldn't be staring at you. It's just that . . . I don't know. I feel comfortable with you, like we've known each other for a while."

I nodded. I felt the same way. My emotions rose in vibrant colors.

Wyatt took my hand again. "Come on, I want to show you something."

I followed him to a gravel path that led uphill. We weren't alone on the path. There were other groups. But I felt like we were alone, dwarfed by the trees and bushes surrounding us. Wyatt told me that the hills we climbed hid giant rocks under their black dirt. He pointed out boulders crumbling off the hills here and there. It was a steep path, one that challenged me after my exhaustion the day before. Wyatt set his pace by the heaviness of my breathing.

As we walked, I explained how I'd lain in bed, consumed by darkness, for months after Dad died. Then I told him what I'd never told anyone. I told him about the hospital—everything about the hospital. I told him how Mom had tricked me into visiting Dr. Jenner and how I'd run over Elly's foot. Then I described how they had to comb all the tangles out of my hair. I told him how hard it had been to stay there, knowing we didn't have the money. I told him about the therapy sessions, the other patients, the bed that felt like a box of air, and my list of goals.

When I finished, he took my face in his hands—right there on the trail as a noisy group of children passed by—and wiped my tears with his fingers. "I wish we could've met earlier. Then I could have been there for you." He pointed to a wild rose that grew beside the trail. "I would have brought you these flowers."

I bent to smell one of the flat pink blooms. It smelled like black pepper and honey. "You're here now. That's what matters."

I plucked off a rose petal. Should I tell him that this was the happiest I'd felt in at least a year? I rubbed the petal between my fingers, releasing its scent onto my skin. "What about you?" I asked. "Have you ever lost anyone close to you?"

"I haven't lost my parents, but sometimes I feel like I have." He put his arm around me as we walked up another hill. We could hear a waterfall now.

I let my arm go around his waist. "Why is that?"

"I'm the youngest of four, which sounds easy enough. Most dads are soft on the younger ones. Not my dad. The more mistakes my older brothers and sister made, the stricter he got. I moved out before I finished high school."

"You moved out before you finished high school? How did you survive?"

"I washed dishes at a Mexican restaurant, but that barely paid for food and gas. I couldn't afford a place to stay. You know California prices. I stayed with my girlfriend's family until we broke up. Then I camped in a one-man tent on the beach. My aunt kept inviting me to stay with her. I always said no. I was too proud."

He looked up at the sky for a moment and then went on, explaining about what must have been the hardest time in his life.

"One day, it was raining when she called. It'd rained for days. There I was in the Laundromat, wishing I could wash myself along with my clothes, and my aunt asked once again if I'd come work for her in the orchard. I scratched a mosquito bite and thought to myself, 'It can't get any worse than this, even if she expects me to go to church with her.' I left that same day."

"And did she expect you to go to church with her?"

"She lets me decide for myself. I've gone a few times."

I didn't want to pressure Wyatt too much by asking any more about church. He'd obviously had some bad experiences. "Have you lived here ever since?"

"No. I've moved around. I go back to California when I feel like it. I still have friends there. I spent a summer in Alaska, a winter in Mexico. I like to see the world, but I always come back here. It's my home now."

"What happened with your parents?"

"My parents?" he said. "They keep their distance."

"Do you ever talk to them?"

"We talk twice a year. My mom calls every year on my birthday, and I call her every year at Christmas." It seemed to me that losing a parent that way was worse than losing one to death.

We crested the hill and saw a gray rock cliff. A waterfall splashed through a crevice on its left side and then ended in a little stream, curving along to our right. Wyatt pulled me off the path. "Come on. I'll show you the best way to get there."

We bounded down the hill, through dead leaves and over rocks. It was a small stream, barely three feet wide. We sat on the bank, removing our shoes and socks. He climbed into the water without flinching and held out his hand for me. I gritted my teeth before making the plunge. The water felt warmer than I'd expected.

"You're used to the Western mountains," Wyatt told me, "where the water comes from snow melt. This comes from underground springs."

My toes gripped the slippery smooth stones as we made our way to the pool at the bottom of the falls. The closer we got to the falls, the more the drops of water rained down from above until we could thrust our hands into the wall of water that fell like living glass.

Wyatt pulled me toward the side of the waterfall and helped me climb up on the rock. The cliff rose at least fifty feet high but cracked and sloped in a way that allowed climbing. Wyatt navigated the angles, leading me along the easiest path to the top. I followed him, grabbing his hand for help in the difficult places.

We sat atop the ridge, gazing down at another couple splashing in the water below.

"My grandmother's trying to pair me up with Colton." After all the little gifts Colton had brought me lately—the bag of food on the trek and the electrolyte drinks afterward—I suspected Grandma was right about him liking me. "He's so much older than I am. Can you imagine if I married him? As soon as I got my children out of diapers, I'd have my husband in diapers."

Wyatt laughed. "His first wife was younger than him too. She was nice, though, and far too good-looking for him. But if you married him, you'd never have to worry about money. That's probably what your grandma's thinking."

"I could never marry for money," I said. "And I could never marry a man who's divorced. A second love is always tainted by the first. That's how it is with my sister Elly—she was engaged for two years before her fiancé dumped her. It's been three years since they broke up, and she's dating someone she really likes. But she's much too cautious. She doesn't even keep a picture of him."

Wyatt touched the side of his foot to mine. "Too many people are logical about love when it's not something you can be logical about at all."

Tingles ran up and down my spine. Was this really happening to me? "Call me naïve—my sister does—but I think everyone has someone who's right for them."

Wyatt leaned back against the rock, resting his head on his hands. "And what if you happened to find him, say, today? Would you live happily ever after?" Something in his voice told me he wasn't playing around. He was serious.

"Then," I said, "I would spend the rest of my life in a happily ever after."

We sat there in silence, listening to the water plunging down into the frothy pool below. Everything felt perfect—the cool breeze whispering across our skin, the children splashing in the creek in the distance, and the tree branches swaying above our heads. Wyatt pointed down the hill. "What's that?"

I gazed in the direction he pointed to a hill opposite the falls, where two easels stood. "It looks like an art class . . . without students."

Wyatt jumped up. "Let's see what they're painting."

As we climbed back down the cliff and walked up the hill, I kept watching for the artists to return. I would've hated for someone to come look at my unfinished painting when I wasn't there. Of course, I wouldn't have left my painting unattended in the first place. In such a busy place as this, the artists would have to know someone would look. Maybe they had only stepped away for a minute to eat a sandwich and could see us from where they sat.

Wyatt stopped a few feet away from the easels. "You look first," he said.

I walked forward to sneak a look at the canvases. "They're blank, but they're primed." I looked down at a box of art supplies. "And these are brand-new acrylic paints." What kind of person would leave brand-new easels and paints out in the woods? I wished I had new acrylic paints. Mine had dried up over the last year.

Wyatt picked up a brush. "The brushes are new too."

I stepped back. "I don't think we should touch anything."

Wyatt picked up a pencil. "Why not? It seems the perfect time for a painting lesson." He sketched a line across the canvas. "You can be the teacher."

I pulled his hand back. "No. They don't belong to us."

He laughed. "The man I got them from said to start with a pencil sketch."

"You mean all these supplies belong to you?"

He drew another line. "I thought it'd make a fun first date."

Tears blurred my vision. He'd bought all this for me. It must have cost over a hundred dollars. "How did you know?"

He brushed my hair out of my face. "You told me yourself you like to paint."

"But I didn't tell you I haven't painted since—" I couldn't finish my sentence. Of all the people who'd tried to console me over the last few months, no one had bought me paints. No one had taken me to a place that inspired me as much as this waterfall.

He took my hands in his, stroking my fingers with his thumbs. "Since your father died?" he asked.

I nodded. "I wanted to paint. I just couldn't."

He put the pencil in my hand. "Let's get started then." He turned me to face my easel. Then, for the first time in fifteen months, I touched a pencil to canvas.

Going back to it wasn't as hard as I thought. I sketched out the scene in a rush, starving for the process of creation. Wyatt imitated my actions the best he could, watching as I mixed the gray paint to resemble the rocks in front of us. The paintbrush seemed an extension of myself, a part of me that had been missing far too long.

Minutes turned to hours as we painted and talked. I told him about my dream to paint for cancer patients. He told me about his dream to start his own business. He had a friend in California who'd gotten rich from her design shop.

"There's no reason why you and I couldn't do something like that," he said.

You and I. I liked the sound of that. Wyatt was what I'd needed all along—more than the hospital visits, medications, and talks with my therapists. Maybe he needed me too.

27

ELLY

MAREN hadn't taken her medicine in over a week. That's what she told me when I offered to pick up her refill after work.

"What do you mean you haven't taken your medicine?" I asked. "Dr. Jenner said you had to keep taking it."

Maren knelt in front of a piece of butcher paper, her paintbrush in hand. She was working late to paint banners for the Cow Festival she and Wyatt had planned. "Dr. Jenner was wrong. Wyatt is all the medicine I need."

I looked at Wyatt, who stood behind her. He shrugged, signaling he wouldn't back me up about the medicine. Something about Wyatt pricked at me. I couldn't trust him. He'd become Maren's guiding force the moment he stepped into her life, despite the fact that he hardly knew her. And he seemed too much like Jake with his easy charm.

"Does Mom know about this?" I asked. Mom had worked late at her catering job almost every night the week before.

Maren painted a shiny, red curve around the letter S. "Tempera always looks better wet than dry," she told Wyatt. "I wish we'd bought paint that wouldn't lose its shine." She was ignoring me.

I grabbed the jar of paint from her hand. "Maren! This is serious. You need to keep taking that medicine." It had been two months since our last big fight—the one where I broke my toe to get her to talk to the doctor. I couldn't let her backtrack on all the progress she'd made since then.

Maren looked at Wyatt and raised her eyebrows. "Can you see what I mean about Elly?"

It would have been better if I'd talked to Maren without Wyatt. The problem was that, except when she slept or took a shower, he was always with her.

The two of them would drive off on his motorcycle every day she didn't work. She told me how they'd driven through the crowded streets of Washington, DC, over the mountains of West Virginia, and along the banks of the Shenandoah River. One evening, after we closed the store, they drove out to the airport and lay on their backs in a field while the planes flew overhead. "You know what it feels like, Elly?" she'd said. "Like scuba diving. Those big planes with their white bellies are like whales swimming over you." Another evening, they drove to Chesapeake Bay and borrowed a sailboat. Last weekend, they visited Philadelphia by moonlight. I was happy she was having fun, but the euphoria couldn't last forever.

"Mom and I need you to be stable." I put my hands on my hips. "As long as you're alive, something is bound to interrupt your happiness."

A customer came through the door, and Maren put on a fake smile. "You need to stop projecting, Elly," she whispered. "Wyatt is not going to abandon me the way Jake abandoned you."

"Can I help you?" I asked the customer.

"Yes," she said. "I need a quart of buttermilk."

"I'll get it," I offered, happy to step away from the conflict. I jumped over Maren's banner and then grabbed the buttermilk in the farthest corner of the refrigerated case. By the time I got it to the customer, Maren had already rung her up.

The woman smiled. "That was fast."

"Yes," Maren said. "My sister's very helpful, even when you don't need it. Have a nice day."

I waited until the door clicked shut behind the customer. "If you're going to act like that around our customers, you do need your medicine."

Maren bared her teeth. "It could be that you're the one who needs medicine."

I should've let it go, but I'd already convinced myself it was a life-and-death battle. "If Dr. Jenner had prescribed medication for me, I would take it. I wouldn't make my family worry about me when they already have so many other things to worry about."

Maren went back to painting her sign. "Did you ever stop to think, Elly, that perhaps my emotional state wasn't that fabulous when I took my medicine?"

"Then talk to the doctor about it, Maren. Or get a new doctor."

Wyatt stood behind Maren with his arms folded. I wanted to tell him not to play bodyguard with me. This had nothing to do with him.

He hadn't been there when Maren had stayed in her nightgown for six months or when Mom had worried that Maren might take her own life. "Don't you ever have to go to work?" I asked him.

He pulled his shoulders back. "I set my own schedule."

Maren stood to put her arm across Wyatt's back. "If you're going to be so rude, Elly, I'll let you close the store by yourself. We have places to go. Wyatt bought me a motorcycle. He's going to teach me to ride."

"You can't—" How could I begin to explain why that was a bad idea? "Mom already has enough to worry about without you racing through the country on your own motorcycle."

Wyatt shrugged. "It's a gift. She won't have to pay for it."

I glared at Wyatt. "It's not that simple. If Maren accepts your *gift*, she'll have to insure it, register it, and pay for upkeep."

"I'm an adult, Elly. I can make my own decisions." Maren took off her hat and apron, dropping them on the floor. "Let's go, Wyatt." They left through the front door.

I hated arguing with Maren, but it had to be done. I didn't trust Wyatt, especially not after the way he'd acted just now—as if Maren didn't need to follow her doctor's orders. I sat on the floor to finish painting the banner. Yes, Maren was twenty-three, but less than two months earlier, she'd been under twenty-four-hour care in the hospital. I couldn't let her backtrack.

I painted way past closing time, trying my best to stay inside Maren's pencil lines. My thoughts wandered to the talk I had with our lawyer earlier that day. He was about to send a letter to Jake about how we could avoid a lawsuit. I was still considering the topic when my phone rang at 8:30, Ethan's normal time for calling. I still didn't want to tell him about the lawsuit, so I let him speak first.

"I've decided I'm going to quit One-on-One USA," he said.

I set down my paintbrush. "What do you mean? You're the founder."

"I'm the *co*founder. My friends are coming home from deployment. It's a good time to make my break." He sounded so sure. "I'll tell the other administrators when I'm in DC."

"What are you going to do with all the extra time?"

"I'll have room for other things. And other people."

By *people*, he meant me. Ethan wanted to make room for me in his life. He wanted to make a commitment. Finally something good was happening because of my decision to move. "Hold on," I said, running to my laptop. "We're going to celebrate." I pulled up the Miss New York video. "I'm putting on my tap shoes." I put the phone on speaker and turned up the volume on the computer as high as it would go.

"I wish I could see this," Ethan yelled.

"Listen for the taps," I yelled back. As the music started, I tried my hardest to make each tap sound on the hard floor. I loved the slippery feel of the floor beneath my shoes. I loved the smell of tempera paint and the husky sound of James Brown's voice.

I didn't stop when Colton peeked his head out from the back. What were the odds he would show up both times I dared to tap-dance at work? I'd been so distracted with the painting and the phone call, I hadn't noticed his truck in the parking lot.

I thought he'd pop back into the back like he'd done before. Instead, he walked out to join me, waving his finger in a James Brown imitation. He grabbed a plastic spoon, gripping it with both hands as if it were a microphone and lip-synched—badly. I laughed. This was not the Colton I knew, the one who shyly watched Maren from a distance. I kept dancing and he kept lip-synching until the music died down. Colton held the spoon out to me.

"So, Miss California, is that long-distance boyfriend stressing you out again?" He didn't know that Ethan was listening to us on speakerphone.

I grabbed my phone to take it off speaker. "I got some good news," I told Colton. "I was celebrating."

"Sorry," Colton said. "I didn't know you were on the phone. When you get a chance, I need you to taste my latest experiment." He pointed to a cup on the counter as he headed back through the door. "Cherry chocolate cheesecake. Maren gave me the idea for the recipe. Maybe you can take her a cup when you leave."

"I'd be happy to," I told Colton. Then, as he walked back to the kitchen, I picked the phone back up. "Are you still there?"

"Who was that?" Ethan asked.

"Colton. My boss."

"Your boss? Should I be worried?" He sounded jealous.

I watched the door close behind Colton. "No. He likes Maren, but he's too shy to do anything about it. He would have never lip-synched around her. It's too bad, really. She would have been impressed."

"And Maren likes the guy with the motorcycle."

"Right."

"So I *should* be worried." It was clearly not the best time to tell him about my letter to Jake.

28

How could I accomplish all I'd planned? Our guests would arrive in a few, short, nerve-wracking hours. The Cow Festival had been my idea, and now I feared it would be a disaster. I knew what everyone would think: *Maren messed up again*. But it was too late to turn back. I had to push on with my dream.

I got to work early, trying to calm myself. The truth was, I loved working at the dairy store—lining up the tubs of ice cream to coordinate like a patchwork quilt behind the glass case, writing the flavors on the chalkboard display in my best calligraphy, and keeping all the equipment shiny. I respected Colton's decision not to have tables. People needed to be outdoors to see where the milk came from and absorb the rays of the sun. Today, especially, they needed to be outside for all the activities.

The Channel Five van pulled into the parking lot as I walked outside. Colton was already inflating the bounce house. His mouth hung open.

"I forgot to tell you about the media coverage," I said. "The Channel Five weatherman is reporting from here this morning." He opened his mouth as if to ask how I'd accomplished such a miracle. I smiled. "I told them we're using the proceeds to help women in Africa buy cows. They wanted to help."

Colton waved to the news crew. "I don't think I'm paying you enough, Maren."

As the crew emerged from their van, Colton and I walked over to greet them. The meteorologist, dressed in a steely gray blazer and jeans, wanted to know about the festival, the dairy, and microloans. Colton explained it all while I poured cups of chocolate milk.

Panic bubbled in my stomach as I looked around at all I had to do. The dunking booth sat empty. The partially inflated bounce house slumped in the grass. A stack of wooden folding chairs leaned against the outside wall of the store. Could I make this a success? I had to prove I could accomplish this, despite my depression. Wyatt, Elly, Mom, Grace, and Grandma were all coming to help. But I'd planned it all. I'd called the news crews. If it turned into a catastrophe, it'd be my fault.

That's when I heard the hum of Wyatt's motorcycle. The sound of it massaged my nerves, rubbing out the tension. I watched Wyatt pull into the parking lot, wearing the cherry red T-shirt I'd designed. It pictured a cartoon cow proclaiming: *Honey Hills Ice Cream Is Udderly Delicious.*

As if the sight of Wyatt wasn't enough to calm me, he pulled me in for his usual hug and kiss. Then he stepped back, looking into my face. I couldn't hide anything from him. He could tell I was as nervous as a mouse in a room full of cats.

"What do you need me to do?" As he said it, his phone rang. He didn't look at it.

"Do you need to get that?" I asked.

He tugged the phone from his pocket. "No." He glanced at the display. "It's my aunt. I'll call her later."

"Are you sure?"

He walked toward the folding tables. "She forgets a lot of things. I told her I'd take her to the bank on Monday, but she wants to go today. It won't be open for hours."

As Wyatt and I set up tables and chairs, we reviewed our plan. Elly and Wyatt would run the store inside. The high school football team would man the dunking booth. Mom would supervise the bounce house. Grandma and Grace would demonstrate how to make smoothies. I would paint children's faces with animal designs. And, most important, Colton would pull groups of children around on wagon rides.

Colton finished talking to the meteorologist and walked toward us. "I'm impressed with how you two have pulled this together. All I've done is hook a wagon up to my tractor."

"The wagon ride's the most important part," I said. "We've pre-sold a hundred tickets for it. The kids can't wait." We watched as the bright orange bounce house rose against the background of the green fields.

Colton's phone rang. *Why were so many people calling before eight in the morning?* He looked at the screen. "Oh, I'd better take this." He walked a few feet away, far enough that I could only hear snippets of the conversation as we finished setting up chairs. He mentioned account balances and withdrawals—the types of things that usually tormented Elly.

"He was like that with his wife too," Wyatt said, screwing the plug onto the bottom of the dunking booth. "He always answered phone calls in the middle of their conversations."

I wanted to ask how Wyatt knew so much about Colton's wife, but Colton walked toward us. "A friend of mine needs help, Maren" Colton said. "It couldn't have come at a worse time, but I have to go."

"Now?" I asked.

Colton's eyebrows slanted, folding the skin above his nose. "Sorry." He took the keys from his pocket. "Do either of you know how to drive a tractor?" I glanced at the twenty-foot wagon Colton had hitched to the back of his green tractor.

Wyatt pressed his lips together. "You're gonna leave now? After all we've done?" It was exactly what I was thinking. We barely had enough people to staff the festival as it was.

Colton glared at Wyatt and then placed the keys in my hand. "I'm sorry to put you in this spot. I have a friend in trouble—probably the only person in the world who needs my help more than you do."

As nervousness surged inside me, I watched Colton run to his truck and drive off. "I can't believe this!" I yelled. I didn't care if the news crew sensed my rage. They could proclaim over the airwaves that Colton Bradshaw was the most insensitive man that ever lived. "What am I going to do without Colton? He's the one who owns the dairy."

Wyatt clasped my shoulders. "You're going to make this work. And I'm going to help you."

"I'm glad you're not the kind of man who answers phone calls in the middle of conversations." I kissed him as if we were the only ones in the parking lot. "Where can I find a tractor driver?"

As I uttered a silent prayer, Grandma's iridescent blue Cadillac cruised toward us. The car rode like a water bed on wheels, bouncing its way into the parking lot. I greeted Grandma as she opened her door. "Do you know anyone who can drive a tractor for the wagon ride?"

Grandma reached for me to help her out of the car. "I can drive a tractor."

I pulled her up to stand. "Not with your bad knees." She held onto the side of the car while I pulled her walker out of the trunk. Whoever drove would have to be a trustworthy driver—they'd be towing wagonloads of children. "Do you know anyone else?"

Grandma smoothed her cherry red T-shirt. "Where's Colton?"

I unfolded her walker. "He had to leave."

Grandma's mouth dropped open. "After all the work you've done for this? I hope he had a good excuse."

Her reaction revived my wrath. "He said a friend was in trouble."

Mom and Elly grabbed bags of frozen berries for Grandma's smoothie demonstration. I showed them the tables and chairs we'd set up for the class. Grandma reached into her purse. "I could drive a tractor if I had some ibuprofen."

"I thought you didn't believe in Western medicine," I said.

"Here it is." Grandma found a bottle of pills in a side pocket of her purse. "My insides are a veritable pharmacy of Western medicine, Maren. I don't like it, but sometimes it's the only thing that works."

"If you're driving, who will teach the smoothie class?"

Grandma nodded toward a yellow pickup pulling into the parking lot with a truck bed full of football players. "It doesn't take a genius to make a smoothie. The recipes are all written out."

Ignoring her implication about football players, I approached a couple of them. After I showed them the ingredients and the recipes, they agreed to help. While they set up their table, I took Grandma for a test drive. I sat in the wagon while she drove. To my surprise, she navigated every turn as smoothly as a limousine driver. "This is easier than the old tractors," she shouted. "It's more like driving a car."

Grandma drove the wagon in a rectangular route around the rolling green hills, bringing us back to the dairy store parking lot after ten minutes. I looked around at the local crafters who'd set up tables to sell their multi-colored wares. The bounce house and dunking booth stood ready. Relief washed over me as I helped Grandma down from the tractor. "I hope everything is going to be okay."

Grandma beamed. "It'll be more than okay, Maren. It'll be spectacular."

In front of us, four football players and the meteorologist crowded around the blender. The meteorologist must have thought it'd be a great setting for his weather spotlight because the camera rolled as he spoke into the lens. "It's going to be a beautiful day for a drink in the shade.

Highs in the low eighties with clear skies. If you're in the neighborhood, come on over to the Honey Hills Cow Festival here in Thurmont." He nodded to the football players. "Now let's see how this smoothie comes together."

The football players tossed in a banana, protein powder, blueberries, orange juice, and yogurt. Then in a rush, one of them pushed the button—without putting on the lid.

"Wait," the meteorologist exclaimed, motioning for the cameraman to step back. It was too late. Orange juice, yogurt, and blueberries flew in all directions.

I covered my face. "Did the smoothie get on the camera? And on the weatherman's clothes?"

"You better get some paper towels," Grandma replied. The blender still whirred, spewing out bits of banana like a tired volcano. "Oh, wait. Wyatt already brought some."

Wyatt lunged to turn off the blender. He fist-bumped the football players and the weatherman. "You couldn't have done any better if you'd planned that," he exclaimed, handing out paper towels. They all chuckled. "I hope you brought a change of clothes," he told the meteorologist.

"Always," the meteorologist responded.

Still laughing, the football players jumped in the dunking booth.

The crowds came a few minutes later. Car after car drove up the little country road and turned into the parking lot. They were the colors of jelly beans—black, red, green, white, blue, and yellow cars lined up in the parking lot and across one side of the lawn. And they kept coming. We hadn't planned for so much traffic.

Once the parking lot filled, I became the face painter *and* traffic director. I couldn't paint a tiger, dog, or butterfly all the way through before someone double-parked. Most people courteously turned around and parked along the street. But one couple turned the whole thing into a battle, yelling that they'd come twenty miles and deserved a parking space.

After ten minutes of arguing with them, I texted Wyatt. He only had to flash his handsome smile and say, "Please park on the street, ma'am." Problem solved.

I returned to painting faces with shaking hands. My anger at Colton grew as the day progressed until it reached pyramid proportions. I clenched my jaw so much that pain radiated through my temples and into my forehead. This was great marketing for Colton's dairy, yet it wasn't important enough for him to stay and help.

Think of the poor African women this is going to benefit, I told myself. *You're doing this for them, not Colton.*

I thought of the African women when a child threw up in the bounce house. I thought of Colton too. I thought of him when we ran out of chocolate ice cream and when the dunk tank stopped dunking people, no matter how hard people threw the ball. Wyatt sat in the dunking booth for most of the afternoon. He taunted all the kids about how they couldn't possibly hit the target. "Come closer!" he'd yell. "I'll bet you can't hit it from three feet away." If the ball even came close, Wyatt dunked himself, crying out with pretend anger. What would I have done without Wyatt?

~

After the festival ended, Wyatt and I counted money while Elly took inventory. She'd noticed some teenagers hanging around the handmade jewelry earlier, and as we suspected, they'd shoplifted thirteen pieces: a $260 loss. Despite the theft and the money we'd spent on advertising, we made three thousand dollars. When I discovered that, I grabbed Wyatt and kissed him with gusto.

"I don't know what I would've done without you. I love you so much."

Elly held her lips tight until Wyatt left the room. "You haven't known him for a month and you're already saying 'I love you?'"

"Dad proposed to Mom after a month."

Elly blew out a breath. "I'm saying you should be careful, okay?"

"And where has careful gotten you and Ethan?" I asked. I didn't wait for her answer. I left her there, sitting alone behind the ice cream case, counting the last few pennies.

29

ELLY

I'D done it. I'd told our lawyer to go ahead and send the letter to Jake. The only problem was telling Ethan. When he called, I didn't answer at first. I waited six rings while I pulled weeds in the backyard. When I picked up, I launched into the whole saga about the lawyer.

Ethan listened without interrupting. When I finished, he said nothing. "You think I'm terrible, don't you?" I asked.

"No, Elly." He'd given me the only acceptable answer. If he thought I was terrible, he couldn't tell me. I waited for him to elaborate. He didn't.

"What's wrong, then?"

His answer was slow in coming. "Candi confided to me that the company's struggling financially."

I didn't hold back my response. "That's no surprise. Their building is too big for a new company. They have too many employees. And Jake has no money sense. I could've told you months ago that they'd run into trouble." I tried to forget that I still hadn't paid Candi back for the upholstery I'd ruined in her car. "They have way too much office furniture. They could sell some of that. They use the most expensive toilet paper and soap in the restrooms. They don't keep track of office supplies. Half of the employees leave their computers on all night."

Ethan interrupted. "Do you want me to talk to Jake about your letter?"

"No. I timed it to arrive while you're on vacation." I sounded more confident than I felt.

"And you think that means I won't have to get involved?" His voice seemed louder than usual. It was hard to tell how angry he was without seeing his face. That was the problem with phones.

I tried to stay calm. "It has nothing to do with you."

I could tell I'd irritated him by how quickly he replied. "Of course it has to do with me, Elly. They know how I feel about you."

I couldn't help responding, "Well, I'm glad someone does. I sure don't."

His volume came back down. "I'll fill you in when I visit."

It was suddenly hard to breathe. "I'm looking forward to it."

"I'd better go," he said. "I have a big project to finish before I leave."

Hanging up, I had that antsy feeling that made me want to cram food in my mouth. I'd upset the delicate balance we'd built over the last few weeks. I'd been a Scrooge, putting money concerns over my relationships.

I liked things organized and predictable. I liked spreadsheets and color-coded file folders. I liked to feel that I knew what would happen next. With Ethan, I had no predictability. With Grandma, I had no order.

I had two more days before Ethan arrived. If Grandma wouldn't let me clean the inside of the house, I'd clean the outside. There might not be room for Ethan on the sofa, but I'd make sure the picnic table had space. I scraped the grease off Grandma's old barbecue grill, fixed the lawn mower, mowed what was left of the lawn, and pulled weeds. One weed, a long vine, seemed to be everywhere. I hacked away at it with a dull machete I found in Grandma's shed.

While I hacked, I thought of Jake and Candi. I'd been in their position before. When our company couldn't pay the bills, I'd cut my own pay to almost nothing. I'd spent months getting up my courage to lay off a few employees. But Jake had one advantage I'd never had—his biggest competitor had already folded. I didn't feel at all sorry for Jake.

As I carted a wheelbarrow load of weeds into the woods, I found Grace sitting with Grandma's Labrador retriever beside the little creek. I took off my shoes and stepped into the water. The dog followed me.

Grace threw a rock into the water. It landed close enough that a few drops splashed my arm. "I want to go home," she said.

It wouldn't help to remind her that we didn't have a home anymore. "Grandma needs us here."

Grace rocked back and forth. "Grandma's food tastes bad."

I picked up a couple big rocks and lined them up in the stream, horizontal to the flow of the water. "Come on. I'll teach you how to build a dam."

Grace put her hands on her hips. "Henry Higgins says that word in *My Fair Lady*. Dad told me we should never say that word."

"I meant the other kind of dam. Take off your shoes and come in."

She took her shoes off and winced at the feel of the rough sand. "It's better in the creek," I promised, holding out my hand for her.

She took my hand and stepped into the water, tipping back and forth to find her balance. "That's not so bad, is it?" I asked.

She stepped back out of the water. "I hate it. I hate everything here."

"You don't hate the dogs." Since she got back from the trek, she'd spent hours talking to the dogs, petting them, brushing their fur, and teaching them tricks. "Let's try to think of the good things. Here's one: Maren's happy here."

"Is Wyatt going to propose to Maren at the Empire State Building?" Grace asked.

Maren and Wyatt had planned a trip to New York City for the Fourth of July. I'd been so busy working with the lawyer, I hadn't paid much attention.

"I don't know. Do *you* think Wyatt's going to propose to Maren?" They'd only dated a few weeks, but it wouldn't surprise me if they got engaged.

30

Could a single moment change your life forever? I was about to find out. While Wyatt and I made waffle cone sundaes for an entire girl's soccer team, a man swung open the door. He stood with his arms folded, looking like a high school principal in his tweed blazer and Dockers. Wyatt held his hand up, acknowledging that he knew him.

"Who is that?" I whispered as I bent to scoop the mint chocolate chip.

"My cousin," Wyatt whispered back.

I let out my breath. "That's a relief. I thought he might be the health inspector." I took another peek at him while I packed the ice cream into the cone. He was much older than Wyatt, but he had the same strong, tall build.

Wyatt didn't smile. Neither did his cousin. As I rang up the last soccer mom, the cousin came up to the counter. "We need to talk," I heard him tell Wyatt.

Wyatt's mouth turned down. "Is something wrong?"

"Yes." The cousin spoke through his teeth. Whatever was wrong made him angry, not sad. I guessed it had something to do with the business, not Wyatt's aunt's health. "Can we go somewhere else?"

"Sure." Wyatt took off his cap and apron while his cousin walked back out the door. Wyatt rolled his eyes at me. "I've never seen him like this." He kissed me good-bye. "I'll see you in the morning, Maren."

"I can't wait." The next day was the Fourth of July, and we were going to New York City in his friend's airplane. Wyatt had hinted more than once that he had something special planned for our visit to the Empire State Building.

I was ready the next morning at 5:30 a.m., exactly as we'd planned. I'd prepped for that day as if I'd be walking down runways with supermodels. I'd done my nails with little rhinestone decals, and I wore Elly's ultramarine blouse. I'd even donned false eyelashes—the expensive kind that looked natural.

"You look like you're going to get married," Grace said as she stumbled out of bed.

I hugged her. "Wyatt and I won't get married without telling you first."

I sat on the front porch, watching for the sun to rise behind the trees as I waited for the sound of Wyatt's motorcycle. Only a few months before, I'd existed in a tunnel of darkness, hardly ever leaving my bed. Now I'd reached the other side, visiting one bright city after another on the back of Wyatt's motorcycle. I whispered a prayer of gratitude, naming blessings that seemed as numberless as the little clover flowers that carpeted Grandma's lawn.

When Wyatt didn't come after a half hour, I decided there was no rush. His friend owned the plane, so he wouldn't leave without us. I sat on the front porch, reading through a stack of Grandma's newspapers. I waited another hour before I called Wyatt's phone. He didn't answer. He must have been on his way to our house.

By 8:00, I started to worry. It wasn't like Wyatt to be so late. What if he'd been in an accident? Some of the roads between our houses were so untraveled, no one would notice if he'd crashed. I called him again. No answer.

I told myself I'd wait five more minutes, and if he didn't come, I'd go looking for him. After the five minutes came and went, I got in our old van. I drove fast on the busy roads, watching to make sure Wyatt didn't pass me on the other side. When I got to the smaller roads, I drove as slow as Grandma, stopping sometimes to look in ditches and down hills. I saw no signs of trouble—no broken headlights or black tire marks on the road.

When I turned into the orchard, I saw a U-Haul truck. I knew it had something to do with Wyatt's cousin. Was he moving back home? If Wyatt had to help, that would explain why he was late. I parked the car and got out. As I did, Wyatt's cousin opened the front door and threw a pile of bedding onto the front steps. Why would Wyatt's cousin throw things out of the house if he was moving back in?

I peeked into the back of the U-Haul. It was smaller inside than I'd thought, barely large enough to hold a queen-size mattress. Wyatt faced the back of the truck, arranging furniture and boxes inside. His motorcycle was in there too. "What's going on?" I asked.

Wyatt turned with a jolt. "Maren." For the first time ever, I saw crimson rise through his face. "My cousin's kicking me out." He tried to smile, but it was a smile of defeat.

I climbed into the truck and wrapped him in my arms. I didn't ask why. I was already on his side.

"I'm sorry we won't be able to go to New York City." He wiped his hand across his brow.

I kissed his cheek. "We can go another day." The front door of the house opened, and Wyatt's cousin threw out a bed frame, letting it crash down the front steps.

Wyatt sighed. "He doesn't understand my business goals. I had to borrow money to fund the vintage apple tree project. I have enough orders to pay it all back and more, but he thinks he could've done better. He can't stand the fact that his mom likes me so much."

"Why is she letting him kick you out?"

Wyatt pulled away from me. "She's an old woman who's losing her memory. She doesn't know what to think anymore."

"Are you sure your aunt's going to be safe with him? He seems unstable."

Wyatt hopped off the back of the truck. "She'll be fine."

I followed him. "Where are you going to go?"

Tears rimmed his eyes as he picked up the bed frame from the bottom of the stairs.

"You could stay with us," I offered. "Grandma won't mind."

He hefted the bed frame into the truck, sliding it along the wooden floor toward the back. "Freeloading isn't my style."

"You could ask Colton for a job."

"I know better than to ask Colton for a job." He shut his eyes for a moment, as if getting up the courage to say what came next. "I have a friend in California who needs my help. The pay's good. I'll go out there until I find something back here."

I felt as if someone had pulled away my chair right as I went to sit down. "California?"

He gathered his bedding from the front steps. "It's only for a few weeks."

I held onto the side of the truck, letting his words sink in. He was going all the way to California. Without me. I wanted to pound my fists into Wyatt's cousin.

The front door opened again and our easels clattered down the stairs. Wyatt drew a sharp breath. Shaking his head, he picked up the easels, but instead of putting them in the U-Haul, he carried them to my van, along with the canvases and the box of paints. "Promise me you'll finish our paintings."

I walked toward him as he opened the back of the van and stowed all the art supplies inside. I reached for the easels. It wasn't like I needed more than one. "They belong to you," I protested.

"I didn't tell you before because I thought it'd creep you out . . . Colton bought it all." He pulled me away from the easels and toward him.

"Colton?" I was still angry at Colton for abandoning us at the Cow Festival. I didn't want the easels to be his idea.

"I expect the paintings to be finished when I get back." He raised my chin with his finger. Then he kissed me. It was the kiss of a dying hero, a long, sad kiss. There was resignation in it, a sort of giving up. "I have to be out of here in fifteen minutes." He stepped back, holding onto my hands. "It'd make it a lot easier if I knew you were painting the falls while I drove out of town." He pulled me toward the front of my van. "Promise you'll paint for me?"

I didn't promise. I got in the van, hardly able to speak for the sobs. Wyatt shut the door beside me. Then he returned to packing. I sat there, watching him. T-shirts, jeans, towels, books, and computer equipment came flying out the door. Without looking at me, Wyatt picked it all up. He stacked all he could into the back of the truck and put the rest in the front.

He came to the van one last time before he left, holding a key out to me. "I forgot. Here's the key to your bike. It's around back anytime you want to come get it."

Then he got in the truck and drove off. He left me.

My body knew what to do without my thinking. I drove home through the familiar roads I'd ridden so many times on Wyatt's motorcycle. It was like the van drove itself. I went straight home, found my ruffled nightgown, and got into it. Then I undid my hair, washed off my makeup, and got in bed. It was nine in the morning. Everyone was leaving the house, but bed was the only place I wanted to be.

31

ELLY

ETHAN was on his way, and welts covered my face. The rash had crept from my ankles to my thighs and from my hands to my face. So much for looking my best.

"You've got poison ivy, Elly," Grandma declared.

"Poison ivy?" I'd never had to worry about poison ivy in California.

Grandma pushed her walker toward the kitchen. "It's a vine with shiny leaves that grow in sets of three. There's probably some in the backyard."

"Not anymore. I pulled it all." In the three days since Wyatt had left, I'd worked out my worries about Maren by removing every last vine from the yard.

It was a group effort to keep Maren out of bed. I woke her every morning. Colton gave her special assignments at work. Grandma found murder mysteries to watch with her. And Mom took her on long drives, trying to get her to talk.

"There's no use pulling poison ivy," Grandma said. "It's as persistent as the devil himself. It always comes back." She turned on the kitchen faucet. "Come here. I'll fix you up." She pushed the plug into the drain, letting water fill her stained enamel sink. "Put your hands in. The hot water takes away the itch." I plunged my hands into the water, but it was so hot, I pulled them out immediately. Grandma pushed them back under. "It'll feel better in a second."

I winced. "There isn't a less painful way?" It was a sticky, hot day already, and the last thing I needed were sweat spots on my dress.

Grandma set the kitchen timer for two minutes. "There's steroid drugs, but they'll make you grow hair on your chest. The rash should go away on its own in a week or two."

"A week or two?" That meant I would look this way during Ethan's entire visit. After a minute of holding my hands in the hot water, I stopped feeling the heat. I couldn't feel the rash either. "I think I'll take a hot shower to get the rest off my body."

Grandma shook her head. "You'd pass out from the heat."

I headed for the closest bathroom. "If Ethan comes, can you tell him I'm almost ready?"

Reaching Grandma's bathroom, I turned the knob for hot water, tore off my clothes, and stepped into the shower. I let the hot water run over my arms and legs while I tapped out one-hundred-twenty sequences of flap-ball-change per body part.

Grandma opened the door. "Just checking to make sure you haven't passed out. I'll have Grace get you another set of clothes. These have the poisonous oil on them."

If we were going anywhere else, it wouldn't be such a big deal. I'd wear whatever Grace brought me. But this was the Kennedy Center, and we were already running late.

Grandma came back to thrust her shower cap into the shower with me. "Use this. That way you won't have to do your hair over." It wasn't like I could *do* my hair anyway, not with all the humidity. My naturally straight hair frizzed as soon as I walked outside.

"Someday I'm going to write an app to help Californians adjust to life in Maryland." I pulled the cap onto my head with a snap and turned my face into the hot water. "Is Ethan here yet?"

"Haven't seen him," Grandma said before she pulled the door shut behind her.

As soon as I finished my last countdown, I hopped out and slipped into Grandma's red satin bathrobe. I raced to my bedroom and grabbed the first matching skirt and blouse I could find. After pulling them on, I tried to cover the rash with makeup. It was no use. Nothing could disguise the swollen, bumpy texture of my skin. I gave up after five minutes.

Grandma stood at the top of the stairs, waiting. "You look pretty, Elly." It was a lie. I loved her for it.

Ethan still hadn't arrived, so I sat by Grace on the porch. She stared at me. "What are those things on your face?"

"Welts from poison ivy." I walked my feet through a time step.

She brought her face closer to mine. "It looks worse than this morning. Yellow stuff is coming out of it."

I bit my lip—one of the only places untouched by the rash—and turned away from Grace. "Grace, if you can go the rest of the day without saying anything about the way I look, I'll buy you a banana split." That was saying something—for me to touch a banana for her.

Ethan pulled into the driveway before Grace agreed to my plan. He drove a black Volkswagen sports car and wore the same white shirt and tie he'd worn to take us to *Annie*. Only one thing was different. He'd grown a mustache. Was he still trying to repel that woman we'd talked about? As mustaches went, it wasn't a bad one. Short and neat, it was confined to his upper lip. I hugged him, breathing in his poolside scent.

His eyes lingered on my face, but he didn't say anything about the rash. "Sorry I'm late." He opened the passenger door for me. "We'd better go if we're going to make the play." His smile lacked its usual enthusiasm.

I leaned back into the cool, dry, leather seat while Ethan helped Grace into the back. When he slid behind the wheel, I started the explanation I'd rehearsed. "I had a tangle with poison ivy. That's why I look like this."

He buckled his seat belt. "Would you rather not go?"

"I want to go. Just try not to look at me too much."

We were so late, I expected him to hurry and pull out of the driveway. Instead, he studied me. "You look great, Elly. I'm more worried about how you feel."

"I'll be fine." We were going to the dress rehearsal for *The Lion King*. Ethan had gone to a lot of effort getting passes. Because it was a rehearsal, there would be fewer crowds, which would make it easier for Grace.

As we drove toward the highway, I asked Ethan whether he'd had trouble finding Grandma's house. He said he hadn't, but I could tell he was thinking of something else while he spoke. Was he angry about the lawsuit?

"Is everything okay?" I asked.

I could tell by the expression on his face that it wasn't. He swallowed. "One of my friends is in the hospital."

"What's wrong? Was he wounded?"

He pondered how to answer. "Sometimes the worst battle scars are in the mind."

I suspected he referred to his depressed friend. "Is there anything I can do to help?"

He sighed. "I wish there were." As usual, he didn't want me to get involved. Maybe he thought hearing war stories would be too traumatic for me, but I could handle it. I could find a way to help. He swallowed. "I won't have as much free time on this trip as I'd hoped."

I watched out the window as we drove past wooded lawns. "When are you going to tell the board of directors you're quitting?"

He rubbed the side of his face as if he were exhausted. "My friend, the one in the hospital, is on the board of directors. That's part of the problem. I won't be able to quit as soon as I'd hoped. It's just the five of us on the board."

Ethan held his jaw tight. Trying to get his mind off his problems, I told him how the cows at the dairy gave more milk when they listened to jazz than when they listened to opera. Then I told him how Colton and Maren had invented a new flavor of ice cream—chocolate pecan pie.

"Colton's the guy who owns the dairy, right?" Ethan asked.

"Right. Every day since Wyatt left, Colton has assigned Maren to help him make up a new flavor of ice cream. He's trying to cheer her up. Not that it's working. Yesterday, Maren sent him on four different trips to the organic grocery store."

Ethan grunted. "Poor guy."

My little story about making ice cream hadn't eased the tension. I squeezed his arm. "Are you angry because I sent that letter to Jake?"

"No." His gaze flickered toward me. "I understand your reasons." He tried to smile.

I knew how much men hated it when people asked about their feelings, so I distracted myself with the scenery while Ethan and Grace carried on a conversation about different breeds of dogs. Dogs were Grace's new obsession, the only thing that could've kept her from talking about musicals or marriage. Since moving to Maryland, she had spent long hours quizzing Grandma about poodles, Labradors, dalmatians, and every other breed she could think of. I tried not to scratch my rash as the two of them debated the merits of each breed.

Maren had gone to the Kennedy Center with Wyatt a few weeks earlier. She'd come home to tell me the building reminded her of an enormous white jewelry box edged with gold. She told me about the velvety red carpets and the chandeliers that hung like strings of pearls in the vast hallways. When we came across the river and Ethan pointed out the Kennedy Center on the other side, it shocked me how much I agreed with Maren's description. The rectangular building surrounded by narrow gold columns did look like a jewelry box.

Once we parked and found our way inside, Grace was all questions: Is this where the president lives? Why is the carpet red? Why is the ceiling so high? How did they hang the lights from the ceiling? Do people get married here? Ethan answered every question as we rushed down the hall to get to the Opera House.

We arrived with a minute to spare. The theater's red velvet seats fanned across a vast red carpet floor. Above us, lights hung in the form of a giant snowflake. They dimmed as we found our seats on the front row of the second tier. Ethan pointed out the presidential insignia below us while we could still see. "That's where the president sits when he comes," he whispered. Though I would've rather sat beside Ethan, I placed Grace between us. We sat on the right side, far away from the other members of the audience, who gathered in the middle. In the privacy of darkness, I scratched the rash on my arms and legs. The shower hadn't helped at all. I needed medicine—whether or not it would make me grow hair on my chest.

When the music began, Grace hummed the familiar tune from the Disney movie. I tapped my toes as actors appeared—some in huge headdresses, others walking on stilts, and still others perched atop baskets. Life-size animal puppets danced around the actors. Except for my poison ivy rash, I forgot about the outside world. I let Grace rock back and forth in her chair.

The characters' problems reminded me of my own. Simba's parents worried about Simba the way I'd worried about Maren and Grace. I couldn't control Maren any more than Simba's parents could control him. Then, as I watched Simba fall into Scar's trap, I thought of the day Check-It-Out closed its doors. I'd also disappointed my parents—along with our employees and clients—because someone betrayed me.

At the intermission, I excused myself to go to the restroom. Like the rest of the place, the bathroom was all elegance. It only lacked one thing: hot water. I was desperate enough to hold my hands under the lukewarm water while I counted to 200. A tween with braids, who waited in line for a sink, gave me a look that said: *This white woman thinks she owns the place*. I apologized, explaining about the poison ivy. She rolled her eyes.

Ethan and Grace waited outside in the red-carpeted hall. Ethan checked his phone while Grace looked on. "Who loves you?" Grace asked, pointing to the screen.

Ethan startled. "What?" He slipped his phone back into his pocket.

Grace still pointed to the phone. "It said, 'I love you.'" Grace looked at me. "Did you send Ethan a text, Elly?"

I shook my head, trying not to scratch the spot on my thigh or the one under my arm.

Ethan laughed in a way that made him seem nervous. He patted Grace on the back. It wasn't that unusual for a guy to get an "I love you text," was it? It was probably from his mother. He looked at me as he brushed a finger over his mustache. "I forgot to ask what you thought of my new look?"

I stepped closer to him. "Since I like everything else about you, I'll let the mustache slide." I couldn't help it—I scratched my neck.

He brushed his finger along the side of my face. "That means I come up short. I like everything about you, Elly." In that moment, I forgot all about the poison ivy. It was the most Ethan had ever said about his feelings for me. We were making progress. He watched me scratch my neck again. "Do you have any cream for that?"

I shook my head. "No. It's not that bad."

He took my hands in his, turning them to look at the rash. "Make sure you only wash in cold water. Hot water feels good, but it opens the sores so they can't heal."

I stared at him, thinking of the open sores that ran up and down my legs.

"You and Grace go ahead back into the theater," he said. "I'm going to find you some cream."

I started to protest, but Ethan was already headed down the hallway. We only had a few more minutes of intermission, so I took Grace back inside the theater. Ethan wasn't there when the lights dimmed. He missed the entire first scene . . . and the second. I began to worry he might miss the entire second half when he sat down in the seat beside me.

"Give me your hand," he whispered.

"But you'll get poison ivy."

"Just give me your hand, Elly."

I put my hand in his and let him massage the cortisone cream into my skin all the way up to my elbow. He reached across me and did the same thing with my other arm. I wasn't sure whether it was the cream or his touch—whatever it was, the itch left. Ethan knew exactly what I needed, and he gave it to me. I couldn't remember the last time someone had done that. It would have been nice to feel that way more often.

32

Maren

What had happened to Wyatt? I had added five origami cranes to my mobile, the mobile I kept to keep track of the days since he left. Five origami cranes in sorbet colors hung from the ceiling of the dairy store. They gave me hope at first, but as day five came and went, something inside me dropped. I'd hoped for day five, telling myself that was the day he'd arrive in California. That was the day he'd have time to call, or at least answer my texts. When he didn't call, I knew something was wrong.

"Have you thought about taking your medicine again?" Elly asked as we restocked the napkins into the dispenser. The medicine was Elly's central theme, repeated over and over again in the symphony of our lives.

"I want to feel how much I miss him. I can't do that when I'm on the medicine." I was afraid to tell her Wyatt hadn't called. I knew what she might think—that he'd abandoned me. It's what I would've thought if I didn't know him so well. And Elly didn't know him well. She hadn't been there when he'd slipped my finger into the ring sizer at the jewelry store. Or when he'd told me he loved me.

My phone had become my constant companion. I had the ringer on the highest volume, even at night when I knew it would wake up Elly. When I couldn't sleep, I sent texts one after another. He never responded.

"I'm worried about Wyatt," I told Elly.

"Why?"

I had to tell her. I couldn't keep it in anymore. "He hasn't called since he left. What if something happened to him?" I couldn't help crying as we spoke.

Concern flickered over Elly's face before she shrugged. "There are all sorts of reasons why he wouldn't call, Maren. He could've lost his phone or forgotten his charger. He's probably fine."

Colton came in from the back to fix a broken hinge on one of the cabinets behind the counter. If I'd been more like Elly, I would have changed the subject, but I couldn't stop the flood of words. "I've been praying for him, but how do I know God doesn't think Wyatt would be better off in heaven?" I asked Elly. "That's what happened with Dad."

"You say a prayer that Wyatt won't die. Then you trust."

"How do I trust?"

"You go on with your life, Maren. You do things you enjoy. You paint."

The paintings still lay in the back of our van, along with the easels and the other supplies. I hadn't finished them like I'd promised Wyatt. "I only feel like painting when I'm with Wyatt." I could feel the darkness creeping back into my life, but considering my loss, that was normal, wasn't it?

Elly wiped off the napkin dispenser. "You always said you wanted to paint for people in hospitals, right?"

I grabbed the bottle of disinfectant to wipe the counter for the third time that day. "Right." But that would never happen. Hospitals had too many regulations.

"Ethan has a friend in the hospital," Elly said. "He's a veteran, and he needs cheering up. You could finish one of those paintings in the van for him."

I wiped the top of the ice cream freezer while I considered the best excuse to make. "I'd have to go back to Cunningham Falls to finish it, and I don't know how to get there."

"I could show you how to get there," Colton offered. He was still trying to make up for deserting me at the Cow Festival. I'd tried my best to give Colton the silent treatment, but, considering he was my boss, it was impossible not to talk to him. "We could go this afternoon," he said.

"Would you?" Elly said. She'd accepted his offer on my behalf—without even looking my way.

In Colton's mind, showing me how to get to Cunningham Falls involved driving me there in his truck and then accompanying me on the hike. He carried the easel and my other supplies while we trudged up and down the crumbling hills. The place looked so different without Wyatt. It seemed a place of shadows. Old bottles and cans lay beside the gravel path. Paint peeled off the wooden signs. The smell of dead leaves drifted around us.

I'd seen a guitar in the cab of Colton's truck on the way there. I wanted to ask if it was a steel string. I loved the sound of the steel strings squeaking in between chords. But I was still mad at him for the Cow Festival, so, instead of asking about the guitar, I asked, "What happened between you and your wife?" It wasn't a question to ask my boss.

"You mean the divorce?" He took his eyes off the trail to look at me for a second before he continued. "The only way to explain it is that I worked too much. My parents left on a mission the first year we were married. They left me the dairy as a sort of inheritance with no strings attached. Allison wanted me to sell it to real estate developers. It was the logical thing to do. We needed the money, and the dairy was failing. Instead, I worked overtime to make it a success.

"Allison helped build the dairy store and got us certified organic. But she was lonely. We barely squeaked by financially. In the three years we were married, I never took her on a vacation. We hardly ever went out to eat. I got her flowers on her birthday and our anniversary. That was it. I didn't realize how bad a husband I was until she handed me the divorce papers. By then it was too late."

I'd expected excuses. He could have said his wife spent too much money or that she refused to work alongside him. He probably could have said a lot of things. The way he admitted his faults made me like him. I didn't want to like him.

"I wasn't the type of spiritual leader in our home that she deserved," he said. "I was casual in my church attendance and in my prayers. I suppose part of that was because I never served a mission, and I felt inferior to the men who did. I should have realized that staying away from church only made me more inferior."

I wanted to tell him that his past didn't matter—Grandma had told me how much he did to serve the members of their ward—but I kept my mouth shut.

Colton went on, answering the questions I was afraid to ask. "We were never able to have a child, but Allison had a little girl after she remarried. They're living down in Atlanta now." He spoke matter-of-factly, as if it were a good thing they hadn't had a child together. Still, I could feel the hurt underneath.

I kept quiet the rest of the way to the falls. I didn't want to find any other reasons to empathize with Colton. If Wyatt didn't like him, I shouldn't either.

Colton set up the easel for me. Then he muttered something about having work to do. He walked downhill to sit on a log, where he opened his laptop and began making phone calls.

I soon forgot Colton was there. Painting the falls made me feel like I was back with Wyatt, reaching my hand inside the falling water. As I painted the rock, I climbed it again with Wyatt. As I painted the creek, I remembered the way my feet had gripped the slippery rocks that lined its bed. In the wind, I felt Wyatt's touch. In the roar of the falls, I heard his voice.

The beauty of the place came back to me. I wanted to capture the leaves rustling in the wind, the water falling in pillars, the great stone crumbling, the pool of water reflecting the clouds. Most of all I wanted to capture the way I'd learned to hope when I first came here. I had to give Ethan's friend a reason to live. He would feel the warmth of the sun in my painting—shining from the leaves and bouncing up from the water. He'd hear the steadying crash in the frothy curls of white at the bottom of the falls. He too would learn to hope.

As I painted I forgot about the U-Haul truck and the unanswered calls. Why had I ever doubted Wyatt's permanency? Our love was as natural as the scene before me.

By the time I finished painting, the shadows grew long, and my back ached from standing so long. At the bottom of the hill, Colton napped on his log. He had never come to check on the painting, like I'd expected. I hated when people did that. I looked at my phone, which hadn't rung the whole time I'd painted. It was 8:00 p.m. I'd been painting for five hours.

Colton lay with his back resting on the log, his arms folded across his chest and his legs stretched out in the dirt. Though I couldn't see how anyone could be comfortable sleeping in that position, his face reflected contentment. When I woke him, he stretched his arms over his head. "Do I get to see it?" He nodded toward the canvas in my hands.

I held it up for him, turning it into the last rays of the sun. He leaned toward it. "It's your best work."

"I was afraid you'd say that." I'd never given away a painting before. Now, here I was, about to give my best work to an anonymous soldier, who probably didn't know a Klimt from hotel kitsch. Would he appreciate it?

Colton read my mind. "You have other paintings you could give him."

"No." I turned the painting around to examine it again. "I wanted to give him the peace of this place. That's part of what made it good. I thought of him the whole time I painted."

"You should write him a note about it." He stood, brushing bits of nature off his back. "I'm hungry. Are you?"

I wanted to say I wasn't, but my stomach growled out its response before I could answer.

"How about a trip to Ireland?" he asked.

I squinted at him.

He laughed, enjoying that I didn't understand him. "You've never eaten at the Shamrock, have you?"

I shook my head. The Shamrock Restaurant sat along the side of the highway. Wyatt and I had passed it a few times, but I'd never wanted to go there. The roadside marquee with changeable letters hadn't inspired my confidence.

Colton walked up the hill to pick up my easel and supplies. I met him on his way back down. "I have a standing reservation at the Shamrock every Thursday night," he said. "It'd be nice to have company this time."

I didn't say I would go, but I didn't say I wouldn't. Truthfully, I would've rather gone home to sleep. But Colton had waited for me for five hours. I owed him something for that.

Colton chatted about the challenges of maintaining an organic dairy as we walked back along the path. He would've taken it the wrong way if I'd told him Wyatt and I wanted our own dairy someday, so I listened as if Colton were a voice on the radio. He told me how he sold the male calves to people who wouldn't raise them for veal, how he avoided using antibiotics, and how he thought pasteurization was unnecessary. If I hadn't felt so tired, it would have fascinated me. Instead, I trudged on, asking an obligatory question here and there until we reached the end of the trail.

Colton kept up the conversation as we drove to the Shamrock. Since he'd never visited California, he asked about the art museums in San Francisco. I told him about my favorite oil paintings at the Legion of Honor museum and how much I loved the Chinese ink paintings at the International Art Museum.

Now that Wyatt was back in California, I missed my home even more. Colton didn't seem to notice. He told me about his visit to the Met, the museum I still planned to visit with Wyatt whenever we got to New York City.

I told Colton about the motorcycle Wyatt gave me. Colton admitted that he had a motorcycle in his garage, though he hadn't ridden it in years.

"Wyatt only had time to give me one lesson," I said.

Colton took his eyes from the road to look at me briefly. "I've mostly given up riding. It's safer to drive a car. But I'll teach you if you want."

I shook my head. "No, thank you."

When we got to the Shamrock, it looked different than I remembered. This time, I looked past the marquee to see a little white house surrounded by trees. Farmland stretched around it on three sides. If I hadn't known it was a restaurant, I would've thought it was someone's home.

Inside, sturdy wooden tables, chairs, and people stuffed the room. Knickknacks and Irish collectibles cluttered the entryway. In a far corner of the restaurant, a man played an Irish fiddle and sang in Gaelic. The waitress, a woman who looked to be around sixty and wore green eye shadow, led us through the maze of tables and adjoining rooms to a back corner table she called Colton's favorite spot.

The savory smell of roasting meat wafted around us, and the cacophony of voices cloaked us in the sort of privacy you can't have in an empty restaurant. Once we'd ordered our food, Colton passed me a pen and notepad. "Did you still want to give that soldier a note? You can write while we wait for our food." He set his laptop on the table in front of us. "I still have some work to catch up on."

My feelings flooded onto the paper. I told Ethan's friend about my experience in the hospital and how I felt while I painted his picture. My depression lifted a little as I wrote. I went through four pieces of paper, explaining it all. When I finished, I looked at Colton. "How do you think I should end this? Should I put my name and phone number?"

Colton didn't lift his eyes from his laptop screen. "If you want him to call you."

I ended the note with my name and phone number. "I hope he'll call." Dr. Jenner always said when you help someone else out of depression, you get yourself out too.

33

ELLY

AFTER our trip to the Kennedy Center, I only saw Ethan at night when he made the two-hour commute from DC.

He would arrive as I closed the dairy store. Then we would bring home ice cream sundaes to eat. One night, we replaced the motherboard in Grandma's computer. The next, we watched a meteor shower. On the third night, we made homemade Pop-Tarts. On the fourth, we went geocaching.

The circles under Ethan's eyes grew darker over the course of the week. By the fifth night, I was so worried he'd fall asleep at the wheel that I pushed him back to his car as soon as he finished his sundae.

On the next to last day of his vacation, he called to say he wouldn't come that night. He would work late so he could spend the next day with me. I did a little tap dance before I began to doubt. "Are you sure the people at One-on-One USA won't find something for you to do tomorrow?"

"I'll turn off my phone. They won't be able to contact me."

"I have to watch Grace tomorrow," I said. "Mom and Maren are working, and Grandma has a doctor's appointment. Is it okay if I bring her?"

"Sure. I'll get another life jacket."

Ethan showed up the next day with a canoe on top of his car. The shadows beneath his eyes seemed lighter. He told me his friend had been released from the hospital.

"Does that mean you can tell them you're going to quit now?" I asked.

He pulled up a map on his tablet. "I resigned from the board this morning before I drove here. Now I have to let my friends know I won't be calling. That'll be the hardest part."

"What about your friend who was in the hospital? You're not going to stop calling him, are you?"

Ethan shook his head as if he had no idea what to do about that friend. I remembered what he'd told me about depressed people sometimes being too demanding.

"Is he doing better?"

He shrugged. "I think so."

I let the subject drop as Ethan pointed out on the map where we'd take the canoe.

We drove separately so I could park downriver and we wouldn't have to carry the canoe all the way back to his car. That meant I had even less time with Ethan. As I drove, I comforted myself with a mental picture of the three of us lounging in the canoe. In my imagination, I may or may not have worn a white dress and held a lacy parasol while Grace sat motionless at the front of the canoe.

Maren called before we got to the river. "I just heard from Ethan's friend—the one I gave the painting to."

"He called you? That's great."

"I hate to tell you this," Maren said, "but *he* is a *she*."

"What do you mean?"

"Ethan's friend is a woman. They released her from the hospital yesterday, and she wants to meet us."

"Oh."

"I told her we can meet her tomorrow morning for breakfast," Maren said. "Are you going to kill me?"

"Of course not, Maren. It's no problem. I can handle breakfast with Ethan's friend." As I hung up, I ached for my tap shoes. I could deal with Ethan having a demanding male friend, but I wasn't so sure I could deal with him having a demanding female friend. And she just got out of the hospital. Shouldn't she be resting instead of coming to visit us?

After we parked the van beside a bridge, Grace and I got in the car with Ethan. My conversation with Maren still tugged at my mind. "Do people ever use One-on-One USA as a dating website?" I asked.

Ethan answered as if he'd heard the question before. "It's not designed as a dating website, but people meet that way sometimes. There aren't any rules against it."

"Have you ever dated anyone you met on the website?"

He kept his eyes on the road. "Why do you want to know?"

"Just curious. You hardly ever talk about your love life."

"There's not much to tell, but yes, I've dated someone from the website."

"And?"

He grinned. "I prefer to meet women at the bishop's storehouse."

We found a place to park where the river swelled wide and trees grew thick along the bank. Ethan and I strapped ourselves into life jackets. We helped Grace with hers and supported her as she walked to the front of the canoe. I sat in the middle. Ethan gave the canoe a shove before he took his place in the back.

Having Grace along for the ride always threw a wrench into idealistic images. No sooner did we get into the canoe than she began to complain about the bugs. She had a point. We paddled through clouds of mosquitoes and gnats. The mosquitoes showed no mercy, biting right on top of my poison ivy rash. I could've kicked myself for forgetting the bug spray.

"Once we get out into the middle of the river, it won't be so bad," Ethan hypothesized. We put all our energy into paddling as Grace kept up her complaining.

"I have to get the bugs off," Grace cried. All at once, she leaned over the side of the canoe. I reached for her as she dove into the water, almost tipping us. Trying to keep the canoe stable, I leaned back to the other side, which was what Ethan had done. We both fell sideways in a rush of water, turning the canoe over with us. As bubbling brown water surrounded me, Ethan's legs tangled with my arms. For a moment, I didn't know which way was up. I could feel my life jacket pulling me, but it didn't pull me toward the air. It pulled me toward the overturned canoe, where I couldn't see or breathe. I pushed and kicked, trying to swim out from under the canoe until something grabbed my leg and, with a great heave, tugged me out. It was Ethan.

"Are you okay?" he asked, still holding onto me as I spat out the muddy water. This wasn't what I'd pictured when I'd imagined Ethan holding me in his arms.

I pushed the hair out of my face and looked around. I wanted to ask where Grace was, but all that came out was a huge burp, the type of burp teenage boys brag about.

Ethan laughed. "I love you, Elly," he said.

Had he really told me he loved me? "Excuse me." I meant it both ways, as in *Sorry I burped* and *What did you just say?*

He was still laughing. "You're excused."

"Where's Grace?" I couldn't see her. Was she stuck under the canoe too?

I was about to dive back under when Ethan pointed. "She's there." I turned to see Grace floating happily a few feet downriver from us. Ethan handed me a paddle. "I'll get her."

He swam to her while I snagged the other paddle. What had he meant when he said I love you? He'd sounded so casual, as if he were speaking to his sister. Should I tell him I loved him too? Outside my family, I'd only said those words to one person, and I'd regretted it. Did I trust Ethan enough?

Ethan caught up to Grace and swam back with her while I floated with the canoe and paddles. "Now all we have to do is turn the canoe over," Ethan said. He explained how we would swim underneath the canoe and raise it over our heads while treading water. It sounded easy enough, but doing it was another thing. My arms were either too weak or too short to lift while treading. I dropped the canoe on my head the first time we tried to turn it over. The next time, Ethan got in the middle and did most of the lifting himself. That did it. The canoe dropped right-side-up into the water.

I held onto one side of the canoe while Ethan lifted himself into the other side. Once inside, he held his arm out for me. I felt like a beached whale as Ethan pulled my body into the boat. He was stronger than I'd imagined. I flailed around in the middle section of the canoe, trying to get into a seated position. "Man, I'm out of shape."

Ethan paddled to steady the boat. "I like your shape." Once I got seated, he reached his arm out for Grace.

"I don't want to ride in the canoe!" Grace yelled.

I looked at Ethan. "The water's calm enough for her to swim," he said.

"Okay, but don't get water in your mouth," I warned her.

Grace mostly floated on her back down the river. Ethan and I paddled to keep pace with her, which meant we paddled backward a lot of the time. I knew it wasn't the date Ethan had imagined for us.

"Thanks for putting up with this," I said. "You're the only man I know who's as patient as my dad." I could have added "I love you" to the end of that sentence. I didn't. It was better to be sure of my emotions first.

Ethan sighed. "If you knew how I'd acted in our board meeting yesterday, you wouldn't call me patient."

I grinned. "What happened?"

"Last year, we set a goal that each member of the board would reach out to the media. So all year I've called radio and TV stations, trying to spread the word that we need more volunteers. Yesterday, in our meeting, I learned the other board members have been turning down interviews. They're afraid they won't look good on camera. When they told me, I stormed out of the meeting."

"I'm a bad influence on you."

Ethan sighed. "It was just the incentive I needed to resign."

I laughed. "Well, it's not as dramatic as breaking a bottle of perfume in someone's car, but I guess it's progress." I wondered if Ethan might be too good for me. I glanced back at him, looking all rugged with his wet hair and mustache.

It was another sweltering day, but my wet clothes made it warm and breezy. The bugs had finally given up the battle and left us to ourselves. We paddled on for a long stretch in silence while I wondered how Ethan had handled media interviews on top of talking to servicemen every morning. Why hadn't he ever told me about them?

Ethan's voice broke into my thoughts. "Would you consider taking a job in the Bay area, Elly?"

"Why? Do you miss me?"

"My roommate Dave is still looking for a head programmer." He said it hesitantly as if he feared my reaction. "And, yes, I miss you."

"I never sent him my résumé, did I?" I'd been too angry to think logically the first time we talked about it.

"I can give you his contact information later."

"Okay." I caught a glimpse of the bridge where I'd parked the car. It was about a mile downriver, closer than I'd thought. "When we get to that bridge, can we keep going? Just float away and never go back to our normal lives?"

"I hate to break it to you, Elly, but if we keep floating down the river, we'll fall hundreds of feet over Great Falls. People die every year doing that."

Typical. I always thought things in the future would be easier than they turned out to be.

34

ELLY

I DIDN'T care that Ethan's friend was a woman. Not at all. But since Ethan had said she was on the board of directors, I looked at the pictures on Ethan's website. There was only one woman, Lanita McChesney. She had long, curly, light-brown hair, full lips, and a perfect oval face. Not that her looks mattered to me at all.

I'd almost finished my makeup when I heard a knock at the door. Though I'd tried to convince myself not to turn this into a competition, I took the time to apply the rest of my mascara before I swung open the door. There, on the front porch with his hands in the pockets of his jeans, stood Ethan. And he'd shaved his mustache.

I hugged him. "I thought your flight left this morning."

He rested his chin on top of my head. "I had to see you again, Elly." He lifted his arm to read his watch. "I only have three minutes. No, two."

I looked up at his face. "You drove an hour to spend two minutes with me?"

He pulled a small wrapped box from his back pocket. "And to give you this."

I tore off the wrapping to reveal a marbled chocolate bar with little black specks. "Let me guess. Ants?"

"You've done your research."

"It'll make the perfect re-gift for Wyatt the next time I see him. Can you believe he still hasn't called Maren? It's been two weeks."

He pulled an identical box from his other pocket. "This one is bug-free. It's chocolate covered caramels."

"Those are my favorites."

He smiled. "Grace told me. It's a bribe to get you to apply for that head programmer job I told you about."

"I emailed Dave my résumé last night." That was before I'd looked at Lanita's picture. "Speaking of jobs, I have an interview in DC tomorrow. I might be working for the government."

He frowned. "Sounds like I might have to move back to DC."

I ran my hand down his arm. "You'd do that?"

He looked at his watch again and sighed. "I'd better go."

As he pulled out of the driveway, a red car came up the street. Ethan stopped his car and stared at the red one. He stayed there at the end of the driveway and watched as Lanita got out of her car. If he was running late, why didn't he drive away? Was he shocked that his depressed soldier friend was out driving so soon after her hospitalization? Or was he surprised that she'd come to see me?

Lanita walked toward me, keeping her eyes on the ground. She wore slim-fitting black athletic pants with a hot pink T-shirt. I could see the muscles in her arms as she extended her hand to me. She glanced back at Ethan's car in the driveway before she smiled. "You must be Elly. It's nice to finally meet you." Her voice had a Southern twang to it. "Ethan's told me so much about you."

Out of the corner of my eye, I saw Ethan drive away. I had the feeling he hadn't told Lanita much about me at all. "It's nice to meet you too." Truth be told, I would've rather kept my distance. "Let me go get my sister."

I walked downstairs to find Maren facedown on her bed, still asleep and wearing the clothes she'd worn to work the day before. I jiggled her arm. "Lanita's here."

"Who?"

I ran the brush through her hair. "Ethan's friend. You told her we'd go to breakfast."

She pushed the brush away. "I don't feel like breakfast."

My phone rang. It was Ethan. I debated whether to answer his call. I handed Maren the brush. "No way are you leaving me alone with her," I said before I answered Ethan's call. "Hello?"

"Since when has Lanita been coming to your house?" He sounded frustrated, almost angry.

I tapped out a time sequence, trying to calm myself. "Maren invited her to breakfast. Is that a problem?"

"I hope not." I could tell by the way he said it, he thought it was a problem. "Will you call me afterward?"

"Sure." I hung up the phone, hands shaking. Why would he be so nervous about me talking to Lanita?

Maren pulled the blankets back around her. I flipped them off again. "You're coming to breakfast with us."

Maren didn't bother to brush her hair or change her clothes. She pushed her feet into her flip-flops and walked upstairs.

"Where should we go for breakfast?" I asked.

"Wyatt likes Subway."

"I didn't ask what Wyatt likes. I asked what you like—McDonald's, Wendy's, the Kozy Inn, or Subway?" We didn't have a lot of choices for breakfast in Thurmont.

"I always love what Wyatt likes."

I'd never thought of Subway as the ideal place for breakfast, but it would be quick. If Lanita's visit turned sour, at least it'd be over in the time it took to make and eat a sub. We drove three separate cars. Maren had the excuse that she had to be to work. I just didn't want to drive alone with Lanita.

I ordered a bacon, egg, and cheese sub. Lanita ordered the same, and so did Maren. The three of us sat at a round table. The Taylor Swift music playing in the background seemed strangely appropriate as Lanita explained how she'd met Ethan.

"We met three years ago—in the same ward. Ethan was trying to find a way to serve people in the military. I helped him come up with the idea for One-on-One USA. We've been together ever since. I couldn't have made it through without him."

They'd been *together*? It sounded like Lanita had a crush on Ethan. Not that I blamed her. She *was* pretty, though.

Maren sorted through her purse. "I think I forgot my phone." She turned to me. "Do you remember if I brought it, Elly?"

"I remember you had it in bed last night." Never mind that she'd woken me twice with the light.

Lanita bit into her sandwich and moaned. "This is so much better than Army food. A girl can get sick of MREs."

I watched her chew while I wondered what an MRE was—some sort of packaged food probably. "What do you do in the Army?" I asked, hoping to talk about anything other than Ethan.

"I'm a sergeant with the MPs—that's the military police. In Afghanistan, we conduct investigations, run checkpoints, do search operations, escort personnel—basically anything to support law and order."

Maren stood to check her pockets for her phone. "You must have seen some horrible violence."

Lanita pulled her lips to the side. "I seen too much. Wish there was a way to get the pictures out of my mind. Last month, I went with some special ops on a raid. The insurgents knew we was coming. They had a kid with a suicide vest and others with IEDs."

"What's an IED?" I asked, reminding myself that Ethan told me he preferred to meet women in normal places like the bishop's storehouse, not through One-on-One USA. Besides that, I doubted he'd find Lanita's grammatical slips attractive.

Lanita stared at her drink. "Improvised Explosive Device. There was ten or twelve of them. I can still hear them going off. We lost four people and a dog. Thirty others were injured. I know God preserved me, but I can't stop feeling afraid. I have nightmares every night. That's why I was in the hospital. I feel like I have to be on guard all the time. Any little thing can set me off—a ring tone, a man with a dark beard, a chemical smell."

No wonder she was depressed. It sounded like she had post-traumatic stress disorder too. "That sounds horrible." I reached to touch Lanita's arm. She flinched, and I withdrew my hand. "Thank you for sacrificing for our country."

Maren wadded up the rest of her sandwich in its paper. "I'm sorry I have to leave so soon, but I'm opening this morning at work."

I gave her the crustiest look I could muster. "Is this about your phone?" She had a good half hour before she had to leave for work.

Maren threw her purse over her shoulder. "I can't go to work without my phone."

"I can bring you your phone later," I called as she walked out the door. Hadn't I told her I didn't want to be alone with Lanita?

The door swung shut behind Maren. I turned back to my sandwich, wondering what to say next. It's not like I could talk any more about Lanita's experiences in the Army. She already seemed a little freaked out from talking about the bombing.

Lanita looked me over. "You're prettier than I expected." I wondered what she'd expected. How had Ethan described me? She nodded at my blouse. It was one of my favorites—peacock blue cotton with a tie front closure. "You got that at Old Navy, right?"

"T.J. Maxx." I'd bought it back before all my financial problems.

"I'm trying to get back in touch with fashion." She looked down at her own clothes. "I bought these yesterday after I got released."

"We should . . . go shopping some time." I wanted to be her friend. Logically, that was the best plan. I could rise above the jealousy.

She dug around in her purse and pulled out a photograph. "I kept this picture of Ethan in my pocket the whole time I was in Afghanistan. It never went through the wash."

She kept a picture of him in her pocket the whole time she was in Afghanistan? Talk about obsessed. It sounded like Ethan's depressed soldier friend and the woman he'd tried to rebuff were one and the same.

I took the picture from her, noticing for the first time that she wore a diamond ring on her left hand. I tapped my foot on the floor, practicing my shuffles. I had to ask. "Is that an . . . engagement ring?"

She looked me in the eyes. "It's a promise ring. That's what I wanted to talk to you about, Elly. We're having trouble with our relationship."

I swallowed. "You and . . . Ethan?"

"That's right. I think my deployment's affected him as much as it has me. He's not the same as he was before. He's so distant."

Why hadn't Ethan told me he'd dated Lanita? Was she the reason we were only friends with potential? Was that what he'd told Lanita too—that they were friends with potential? She said something had changed. *He's not the same as he was before.* "What was he like before?" I asked.

"We dated a few months before I left. We was friends before that, though. I loved him from the start. That's why I proposed the day I left. I asked him right there in the airport if he'd marry me. I think, if it was any other situation, he'd have said yes. But it scared him that I'd be gone for a year, so he said, 'We'll decide later about marriage.' He promised he'd stay faithful through my deployment. Afterward, we'd pick up where we left off."

The way Ethan had talked about his volunteer commitment, the mustache, and the *I love you* text message suddenly made a lot more sense. He'd made a commitment to Lanita.

"He kept his commitment, didn't he?"

"Yes, but I wasn't my best self when I was there. I got all depressed. He forgot the way things used to be. We had something good going, him and me. I don't want to lose that because I served my country. Ethan's the only reason I have to live."

I tried to keep my feet from tapping the floor. Ethan's relationship with Lanita was starting to sound a lot like my relationship with Jake, and I was starting to sound like Candi. No way would I be able to finish my breakfast sub. I stared at the photograph in front of me. It was the old Ethan, before he grew a mustache and stopped sleeping.

Lanita took the picture back from me. "I'd look at this picture on all my hard days. Sometimes you see things you wish you hadn't, children in pain and such things. This picture could replace those other pictures in my brain."

As I imagined Lanita in her uniform, staring at Ethan's picture, I caved. I couldn't compete with her anymore, and yet I felt so angry. I had to leave before I threw my bacon, egg, and cheese sub against the wall.

"It was nice to meet you, Lanita. I hope we can get together another time." I needed time to think. I needed to be alone, so I wrapped the rest of my sandwich and shoved it into my purse. Then I made an excuse even worse than the one Maren had made.

"I'm sorry I have to go. I have to watch my younger sister today." What did it matter that Grace wouldn't be awake for another two hours?

I drove home, trying to make sense of the situation. I wanted to blame Lanita for loving Ethan, but I couldn't. She had every right to love him. I wanted to blame Ethan for leading me on, but he never had. He'd always said we could only be friends. And though I knew he didn't love her, I couldn't blame him for keeping his commitment. That was something I'd always admired about him: he sacrificed to help others. Clearly, he couldn't abandon Lanita now. Her deployment hadn't ended. She still lived it in her mind.

Maybe there was hope for me. Maybe there wasn't. The only thing I knew for sure was that I couldn't keep being his friend. Good thing Ethan would be on a plane all day. That would give me ten more hours to decide what I'd say to him.

I drove home to find Ethan's car parked in front of Grandma's house. I didn't stop when I saw him standing in the living room beside the broken vacuum. I walked right past him, grabbing the vacuum. "I thought you had to catch a plane."

"I had to talk to you."

I carried the vacuum into the kitchen, where I found a screwdriver in Grandma's junk drawer. "You missed your plane?"

"There's another flight this afternoon. I rescheduled." Ethan followed me as I walked back through the living room and headed out the back door. "I should have told you about Lanita," he said.

"You think?" I turned the vacuum upside down on the grass to take apart the roller assembly. "This needs a new belt."

I unscrewed the plate on the bottom, took out the roller, and looked up into the hose. "There's a clog too. This happens every time Grace vacuums." I jammed the screwdriver into the opening, trying to pry out the debris. Dust floated around me as I pulled out hair and scraps of paper. I turned the vacuum over to get out the rest of the dust. Then I took off the hose, shaking out dirt until I had to sneeze.

Ethan watched me. "If I had told you about Lanita, you would have rejected me for sure. It was hard enough being Jake's brother-in-law."

I pushed the handle of Grandma's rake into the vacuum hose, forcing out more debris. Tears pooled in my eyes. "I don't think we should see each other anymore. I get the whole life and death thing now. She needs you."

"And you don't?"

I shook my head. "I'll be okay."

"Look, Elly, I didn't expect you to come along when you did. Meeting you threw a wrench into my plan."

His plan? He sounded like Jake. I jammed the rake handle so far into the hose, the nozzle popped off the end. "Sorry to interrupt your plan."

Ethan reached for my arm. "I wish I hadn't ever made a plan."

I pulled away. "You should leave now." I took the bagless canister off Grandma's vacuum and walked toward the garbage can.

"I'm sorry, Elly," Ethan yelled as I walked across the yard. "But I'm not sorry I didn't tell you about Lanita. The last few months have been the happiest—"

"I said you should leave!" I yelled back as I flung a load of dust into the garbage.

He caught up to me on my way back to the vacuum. "Have you ever heard that story about a hiker who got his arm caught under a boulder?

He was out in the desert where no one would find him for days. He had to decide between keeping his arm or cutting it off so he could live. I feel like that man right now. I have to choose between saving a life and losing you."

I couldn't see through my tears to fix the vacuum. As much as I understood why he shouldn't break up with Lanita, he needed to do it. He'd kept his commitment. She was home now, and I was done waiting.

"Since you can't seem to choose between us, I'll choose for you. Please don't call me anymore or text me or talk to me." My words rushed out. I'd raised the stakes. If he wanted me, he'd have to take action.

Ethan stood there, watching me put the vacuum back together. His voice sounded hoarse. "I'm sorry you feel that way." It wasn't what I'd expected. I'd expected him to say he'd break up with Lanita. Instead, I'd lost my gamble. Too startled to speak, I put the hose back on the vacuum. Then I replaced the roller assembly. Ethan handed me the screws. "I have one more thing I need to say."

I turned toward him, trying my best to look impatient instead of heartbroken.

"Jake called me on the way to the airport. He got your letter. He wants you to come to San Jose."

35

When you love someone, is it possible to stop thinking about them? I couldn't. At work, I spent all the time I could looking out the window, praying that Wyatt's motorcycle would appear around the bend of the road. I needed him beside me. Our love wasn't static, like some painting in a museum that could be completed and hung on a wall. It was something we created every day. And every day was missing half the colors when Wyatt wasn't with me.

As I watched out the window, waiting to open the store, Lanita pulled into the parking lot. I'd thought I'd never see her again after our breakfast with Elly. Now here she was once more, less than a week later. She got out of her car, but she didn't try to come in. She cycled through a routine of exercises—a hundred sets of push-ups, burpees, mountain climbers, and jumping jacks. At 9:00 a.m., when I opened the store, she held herself in a full plank position with her long sinewy muscles tensed. I walked out to her. "Would you like to come in?"

"After I finish with my exercise." She had plenty of breath to speak, despite having held herself up with just her hands and toes for at least a minute.

"How long are you going to hold that pose?"

"To the count of three hundred. That's my usual." She spoke with a heavy Southern accent.

I hungered for someone to talk to, someone who could give me a different opinion than my family members. Elly had been unusually distant since Ethan left. I had to find out from Mom that she planned to go to San Jose next week to meet with Jake. Meanwhile, she obsessed about fixing Grandma's computer, the lawn mower, and the torn upholstery on the sofa. When she wasn't doing that, she was on the computer, searching for jobs.

There were no customers, so I leaned against the outside wall, watching Lanita and the road. With my head near the window, I could hear the phone inside if it rang. "Did you need to talk to me about something?"

Lanita held her plank. "I came to thank you for the painting."

That didn't seem likely. If she only wanted to thank me, she could've sent me a note. I recognized the need in her face—the need for understanding that came from depression.

"I know what it's like to be cooped up in a hospital," I said. "That's why I gave you the waterfall painting."

She moved to a side plank. "I didn't miss being outdoors at all. I feel safer when I'm inside."

"Would you feel better inside the store?" I asked. "As long as there aren't any customers, you can do your exercises there."

She followed me inside. While she moved through the exercises, we compared our experiences with the doctors and the medicines. I could tell they hadn't helped her much. When I accidentally slammed a cabinet door, she startled, covering her head as if someone had attacked her.

I touched her shoulder. "Are you okay?"

She nodded. Then she went back to her mountain climbers. I stood as still as possible after that. I didn't want to scare her again.

She asked how I'd gotten to know Ethan, so I told her how Ethan and Elly worked together at LibraryStar before his sister fired her.

Lanita stopped exercising to look at me. "Ethan and Elly are just friends, right?"

"Ethan's shy. For a while, Elly thought he didn't like her all that much, but he always found excuses to be around her. You can tell by the way he looks at her that they're more than friends. The rest of us might as well be invisible when she's in the room."

Lanita drew her eyebrows together, folding the crease above her nose. "So they're dating?"

"They've gone on a few dates. And he calls her three or four times a day. Next week, his company is flying her to San Francisco for a business meeting. I wish I could go. My boyfriend's there too."

I told her about Wyatt as she went through another round of exercises. I told her how we'd met on that gravel road after the rainstorm left everything shiny and green. I told her about the next day we'd spent together and then the next. I told her the things we'd said and felt. I told her about the paintings, the road trips, the Cow Festival, our plans to go to New York City, and the day his cousin kicked him out.

She finished her jumping jacks and bent with her hands on her knees to catch her breath. "So you think Wyatt's in San Francisco?"

"That's where he said he was going."

"I've always wanted to go to San Francisco." She sipped from her water bottle. "I got another three weeks of leave before I'm back on duty. We should go together."

"I'd do anything to see Wyatt, but I don't have any money." If I left now I'd probably also lose my job. I'd agreed to work double shifts while Elly was out of town.

"Don't worry about money, Maren. If you'll show me around San Francisco, I'll pay your way." Lanita picked up her phone. "When did you say Elly was leaving?"

36

ELLY

IT was bad enough Lanita had followed me to San Jose. She and Maren had come out on the same flight and stayed in the same hotel. Now Lanita wanted to follow along on my visit to LibraryStar. As if that wasn't bad enough, the hotel hair dryer didn't work. Now I had ten minutes to arrange my wet hair into some kind of style, using only the three bobby pins I'd brought in my suitcase. "Wouldn't it be better if Ethan showed you around LibraryStar?" I asked Lanita.

She sat on the edge of my bed, her hair perfectly arranged in long curls. "I'm planning to surprise him. If he's not there, I'll need someone to introduce me to his family."

I attempted a French knot. "My relationship with Ethan's family isn't the best. I think you're better off introducing yourself."

Lanita picked up my comb. "Why don't you let me French braid your hair?"

No way was I handing my hair over to my arch nemesis. "You don't happen to have a hair dryer I could borrow?"

"Nope. Maren took both key cards when she went out looking for Wyatt." Lanita turned sideways to check her outfit in the mirror. She wore skinny jeans with a bright pink asymmetrical top. She hadn't worn her promise ring since our breakfast together. "I'd still like to tag along. If I've learned anything in the military, it's that any connection's better than no connection."

I wrestled the three bobby pins into place while Lanita awaited my answer. What could it hurt to take her along? "I'll drive," I finally said.

Jake had gotten me a rental car for the day. Lanita had one too, but I didn't trust her to drive. She startled too easily.

While we drove, Lanita kept her eyes closed. She couldn't stand busy roads. How she could live in DC was beyond me. To keep her mind off her fears, I asked her where she'd grown up. She told me about her childhood in Appalachia. Lanita claimed she was the first woman in her family to complete high school, the first to drive a car, and the first to travel outside the state of Kentucky.

I'd heard of mountain people, but I'd never met anyone who came from that background. I wasn't sure I believed her. "So you grew up in a cabin?" I asked.

"No indoor plumbing, no phones, and no electricity."

"How do you keep in touch with your family?"

"I write letters. My younger brother reads them to my parents. He wants to join the Army, same as me. Just has to finish high school. It's a lot of work for him now, having to do his chores and his homework and walk to the bus stop." She explained how, as a child, she started the fire in the stove every morning, did all the cooking, and took care of the animals. "Mama always told me if I worked hard enough, I could get to a place where I'd never have to work again."

It was a short drive to LibraryStar, and I still asked questions as we walked into the building. "Do you ever go home?"

Lanita followed me to the reception desk. "Sure. I took Ethan with me last year. I'll probably take him again this fall."

I told the receptionist I'd come to see Candi. Then I pushed back my shoulders and headed for her office. Lanita followed. When I passed my old desk, I pointed her in the direction of Ethan's cubicle. Then, doing my best to avoid seeing him, I hustled to Candi's office.

I took a stack of bills from an envelope in my purse as I walked through Candi's door. It wasn't much, certainly not enough to pay for new leather upholstery in a car, but it was all I had to give: $225. If I expected Jake to compensate me for my losses, I'd do the same for his wife. Besides that, I didn't want Jake and Candi to feel like I owed them anything.

Candi stood up from behind her desk. Her belly stuck out round and high in her red wrap dress. "Hello, Elly."

I laid the bills on her desk. "This is for the damage I did to your car. Sorry it's taken me so long."

She stared at the bills. "You didn't have to do that. Ethan told me it was an accident. I'm sorry I misjudged you before."

I shrugged. "I *was* angry, but I didn't do it on purpose."

She looked at her watch. "I'm starving. Let me go get Jake."

She waddled off, leaving me there with her peace lilies, my money, and the view of the palm trees outside. I sat in a chair opposite her desk and plucked little balls of pilling off my old black skirt, trying to keep my feet from tapping out a time step.

Ethan appeared in the doorway. "Hi, Elly." I jumped in my seat. "Candi told me you were here."

I stared at him, not knowing what to say. Though I hadn't answered his calls and texts for a week now, seeing him made me want to take back everything I'd said about never speaking to him again. I could accept just being his friend.

Lanita must have found out Ethan was with me and had come running from the cubicles. She tackled him with a hug while he watched me over the top of her head. I wasn't sure, but I thought I saw disappointment in his eyes.

She looked up at him, smiling. "Are you surprised I came to visit you?"

He coughed. "Yeah."

"Maren and I flew with Elly."

He looked from her to me. "You came together?"

I folded my arms and raised my eyebrows. I didn't have to speak. He knew what I meant.

Jake burst through the door. "Hey, Elly, it's good to see you." He extended his hand to me. Then he turned toward Candi, who was just now waddling into the room. "Did you hear Candi and I are gonna be parents? A little girl." He was full of that same nervous enthusiasm he'd had when my dad hired him.

I stood to shake his hand. "Ethan told me. Congratulations." I could feel Ethan watching me, but I didn't look his way.

Jake adjusted his cuff links. "Thanks for coming to meet with us. I thought we'd take you to lunch first . . . before we talk business." It was his standard mode of operation: any time you have something unpleasant to say to someone, buy food first.

I smiled. "Sounds good." I had my plan in place too. No fancy lunch would change it.

"Let's get going, then." He turned to Ethan. "You want to drive her, Ethan? Or do you want to ride with us?"

"I'm afraid I'll have to cancel," Ethan stammered as Lanita hung on his arm. "I should probably introduce you. Candi, Jake, this is Lanita. She's an old friend from DC. I didn't know she was coming into town."

Candi tilted her head to the side, smiling, as she took Lanita's hand. "It's so nice to meet you." There was nothing in Candi's reply to suggest she'd ever heard of Lanita. Had Ethan kept her a secret from his family too? Was he embarrassed by her?

Jake shook Lanita's hand. Then he turned to me with an eye roll. "You can drive with us if you want, Elly."

Jake had a new car, a black Audi sedan he called a family car. No sooner did we get in than Candi announced she'd felt the baby kick. Jake put his hand on her belly and waited. "I missed it again."

"You have to be patient," Candi said.

Jake kept his hand on her belly as he pulled out of the parking lot. "I never thought I'd enjoy being a father so much," he said. "You should see me, Elly. I keep ultrasound pictures in my wallet."

Candi giggled. "Jake's bought more clothes for the baby than I have. And he's already got the nursery set up. The baby isn't due for another four months." Candi went on to describe the decorating scheme in the nursery—complete with a hardwood floor, wainscoting, and a sheepskin rug. Not that I cared. The furniture was all solid oak and meant to grow along with their little girl. It sounded cute but expensive.

The restaurant they took me to also seemed expensive. The airy Italian place featured high ceilings, linen tablecloths, and real flowers. Jake told me it was Candi's favorite. He'd reserved a table in the back by the floor-to-ceiling window. Once we ordered our food, the conversation turned more serious. "Before we talk about the letter from your lawyer, I have to tell you it hasn't been easy starting LibraryStar," Jake told me. "It's not like it was for your dad. This economy isn't favorable for start-ups."

It's not like it was for your dad? It was all I could do not to haul off and hit him. I tapped my feet through three cramp rolls under the table. "Dad started out with five employees, working out of an old car-mechanic's shop. He didn't have a rich father-in-law either." I'd always suspected Candi's father had invested heavily in LibraryStar, and the way Jake looked down at the table confirmed my suspicion. "My dad stayed in business because he knew how to handle money."

Jake sipped on his soft drink. "But inflation drove him out of business, and it's going to drive me out of business, too, if I'm not careful."

I sat taller in my chair. "Inflation didn't drive him out of business. You did. You stole the programs we wrote, made a few improvements, and undersold us. That's why he went out of business."

"It's a free market system, Elly. Competition is part of the game." Jake shook his head as if I could never understand. "I didn't mean to talk business during our lunch. I meant to ask how your mom's doing. Is she enjoying Maryland?"

That was it. I knew what I needed to say, and I couldn't avoid it any longer. "I don't mind discussing business. I came here to discuss business. And since you asked about my mom, I'll tell you how she is. She's living in her mother-in-law's basement. That's why I'm here, Jake. I'm not here for me. I don't need the money. I can spend the rest of my life paying off my father's business debts, but Mom and Grace deserve better. Dad built his company to provide for them. Because of you, they lost their home."

Jake scratched the back of his neck. I kept going. "You know you copied our programs. We shouldn't have to spend a lot of money for lawyers to fight about it. I'll give you two weeks to decide how you're going to make it up to my family. If I don't hear from you by then, there will be a lawsuit." I'd delivered the ultimatum like I'd planned, but I hadn't planned what to do afterward.

Candi looked at Jake. "Is it true, Jake? You copied the programs?"

Jake rolled his eyes. "Programmers copy code all the time."

I couldn't keep sitting there, waiting for my lunch to arrive. I stood up from the table. "Please tell the server I won't be eating here after all." With that, I walked straight out of the restaurant. I had plenty of other things to worry about, number one being Lanita.

37

ELLY

SO much for Maren playing tour guide. Lanita hadn't enjoyed the previous day's visit to Wyatt's old high school or her tour of motorcycle hangouts. When Maren begged me to take over her tour guide duties, I'd agreed to it. I didn't want to spend any more time with Lanita, but I was curious to know what had happened between her and Ethan. On top of that, I'd returned the rental car Jake got me, so tagging along with Lanita in her rental car was a way to get out of the hotel. That's how I ended up with her in Muir Woods.

I walked with Lanita along the path that led into the redwood forest. These weren't the giant redwoods she'd expected. You couldn't drive a car through one. Still, their trunks were bigger than any I'd seen in Maryland. I'd spent time here as a child with my parents. Back then, it'd seemed so far from the city.

I loved to watch the tourists. Busloads of people from China milled around us. They carried expensive cameras and wore mismatched clothing. A toddler threw a fit because his parents bought him the wrong flavor of ice cream. Gray-haired couples walked arm in arm.

"I worry about Maren," Lanita said.

"Me too." Maren had spent every minute of our trip either searching for Wyatt or crying about how she couldn't find him.

"Do you think Wyatt's avoiding her?" Lanita asked.

Her words stung more than anything she could have said about Ethan. I pretended to watch a bird peck at something on the ground. "If you'd seen Wyatt and Maren together, you'd have a hard time believing he'd ever avoid her."

Lanita shrugged. "Not all men are as committed as Ethan."

"You might be surprised," I said, failing to keep the anger from my voice.

Lanita looked at her watch. "Maren told you Ethan's meeting us here, right?"

"No." I couldn't show emotion. It never did any good to show emotion.

"He's taking a long lunch." Lanita pointed back the way we came. "He said he'd meet us at the gift shop at noon. We should head over there now."

She acted as if it were the most normal thing for the three of us to hang out, but I knew what it was—an act.

I refused to take part. "You go ahead. I'm sure you two would rather be alone. Just call me when you're done."

I walked down the path, hoping to put Lanita and Ethan far behind me. It felt colder than I'd planned for a morning in July. I folded my arms close to my body. I'd be warmer if I moved—and the faster the better. Keeping my eyes on the path ahead, I wove around groups of tourists.

It wasn't fair that I'd been through the same rejection twice. Two times the men I loved had chosen someone else. Did Heavenly Father think I was strong enough for this? Why did I need a man anyway? I was better off on my own. I had too many responsibilities to even think about getting married and having a baby. And what if Lanita was right about Wyatt? Maren definitely wasn't strong enough.

As I walked deeper into the forest, the crowds thinned out. It was just me and my thoughts. I plodded on until my footsteps became a mantra: *no more men, no more men*. I was happy enough to be single. I had my family. I had the Church. Now that I wasn't calling Ethan, I'd have time to do more at church than sit on the back row once a week. I had my tap dancing. I had my job at the dairy store. Thanks to Maren's request, Colton had hired temporary workers to replace us during our absence.

I didn't notice the sound of footsteps behind me. "Elly!" I turned to see Ethan running to catch up with me.

So much for keeping my emotions in check. Being near him sent my heart racing. "Lanita's waiting at the gift shop," I said.

His eyes pleaded. "I need to talk to you."

My "no more men" mantra hadn't done any good. "Okay."

He wore a plain, blue T-shirt with jeans. "Dave's been calling you all week about that job. I know he doesn't seem like much, but he's a top manager. Don't judge him by the fact that he's my roommate. He pays a lot in child support."

That's what this was about? My job hunt? I continued walking, keeping my eyes on the path ahead. Looking at Ethan would only weaken my resolve. "Thanks for letting me know." I hoped he would leave then. What more could he have to say to me? I quickened my pace. He kept up. "Lanita's waiting for you," I reminded.

"Do you think she's getting better?"

It took me a few seconds to process what he'd said. I stopped. "You're asking *me* if she's getting better?" If I had to guess, I'd say she was getting worse.

Ethan stopped. "You don't think she's faking, do you?"

"What do you think she's faking? Her illness or getting better from it?"

He stuck his hands in his pockets. "I don't know."

I remembered the way I'd had to coax Lanita from her rental car earlier. And while she drove us here, she'd panicked at the sight of a bearded man. I'd grabbed the wheel to keep her from running us off the road.

"She definitely isn't faking the illness, but you'll have plenty of time to figure it out for yourself," I said. "She's staying another week."

He combed his fingers through his hair. "I thought she was leaving tomorrow."

"Maren and I are leaving tomorrow. She's leaving next Thursday. You know she's throwing a baby shower for Candi, don't you?" I still couldn't look at his face. His disappointment would show too clearly. "Is it true Lanita grew up without electricity?"

He groaned. "It's true. I've seen her parents' house." He stepped closer. "Thanks for being her friend, Elly."

I finally looked at him. "Are we the only friends she has?"

"She has her Army buddies, but I'm the only one outside the military and her family." He looked at the top of my lip and smiled in a sad way. "I always meant to ask how you got that scar."

I ran my finger along the old wound. "I was four. I went headfirst down a slide and crashed into a boy wearing cowboy boots. My lip hit the heel of his boots. Maren says I should get it fixed."

"Don't fix it." He moved as if he were going to touch me.

I wanted to kiss him, but I also wanted to wring his neck. I stepped back.

"Lanita needs to know how you feel about her. And how you feel about me." I'd never told him I loved him. Would it have made a difference?

"I've already told her." He took a breath, held it, and then let it go with a sigh. "She isn't strong enough to accept it."

"Do you think she'll ever be strong enough?"

"I hope so." His eyes searched my face. "We were good friends before her deployment. I didn't realize she had any other feelings for me until the day she left for Afghanistan. When she asked me to marry her, I thought she was joking. But she didn't laugh. That's when I saw I'd made a mistake spending so much time with her. She loved me and thought I felt the same. I held her life in my hands, Elly. If I broke her heart, she might take unnecessary risks during her deployment. If I didn't break her heart, she might think we were engaged. So I chose a middle road. I told her I'd still be here when she got back and we'd pick up where we left off. Considering the circumstances, I did the best I could."

It helped to hear Ethan's side of the story. Lanita had implied they were more than friends when she proposed. "So you weren't dating her?"

Ethan dug his hands into his pockets. "We hung out some. I never bought her dinner or anything like that. For me, it was about supporting the troops."

"What about that diamond ring?"

"I didn't know about it until yesterday. She bought it for herself." He didn't know about the ring? Ethan wasn't as guilty as I'd thought. He stepped closer to me. "I wish I could drive away with you," he said. "We could spend the day together."

My phone's ringtone sounded. His offer *was* tempting. I considered it for a moment before my rational side took over. My phone rang again. "Lanita's waiting," I said. "You can't leave her. You told her you were coming."

I expected him to argue his point. Instead, he turned and walked toward the gift shop with his head bent low. I remembered how he'd said his volunteer work was about saving lives. What he felt for Lanita was more obligation than love. Surely, it would end soon.

My phone rang for the fifth time. I answered. It was Maren. "I just talked to Wyatt's sister. She told me where he's working. I'll need to borrow Lanita's rental car to get there. It's up in Sonoma."

Her voice radiated excitement. I wanted to share in her triumph, but my questions about Wyatt held me back. We might finally discover the answers.

38

Maren

Have you ever felt terror and elation at once? My stomach churned with both emotions as Elly and I stood in front of the white clapboard building with black shutters. A sign above the door read "Silver Linings," but we didn't have to read the sign. I saw Wyatt's red Ducati with its Maryland license plate parked off to the side of the store.

My breathing relaxed for the first time since Wyatt left in the U-Haul. He wasn't lying dead on the side of the road somewhere. Still, my worries gnawed at me—if he wasn't dead, why hadn't he called?

The red door set off a buzzer as we entered. At the back of the store, a woman perched on a high stool behind a tall counter, arranging fabric samples. She wore her smooth blonde hair in a tight bun like a ballerina.

"Can I help you?" she asked.

I rushed across the store, almost knocking over a table lamp. "Yes, please, I'm looking for Wyatt. I'm Maren. I'm sure he's told you about me."

The woman's eyes widened. "Just a minute." She went through a Venetian red door to the back of the store.

Looking around, I could tell this was the kind of store for people with money. Lots of money. Furniture in shades of gray and white stood in groups, creating tableaus with different colored accessories throughout the room. One arrangement highlighted the color orchid, another played up a spicy orange cayenne. It reminded me too much of all our financial problems. For Elly and me, holding onto money was like carrying a handful of sand. Eventually, it all sifted through the cracks between our fingers, leaving only the gritty memory of its weight.

Had I done the right thing, coming here?

Elly pointed out some sheets draped over a table next to us. "These would look pretty in our room."

Any other day I would've studied the French toile design, but today I kept my eye on that back door. I strained to hear the slightest hint of conversation as Elly asked, "Who would pay seventy-nine dollars for a flat sheet?"

I stood on tiptoe to peer behind the counter. There, next to a bolt of fabric, lay Wyatt's black helmet. I recognized the scratch on the side. "He's here, Elly. His helmet's right there."

Elly wandered to a display of handmade soaps, holding each one to her nose and telling me whether they smelled of lavender or cloves or something else. "We could probably afford one of these. They're only twenty dollars."

I felt as if I might be auditioning for a performance. Nervous and breathless. It wasn't how I'd expected to feel. "I wonder what's taking so long," I said.

"Relax, Maren." Elly rolled her feet through a tap move that sounded like a gallop. "He's probably busy. We can wait."

I picked up a business card: *Silver Linings, Jillayne Stirling, Designer,* it read. A sign at the counter advertised custom-made invitations.

We waited ten minutes. An agonizing ten minutes. Elly walked around the store, pointing out things she thought we could make ourselves—a throw pillow here, a swag of pendants there, a hanging lamp embellished with colored glass disks, and a table made from a tree trunk. "Can you believe this is $3500?" She said, touching the table. "I could make this in a day. All I'd need is power tools."

The woman finally came back through the door, smiling one of those false, retail smiles. "I'm sorry. There's no one here by that name."

I leaned against the counter, pointing to Wyatt's helmet. "Then I'd like to see the man who owns that helmet. Can you please tell him Maren came to see him?"

The woman's facial muscles contracted until she wore an expression as tight as the bun in her hair. "That's my helmet."

Elly stood behind me. "What about the motorcycle beside the store?"

"That's mine too." The woman stood stiff. "Is there anything else I can help you with?"

"No, thanks." Elly's feet moved through a dance step. Brush. Brush. Tap. "We're just going to look around a little more."

Why was this woman lying? I knew it was Wyatt's motorcycle, and, even if she'd bought it from him, she couldn't have driven it here in that pencil skirt. Wyatt had told me about a friend who owned a design store. This woman had to be that same friend. But, if she were his friend, why would she keep me from seeing him? She'd have to know he loved me.

"It's a nice store." Elly pulled me toward a display of gilt-edged dinnerware. "I think we'd better go, Maren," she whispered. "Remember Lanita's waiting in the car."

The darkness seeped into me, casting doubt on my choice to come. "He's here. I know he's here." Why didn't he come running?

"I guess we can wait a little longer." Elly looked at the price tag on a turquoise candelabra. "But we can't afford to buy anything. Not with these prices."

We made our way around the store, pretending interest in every piece of furniture and accessory. I couldn't think of anything but Wyatt. I was so close. I couldn't leave without seeing him.

We'd started our second lap around the store when the woman approached us. "If you're not interested in buying, I have to ask you to leave."

Elly clasped my arm, willing me to keep quiet. "Of course we're interested in buying," she said. "It's just taking us a while to decide."

"Maybe I can help," the woman said, sounding bored. "What are you most interested in?"

While Elly said something about handmade soaps, I made my break. I maneuvered around the displays with the speed of an Olympic hurdler, dashed past the counter, and threw open the Venetian red door that led to the back room. I heard the woman yell, "You can't go back there."

It was too late. I stood at the threshold, looking into the poorly lit room. Shelves lined the walls. Assorted furniture took up the center of the room. At the end of the room, beside an unfinished table, Wyatt stood with his back to me. He held a can of wood stain in one hand and a brush in the other.

No sooner had I seen him than someone pulled me back by my arm, keeping me from entering the back room. "I said you can't go back there," the woman said. Wyatt turned as she shut the door, separating us once again. Had he seen me?

"Wyatt!" I yelled. I didn't care about his job. I needed to talk to him.

The woman turned a key in the lock. "I'm calling the police."

I watched her take her phone out. "Wyatt!" I yelled. If he had seen me, he would be here already. I pounded on the door. "Wyatt! It's Maren." I felt as if I were in someone else's body, living someone else's life. Darkness soaked into me, the way it had when I'd run over Elly's foot. This wasn't me. I wasn't a woman who yelled in stores.

Elly stood on the other side of the counter, apologizing to the woman. "Maren," she said. "We should go. Lanita's waiting in the car."

I hadn't come this far to give up. Wyatt was the man I loved, and something was wrong. Our relationship was dissolving like a watercolor painting left in the rain. I couldn't let it fade away. "Wyatt!" I yelled. I yelled his name again and again as Elly pulled on my arm, trying to get me to leave.

I don't know how long I stood there yelling. After my voice grew hoarse, I heard a man behind me. Jillayne said something to him about a disturbance, and Elly said something about depression.

A police officer stepped into my periphery vision. "Ma'am, you'll have to come with me."

I clung to the door handle. "Please, I need to talk to my boyfriend."

The police officer took out his handcuffs. He was an older man with gray hair in his mustache. He had a weary look, as if he'd lost his patience long ago. "Either we do this the easy way and you walk out on your own," he said. "Or we do this the hard way. Which will it be?"

I needed more time. "This is a free country. I have every right to be here."

"This is private property. You've been asked to leave." He clipped the handcuff onto my wrist. Then he forced my arms behind me, clamping my other wrist into the handcuffs.

Elly stood behind us. "You're not arresting her, are you?"

He grabbed me by the elbow. "Yes, ma'am, I am."

"Wyatt!" I yelled. "The police are taking me away. Please tell them you're my friend."

I was so shocked to be in handcuffs, I allowed the officer to lead me from the store. How could Wyatt do this to me?

"What's wrong with Wyatt, Elly? Something has to be wrong with him."

Elly stood back from the police car as the officer forced me inside. I watched Lanita come out of her rental car to join her. I wished I could have heard what Elly told Lanita and then what the officer said to them both as they stood beside the police car.

Elly almost never cried, but I saw her wipe a tear from her cheek. I couldn't believe our visit had ended this way. Now I had more to worry about than ever.

39

ELLY

WITH all the stress of Maren getting arrested, I forgot to call Ethan's roommate about the head programmer job. After the officer released Maren and we drove back to the hotel with Lanita, I phoned Dave to apologize, explaining that our flight left in the morning, so I couldn't come for an interview after all.

"That's okay," he said. "I can interview you tonight at my apartment. I'd do it at the office, but I've got my kids today." If things worked out with Ethan—like I hoped they would—I might regret skipping the interview.

Lanita went shopping with Candi that evening, and I couldn't leave Maren alone in the hotel room. "Come on," I told her. "I need you to play with some kids during my interview."

Despite the fact that she had a migraine, Maren agreed to come. After a fast-food dinner and a taxi ride, I dragged Maren into Dave and Ethan's apartment. She held a hotel washcloth to her face as she flopped down on the microfiber sofa. So much for her helping with the kids. They zoned out in front of the television while Dave interviewed me at the kitchen table.

The last time I'd sat at this kitchen table, I'd felt like Ethan had brought me into his inner circle. How was I to know that his inner circle included one more person he didn't want me to meet? I looked around, checking to see if Ethan might be home. He wasn't.

"I can see you're busy, so we'll keep this short," Dave said. "I already know from Ethan's description that you're the perfect candidate for the job." He listed the responsibilities, letting me know I'd only be working on the most challenging programs. The rest of the time, I'd manage my team. It was the exact job I'd wanted.

As we talked salary and benefits, Maren interrupted. "I think I might have to throw up in your bathroom." She ran for the bathroom, not waiting for his reply.

Dave blinked. "That's fine." We went on talking, trying to ignore the sounds coming from behind the bathroom door. The salary was more than I expected—enough to pay off our debts in a matter of years rather than decades. I would have health insurance again and a retirement plan. Still, I would've rather talked about what was happening between Ethan and Lanita.

Dave offered me the job as Maren emerged from the bathroom, wiping her mouth with her washcloth. I watched her walk back to the sofa. "I'd love to accept," I said. "But it's not as simple now that I've moved. I'll have to think about it."

Dave pulled out his phone. "Let me talk to my boss about the salary. I'm going on a Disney cruise with my kids next week, and I want to work something out with you before I leave." The doorbell rang. Dave punched numbers into his phone as he went to answer it.

Ethan's phone sat on the counter. For a second, I wondered why he'd left it home. Then I heard a familiar voice at the door. I looked up to see Candi biting her nails as she spoke to Dave. Lanita stood behind her.

"Is Ethan around?" Candi asked. "We wanted to show him something . . . and use your bathroom if that's okay."

Dave opened the door wide for them to enter. "Ethan's not here, but you can use the bathroom." Candi bolted past us as Dave spoke on the phone.

Candi wanted to use the bathroom? I stood, trying to block her path. "Umm, Candi, before you go—"

"I cleaned up after myself," Maren said, still holding the washcloth over her face.

I sat back down in the kitchen chair. "Never mind."

Why did the sight of Candi and Lanita together make me more nervous than a job interview did? My feet tapped out cramp rolls beneath the table.

Lanita sat on the love seat across from Maren. "Candi and me did a little investigating at Silver Linings."

The look on Lanita's face sent panic through me. She seemed like she couldn't wait to tell us what she'd discovered. I walked closer to the sofa, where Maren lay.

Maren sat up and lifted the washcloth from her face. "Was Wyatt there?"

"Jillayne was helping someone else, so she had Wyatt come design our invitations. They have the cutest invitations. Anyway, while he worked, I told him I'm a friend of yours and that I was waiting in the car this afternoon when you got arrested. He said he's sorry about that whole police thing." Lanita seemed like she was on our side, but was she really?

Maren held the washcloth to her forehead. "So he knew I was there?"

"Him and Jillayne have some sort of partnership going on. That's why he couldn't talk to you. He'll be part-owner of a store they're opening downtown. He was embarrassed Jillayne found out about you." Lanita smiled.

I wanted to slap that smile off her face. "Embarrassed?" I asked. "Why would Wyatt be embarrassed about Maren?"

Lanita looked at me with a certain significance. "A woman doesn't like finding out her man's seeing someone else on the side. Wyatt told me Jillayne and him have been together off and on since high school."

Maren stared straight at the blank wall in front of her. "That doesn't make any sense," she whispered.

It made sense to me. Wyatt needed money, so he went running back to his old girlfriend. What didn't make sense was the way he'd treated Maren.

Despite Maren's reaction, Lanita still seemed to be enjoying herself. "Candi gave him a piece of her mind about how Maren needs to know one way or the other how he feels about her. He promised he'd be in touch."

Candi emerged from the bathroom. She cast a worried glance my way before she turned to Lanita. "We should get going."

Lanita opened her purse. "Okay, just let me show them the sample invitation Wyatt made."

"Why don't we wait and show it to Ethan first?" Candi bit her lip, and I had the feeling that, for the first time in her life, Candi was on my side.

"I *would* like to see it," Maren said, reaching her hand out. Lanita passed her the invitation. Maren stared at it, confusion growing in her face. "I thought this was an invitation for Candi's baby shower."

Lanita laughed. "Candi already has invitations for her baby shower. I had to come up with something else."

I leaned closer, trying to get a look at the invitation. I couldn't stop my right foot from tapping out a flap ball change.

"I think we should go now," Candi interrupted. She stood in the doorway.

Lanita kept talking. "So I planned an engagement party for me and Ethan." As she said it, Dave laid a protective hand on my shoulder. I hadn't noticed he stood beside me. He was still speaking on the phone with his boss, saying something about a company car.

Maren held the sides of her head as if trying to keep the room from spinning. "But you aren't engaged to Ethan."

Lanita headed for the door. "Ethan doesn't want me to have to make any big decisions while I'm readjusting to normal life. But I've wanted to marry him for the past three years. All we need now is for Ethan to find a job in DC. I can't up and quit the Army."

She held her hand out, flaunting her diamond ring as she walked to the door. Clearly, Ethan hadn't found a way to make her understand his feelings. If he cared about me, wouldn't he have broken up with Lanita already? I was so glad I hadn't told him "I love you."

"Wyatt should be in touch soon," Lanita said.

"You go ahead to the car, Lanita." Candi waved her off. "I forgot something."

Candi came back into the living room, shutting the door behind her. Looking like a schoolgirl about to give her first speech, she stared at me. "I just wanted to say Jake and I talked about . . . what you told us. We're going to work something out." She reached toward me, thrusting a fistful of bills into my hand, the same bills I'd given her. "I think we owe you much more than you ever owed us."

I didn't know what to say. It wasn't like Candi to be so accommodating. Was this a ruse? I looked into her face. She seemed sincere. It was more than that, though. She felt sorry for me. "Thanks," I said, watching Candi pivot with the grace of a beauty pageant contestant and exit the apartment. But I didn't want her empathy. I wanted her respect.

Maren pinched the bridge of her nose. "I cannot believe I gave Lanita my best painting."

I wished I could throw my arms around Maren and have a pity

party for the two of us there in Ethan's apartment, but I turned to Dave instead. "Sorry about the interruption."

When he spoke next, his words bounced off my brain. I didn't know whether he offered me a higher salary or apologized for Ethan.

"We need to go home now," I said.

By *home*, I no longer meant San Jose. I meant Grandma's house. For the first time, I longed to sit on Grandma's couch beside the piles of laundry and pet her dogs while she filled me in on the latest neighborhood gossip. I'd much rather hear about her neighbor's hip replacement than anything about Ethan Ferrero.

40

Maren

Was it really all that horrendous to hold flowers on my lap during take-off and landing? Perhaps they were too large, but they were a gift from Wyatt, white gardenias. Their delicate, bridal blooms made no sense when paired with his note: *I'm sorry if I led you to believe I felt more for you than I did.* That was all it said.

He hadn't come himself to deliver them.

I watched the gardenias wilt as we flew from San Francisco to Baltimore. They were too delicate, too easily bruised. I tried to save them, wrapping the stems in wet paper towels from the restroom, but nothing I did could keep them from dying. In the end, every time someone walked down the center aisle of the airplane, a petal fell off. I'd lost my first love, and nothing would ever be so fresh and pure again.

Elly had slept the whole way in the seat beside me. She'd stayed up the night before, telling me about Ethan and Lanita.

"Why didn't you tell me about Ethan and Lanita before?" I'd asked.

Elly yawned. "You were so upset about Wyatt that I didn't want to stress you out."

It was strange how she could be in the same situation as I was, and yet she could be so calm. I was the one who cried all night. I threw up in her friend's bathroom. I got arrested for making a disturbance and now had a $125 ticket. Why couldn't I hold myself together the way Elly did?

I didn't read, or watch the movie on the airplane. Hours passed as I replayed in my mind everything that happened with Wyatt, searching for what I'd done wrong. I wasn't as professional as Jillayne Stirling. I probably wasn't as beautiful either, or as educated. I hadn't taken Wyatt anywhere he hadn't gone before. In all the time we dated, I'd only taught him one new thing—I'd taught him to paint, but that was nothing compared to what he'd taught me. I'd done so many things wrong and shown myself weak in so many ways. I couldn't tell Elly how I felt. She would say it was the depression talking and that I should take my medicine.

My bags felt heavier as I carried them off the airplane. I battled with all my strength to get through the baggage claim area and out to where Grandma and Grace waited in the Cadillac. Grandma wore an orange, cotton dress in an African pattern and hobbled out of the car to hug me. "It's always darkest right before the dawn, my dear. You'll find someone new."

I slumped into the back seat while Elly lugged the suitcases into the trunk. "Please don't say anything about Colton," I warned.

Grandma clasped my knee with her bony fingers. "I wasn't going to say anything about Colton, but since you mentioned him, I'll say this. The way a man treats animals is a good indication of how he's going to treat his wife. I'm sure you've seen the way Colton treats those cows."

"I'm not a cow, Grandma."

It took another hour of driving before we arrived at Grandma's house. The sky glowed peach and pink from the sunset as Mom greeted us on the front porch. She'd just come home from work and still wore a white apron over her black uniform.

Elly did her best to sound cheerful, emphasizing her successful job interview and the negotiation with Jake, but I knew she felt the same way I did. She didn't want to come back to a place that reminded her of things she needed to forget. We could never come *home* anymore.

I handed Mom my bedraggled gardenias. "Oh," Mom said. "The poor things."

At least I still had my nightgown. I'd slip into it, swallow one of my pills, and wait for the numbness to return.

Hefting my carry-on bag onto my shoulder, I dragged my suitcase through the garage, into the kitchen, and down the stairs. When I opened the door to our room, I found the room rearranged. Someone had cleaned it. My nightgown, normally tucked beneath my pillow, wasn't there. Instead, I found a pair of pink pajamas. I looked in the dresser drawers, now full of our clothes. My nightgown wasn't there. Mom appeared in the doorway.

"It looks better, don't you think? Grandma let me donate some of her things to a family whose house burned down."

"I can't find my nightgown."

Mom sat on the edge of Elly's bed, facing me. "I threw it away. It was so worn out."

I tried to remember what day the trash truck came. "When? When did you throw it out? Is it still in the trash can?"

"The trash truck came this morning. It's gone. I'm sorry."

There, on top of my dresser, lay the key that Wyatt had given me, the key to my motorcycle. I could feel the darkness coming back, the darkness that wasn't me. I had to get out before I did something else I regretted.

Mom patted my knee. "I found you a new doctor. I think you'll like him . . . Can I get you something to eat?"

"No, thank you. I'm going to sleep." I lay down with my clothes still on, and Mom turned off the light. I listened as she walked up the stairs, each one creaking. Then I got out of bed and grabbed the key. Mom wouldn't understand.

While Grandma, Grace, and Elly ate bowls of Mom's rice pudding at the kitchen table, I took the keys to the Subaru. I wasn't hungry. My body only needed to drive.

As the sky turned lavender, I drove and prayed. My situation seemed impossible, but God could work miracles. He could bring Wyatt back to me if I only had enough faith. I felt myself pulled toward the orchard as if by a migratory instinct. Some people ate chocolate on their bad days. Elly tap-danced. I had to drive a motorcycle.

The shiny new Kawasaki still waited beside the barn. My helmet sat on a shelf under the eaves. I put it on with my heart racing. Was I going to ride all by myself? In the dark? I'd only driven the bike once, enough to know that it wasn't at all like riding a bicycle. Driving wasn't so much of a problem. It was starting. The first time I drove, I'd stalled the engine at least thirty times trying to get it into first gear.

I threw my leg over the bike and turned the key. The two red lights flashed on, and Wyatt's training came back to me. I twisted the throttle with my right wrist and the engine sputtered to life. A sense of power came from sitting on top of the engine. And vulnerability. I didn't have Wyatt to hold onto anymore.

I squeezed the clutch the way Wyatt had taught me—slow and steady. Then I clicked down with my left toe on the gear. It caught. I eased forward. All on my own, I'd started the bike.

I drove down the long gravel driveway in first gear with the headlights lighting my way. Driving at night wasn't the best idea for my second solo ride, but I didn't plan to go far. This was a practice ride. I turned onto the road that ran beside the orchard. I'd drive to the place where Wyatt rescued me, and then I'd come back. The brake nestled under my right foot, just like in a car. I had nothing to worry about.

On the pavement, I gave it throttle and shifted to second gear. From there, it felt easier to drive. I shot up to third gear and then fourth. I was the only one on the road, alone with the trees and the grass.

It felt like flying, the way I pushed through the wind, going faster and faster. Wyatt hadn't let me go this fast while he taught me. Wouldn't he be surprised if I drove all the way to California? He'd want me back if I could do that.

Only one stop sign marked the little country road. I stopped at it, kicked the gear down to first and squeezed in the clutch. Once again, I eased it into first gear without a problem. My bad luck had turned.

I raced on ahead. Not wanting to slow down, I passed the dirt road and turned instead onto another paved road, one I'd traveled a few times with Wyatt. It was narrow, curvy, and surrounded by trees—the kind of road Wyatt liked best. The sky darkened to an inky blue. Here beyond the city lights, the stars twinkled in their nakedness, fully exposed to the darkness.

The Kawasaki engine roared as I gave it throttle, forcing the bike to speed up the hill. I leaned into the curves the way Wyatt had leaned. With each curve I went faster and the engine roared louder. I remembered Wyatt telling me to shift up when the engine sounded too loud. I kicked the gear up as I headed into the next curve, but something felt wrong.

The back tire skidded to the side. I steered to the left, trying to straighten the bike, but it tipped. I pushed on the brakes, unable to keep the bike from falling sideways and unable to steer away from the rocks ahead of me.

41

ELLY

SOMETHING was wrong. The clock read 3:00 a.m. and Maren still hadn't come home. She'd taken the Subaru, so I knew she wasn't somewhere in the house. I'd seen that look on her face, the same look she'd had the day we met Dr. Jenner—a blank look, as if nothing mattered to her anymore.

I called her phone. She didn't answer. The only message was from Ethan, asking me to call him about the job. I deleted it. If I ever called him again, it would be after he broke up with Lanita.

I walked out to the van three times and turned back three times before I got in. Where could Maren have gone? It would probably be someplace where she'd spent time with Wyatt. Not that I knew how to get to any of those places. I drove to the dairy store. It was empty. Feeling powerless, I parked the van and prayed.

I needed to find Maren, but I couldn't do it alone. I needed to tell someone, someone other than Mom and Grandma—they would only worry. I started to dial Ethan's number. Then I stopped. Who else could I call? The answer seemed clear: Colton.

I took a deep breath and dialed Colton's number. It rang five times. Then I hung up. What was I thinking, calling Colton at 3:00 a.m.?

A second later, my phone rang. "Is something wrong?" Colton asked.

My voice broke. "It's Maren." I couldn't say anything else. All the emotions from the past month had caught up to me.

"What can I do to help?"

I took a breath, willing myself to stay calm. "She took the car a few hours ago. I don't know where she went, but she shouldn't be alone."

"I have an idea where she might be." He sounded confident, as if he had much more than an idea.

I drove down the road to his house. I knew he lived across from the dairy in a home that had belonged to his parents, but I'd never driven past the crop of trees that sheltered it from the road.

Colton flipped on the outside lights for me. As I pulled into the driveway, I could make out the shape of his house. Grandma had told me how Colton drastically remodeled his parents' former home, but this wasn't the country home I'd expected. It was whimsical—a cross between a log cabin and a tree house that rose three stories high. If I hadn't felt so nervous, I'd have taken more time to admire the architecture. Instead, I parked the car and made a beeline for the arched entry, noticing only a stained glass detail on the front door.

Colton opened the door before I had a chance to knock. I could see a few wrinkles on the side of his face where he'd slept. Other than that, he looked ready for an ordinary day at the dairy. He had on his work boots and jeans. "I'll drive," he said, pulling the door shut behind him.

I followed Colton to his truck. "I'm sorry I had to bother you. I should have stayed with Maren after we got home from the airport."

Colton opened the door for me. "My dad always said there are two kinds of people in the world—those who blame themselves for problems and those who blame others. Most of the time it's a good thing to take responsibility, but you're blaming yourself for something that's not your fault."

I waited for him to get in on his side. "Yes, but I should have predicted this would happen."

Colton started the engine. "It's more my fault than yours." In the dim light, I saw his Adam's apple go up and down.

"Why would you think that?" As far as I could tell, Colton had done nothing but help us since we'd moved in with Grandma.

"I'd rather not go into it." His eyebrows pulled in.

Now I was curious. "I wish you would." I could at least alleviate his guilt.

He sighed. "On the day of the Cow Festival, Vera Mills called me. She's Wyatt's aunt."

"Wyatt's aunt?" What did Wyatt's aunt have to do with any of this? As far as I knew, Maren had never even met her.

"Her bank account was overdrawn. Wyatt told her someone had hacked into her accounts and that he'd take care of it. But that didn't make sense to Vera, so she called me. I'm her home teacher."

Colton shook his head. "Once I got to her house and started going through her accounts, it became clear it wasn't a hacker. It was Wyatt. And we're not talking a few hundred dollars. We're talking tens of thousands on top of his salary."

"Wyatt?" My instincts told me Colton wasn't lying. The whole time I'd known Wyatt, I'd wondered how he could spend so much time with Maren and still throw cash around as if he worked nine to five.

"I didn't want to believe it at first. I thought my own feelings for Maren were getting in the way." Colton spoke Maren's name with reverence. "I also worried how Maren would react when she found out I was the one responsible for Wyatt leaving."

I touched Colton's arm. "I won't tell her."

"It might be better if she finds out," Colton said. "Wyatt isn't what he seems. She needs to know that."

I folded my arms across my chest, trying to ward off the shivers. Wyatt meant everything to Maren, but if he stole from his aunt, Maren couldn't be happy with him. "You did the right thing."

"It was a clear case of elder abuse. He took advantage of Vera because she'd lost her memory. She feared him. Even after she found out he'd stolen from her, she didn't want me to tell anyone."

I watched the headlights illuminate the trees and fences ahead of us as I thought through the situation. Was this why Wyatt broke off contact with us? Did he think we knew what he'd done to his aunt?

Colton explained that we would drive to Vera's house first to see if Maren was there. While we drove, I told him what had happened between Maren and Wyatt at that store in Sonoma.

Colton clenched his jaw. "Wyatt stood by while she got arrested? He's more of a jerk than I realized."

It untied a few knots inside me to hear him say it.

"There was a time when I trusted Wyatt," Colton said. "He hung around with my ex-wife all the time at the dairy store. That was before she was my ex. I didn't think much of it. The two of them had similar interests."

"Your ex-wife sounds like Maren."

"She was a lot like Maren." Colton swallowed. "I didn't find out until later—when we were in counseling—that Wyatt told Allison things about me that weren't true."

"Like what?" I asked.

Colton shook his head. "That I flirted with customers when she wasn't around and that he'd seen me take another woman out to lunch. He also told her I'd dumped waste in the creek. I hadn't done any of it, but his lies still caused a rift in our marriage."

"Why would Wyatt want to hurt you that way?"

Colton drew in his breath as if the memory still pained him. "The only thing I can think of is that he wanted my wife. After we divorced and she went back to stay with her parents in Georgia, he followed her there."

"So he dated her after your divorce?"

Colton stared straight ahead at the road. "I don't know. I never asked."

We pulled onto the dirt road that led to the orchard. There, in front of the barn, was our Subaru. I hopped from Colton's truck to open the door, expecting to find Maren sleeping in the backseat, but the car sat empty. "She must be around here somewhere," I said. "Maybe she went for a walk through the orchard."

"The motorcycle's gone," Colton said, pointing toward the barn.

"What?"

"Wyatt gave her a motorcycle. Didn't she tell you? It was parked there when I came last Sunday."

Panic filled me. "I forgot about that."

"She'll be okay. She knows to stick to country roads." His voice lacked conviction.

We got back in Colton's truck. I rolled down my window, listening for the sound of a motorcycle. "She could be hours away for all we know."

He started the engine again. "I don't feel like she's hours away."

Feel? I didn't feel anything but panic. "We should say a prayer," I said. He folded his arms, and I launched into my prayer of desperation. It consisted of the same sentence, repeated twice. "Please help us find Maren."

After the amen, Colton squeezed my hand. "We'll find her."

I muttered my prayer over and over as Colton drove. We drove past the orchard, watching for the lights of other vehicles. Nothing. Our headlights were the only lights I could see for miles around.

After a few minutes, we turned onto a ramshackle dirt road, where Colton explained that Wyatt had found Maren on the last day of their trek. It seemed like the kind of place she'd go. We bumped along, following it all the way to the end, before turning around and following it back to the paved road. "Where should we go next?" Colton asked.

Why was he asking me? It's not like I'd made any good decisions since my father got sick. I closed my eyes, trying to feel the Spirit. "Let's go left." Was I crazy to be up in the middle of the night searching for Maren? She was probably home in bed by now with the motorcycle parked in Grandma's garage.

We drove a few more minutes before we got to another road, veering off to the right. Colton turned onto it. He followed the narrow road through several curves before we saw a sparkle of metal. Colton stopped the truck and grabbed his flashlight from the glove compartment. "Stay here," he ordered in a voice that didn't sound at all like himself.

I watched as he walked behind the truck, moving the beam of his flashlight until he found what looked like a rearview mirror along the shoulder. As much as I wanted to obey my boss, I couldn't stay in the car any longer. "Maren!" I called as I jumped out.

There was no answer.

Colton swept the beam of the flashlight along the edge of the road, lighting trees and boulders, until he stopped on a large piece of black and silver plastic. I couldn't ask the question in my mind. *Was that a piece of Maren's motorcycle?*

Colton ran toward the plastic, pointing the flashlight ahead of him. I followed, rationalizing that it couldn't have been Maren's bike. It was more likely a piece of a car's bumper. We stopped in front of it long enough for me to see it wasn't a car's bumper.

Colton grabbed me above my elbow. "You should be in the car." He pointed his flashlight down the embankment in front of us. There, laying on its side against a tree, was a motorcycle. "It's a Kawasaki," Colton whispered. "A new one like Maren's."

I peered through the darkness at the crashed bike. Could Maren have walked away from that? "Maren isn't on it. Do you think she—"

Colton's grip on my elbow tightened. He put the flashlight in his pocket and reached toward my opposite shoulder, trying to turn me from the scene. "Let me take you back to the truck." His hands shook.

I pushed his hand from my shoulder. "If she's here, I need to see. I need to be here."

Colton let go. We stood side by side in the light of the truck's headlights, peering down the dark embankment. I strained to hear crying or moaning, but I heard only the sound of crickets chirping. It was too quiet. As Colton swept the beam of the flashlight down the grassy hill, I heard his breath catch.

She was there, a tangle of hair, helmet, and mud pushed up against a large rock. I recognized the light flowery pattern of her blouse, now stained dark. "Stay here," he ordered, running down the bank.

Colton held the flashlight on Maren as he ran. I couldn't tell whether she lay faceup or facedown. Grass covered her, and her limbs jutted out in unnatural angles. Colton knelt beside her, holding the flashlight in his mouth as he felt for a pulse.

I couldn't move. In my mind, I heard Ethan tell me about the day Candi almost drowned. He had stood there, watching his neighbor save his sister. Now I was doing the same thing. I took the phone from my pocket, but I couldn't look at it. I couldn't dial until I knew.

42

How had Wyatt gotten here so quickly? I heard his voice, breaking through my dream.

"I think she's alive. She's cold, but she's alive."

I felt his hand on mine. This was what I'd prayed for. Wyatt had come back to me.

"Can you hear me, Maren?" He yelled for someone to bring his coat and call 911.

I opened my eyes. Everything was dark and hazy. "I can't see you." I could only see the shadow of his head.

"Your helmet's all scraped up. Just lie still. The ambulance is on its way."

Everything hurt—my head, my back, my arms. I closed my eyes and let the sleep take me again. It was only for a little while. Wyatt came back. I had to live for Wyatt.

I woke again as someone lifted me. I lay strapped to a board, forced into rigidity. Pain shot through my spine and out my limbs. Straps held me down. I couldn't make myself more comfortable. People carried me up the hill, tipping the board as they walked. Someone had lifted the visor on my helmet. All lights focused on me—blinded me—but I had to open my eyes. I had to see Wyatt. As I squinted into the light, Elly stood over me. I couldn't move my head to see anyone else.

"Where's Wyatt?" Everything was dark outside the lights—a chiaroscuro.

Elly bent toward me. "We're going to the hospital with you, Maren. You're going to be okay."

"Where did Wyatt go?" I wanted to see him, to tell him how sorry I was for the scene I'd caused.

Elly looked away from me as if trying not to cry. "I'll make sure Wyatt knows what's happened. I'll call him."

What did she mean? Wyatt already knew about the accident. He was already here.

"Your mom is on her way," another voice said. It was a woman's voice. "She'll meet us at the hospital."

They carried me into a vehicle, an ambulance.

Every jostle pained me. I closed my eyes as the two paramedics, a man and woman, worked around me, asking questions. Did I have any allergies? Did I use any drugs? What did I remember about the accident? Was there another vehicle involved?

I stared at the white ceiling of the ambulance, unable to move. It seemed a hazy dream, as if I weren't really there.

"Am I going to die?" I asked.

The man bent to look in my eyes. "You're *not* going to die. Your vital signs are good."

My back and hips shrieked with pain at every bump in the road. It was too much. My eyes wouldn't stay open. I drifted in and out of the darkness as we rode to the hospital. Sometimes I heard the paramedics talking. Sometimes I heard Wyatt.

"You waited too long to shift up. The RPMs were too high," he said.

It seemed familiar. Had he told me that before? Or was it that he kept repeating himself? *The RPMs were too high. The RPMs were too high.*

The pain shot through me again as the paramedics carried me from the ambulance. Were we already at the hospital? Had I slept the whole way? I still lay strapped to the board, the board that never seemed level with the ground. Other people came now, meeting us. They lowered the board onto something level and smooth. Every inch of me burned with pain. I could hear Mom crying out a prayer in Portuguese.

"It's okay, Mom," I wanted to say. "Wyatt's back now. Everything is better." But she couldn't hear me. I spoke from my dreams.

When I woke again, I lay inside a tube. Had someone screamed? "It's not as bad as it looks, Ms. Goodwin," a man said. "The dark area is bruising. She has a concussion."

Pain consumed me—the pain along my spine from lying flat on a board, but also a burning, searing ache through my hips and legs.

"What are you going to do about her hip?" Grandma asked.

"Our best surgeon is on her way."

Surgeon? Did that mean I needed surgery? It came to me again. The curve in the road. The way the bike tipped. What happened to the bike? I wanted to know, but I was too tired to speak.

Mom said something in Portuguese, something about the priesthood. Then I heard Elly's voice. "Would it be all right if our friend came in to give Maren a blessing?"

My mind felt foggy, but I had to wake up. "What happened to the bike?" I asked, sounding hoarse and slow.

"You're lucky to be alive," a man said. His voice sounded familiar. Who was he? "The bike's replaceable. You aren't."

I opened my eyes to see Colton staring down at me. His light brown hair curled up from his forehead and caught a glow from the hospital lights. A smudge of dirt ran along the side of his tanned face. He looked alive, much more alive than I felt. "Is it okay if I give you a blessing?" His pupils expanded inside his hazel eyes.

"Yes." I squirmed against the straps.

His hands barely touched the top of my head. I listened to him say my name, but I couldn't stay awake long enough to hear the rest. I would ask him about the bike again when I woke up. It would only be a few minutes.

I woke in a different place, a bigger room with a nurse standing beside me. My head pounded. I could feel a bump behind my right ear, bigger and wider than any bump I'd ever had.

"The surgeon placed an external fixator on your pelvic bones," the nurse said. "It holds the bones in place while your other injuries heal."

My throat and mouth felt dry as chalk, but I was too nauseated to drink. "I feel sick."

The nurse put something in my IV, telling me it was for the nausea. "We can take you to your room now. Your family's waiting for you there."

While the nurse pushed me down the hall, she told me that a surgeon had also treated a tear in my shoulder, my broken elbow, and my broken leg. I had never broken a bone in my life, and now, here I lay with three. Wyatt would have to learn to love driving my Subaru.

In a flash, I recalled what had happened in that store back in Sonoma.

Wyatt would have to explain why he'd ignored me. He had to have a good reason.

The nurse pushed my gurney into a tiny room, where Elly, Mom, Grandma, and Grace waited. They stood silently watching as the nurses transferred me to the bed. I must have looked a mess with my IV and my little throw-up basin, but I had to see Wyatt.

"Is it okay if my boyfriend comes in?" I asked the nurse.

She smiled. "Certainly."

"He's here, isn't he?" I asked Mom.

Mom adjusted my dull gray blanket. "Who, *querida*?"

"Wyatt. I saw him last night. He rescued me."

Grandma patted my bandaged hand. "You need to forget about that good-for-nothing."

Mom, the nurse, Grandma, Grace, and Elly surrounded me, framing my bed with their bodies.

"But he came back," I said. "He's home now. I saw him."

Elly squinted at me. "Are you talking about the man who rescued you? That wasn't Wyatt. That was Colton."

At first, I thought Elly had missed seeing Wyatt, but then I realized I'd never seen him either. I'd imagined it all.

43

ELLY

THE hospital's vinyl easy chair was anything but easy to sleep in. It was my third night on the thing. And I probably wouldn't sleep, not when I knew I might lose my sister.

The doctors hadn't held back when they told us about her condition that morning. They'd discovered that Maren had somehow picked up a staph infection called MRSA—it didn't respond to antibiotics. The sores had spread along the road rash on her arms and legs. Now the doctors worried the infection would also spread to her surgical wounds.

Mom, Grandma, and I fasted and prayed all day, hoping for a miracle. So far, the miracle hadn't arrived. Her fever continued to rise, and her sores burned redder.

I watched her, lying pale against the white hospital sheets. Bandages and splints encased her limbs. IVs dripped steadily into both her arms. She'd refused all offers of food and drink. No juice or Jell-O had passed through her lips since her arrival. The bruises on her face had faded to a grayish blue, making her look even more on the verge of death.

We'd hoped that by now, she would be well enough to transfer to the hospital in Baltimore, where specialists could permanently repair her broken pelvis. Three days before, when the nurse brought her back from her first operation, Maren had smiled through her pain.

Then I'd told her the man who rescued her was Colton, not Wyatt, and she returned to the blank look. She'd given up. The psychiatrist hadn't helped much either. He'd only offered another prescription to add to Maren's long list of medications, only this one she couldn't take through her IV.

Maren slept fitfully, moaning and crying out in pain. When she spoke, she asked me the same questions she'd asked the hour before. "Have you talked to Wyatt?"

"Colton talked to him." It was no use telling her Wyatt didn't deserve her. She was delirious half the time and couldn't look at the situation logically. She must have forgotten about the gardenias.

Maren flinched with pain as she turned in the bed to look at me. "Is he angry about the bike?"

"It was insured. He can get a new bike. He's just glad you're okay." Wyatt hadn't actually said he was glad Maren was okay, but he'd cooperated with the insurance claims process. It seemed fitting that he should pay for all of this. He caused it.

At 10:00 p.m., after Maren fell asleep, Colton texted me, telling me not to worry about coming into work the next day. I figured that meant he hadn't gone to bed, so I called him. It was getting to be a habit. I'd called him the two previous nights also. It didn't fill the void I'd created when I'd stopped answering Ethan's calls, but it relieved me to have someone outside the family who understood the situation.

"Why don't you meet me down in the cafeteria?" Colton said.

"You mean the hospital cafeteria?" Though he hadn't seen Maren since that first day, it was clear he was as worried as I was. He'd have to drive twenty minutes from his house to meet me.

"I'll bring you pie," he offered.

I couldn't say no. I needed a break. Though I'd started my fast that morning, I hadn't eaten since my dinner with Grandma the night before, which meant I'd fasted for over twenty-four hours.

After Colton texted to say he'd arrived, I removed my protective gown and gloves, depositing them in bins by the door. I didn't want to leave Maren, but I didn't mind leaving her pasty-white room.

How could anyone think a stark little square room was the right place for someone to heal, especially someone like Maren? Maren's nurse stood at the end of the hall.

"I'll be back in fifteen minutes," I told her. Then I wandered through the maze of hallways until I found the brightly lit cafeteria.

A blueberry pie sat on the table in front of Colton—the same kind of pie I'd eaten in Ethan's apartment. That, in itself, would have made me cry. Combining it with my worries about Maren made me sob out loud.

"She's not better. She's worse." My voice came out high pitched and broken. I wasn't sure Colton could understand much of what I said, but I did my best to explain all the medical jargon about internal bleeding, pelvic fractures, road rash, and the staph infection. "I know I shouldn't have, but I looked up all her conditions on the Internet."

My sobs prevented me from saying the things I'd learned—the worst being that fifty-five percent of people who break their pelvises in motorcycle accidents die.

Colton leaned toward me. "Elly, she's going to be okay. I felt it when I gave her the blessing."

I remembered the peace I'd felt that day. Then I recalled a discussion Maren and I had when Wyatt stopped returning her calls. *Everybody's okay when they're dead* was what she'd said. If we felt like Maren would be okay, that could mean anything.

"But is she going to live?" I asked.

"She's going to live, Elly." He sounded so sure.

I took a breath, holding it until I felt calm enough to speak. "She's in so much pain."

Colton looked at the table for a long time before he shifted his gaze back to my face. "What can I do to help?"

I hated to say it. "If she's going to live, she has to fight this thing on her own. I'm afraid the only way she'll get better is if Wyatt comes back. Without him, she doesn't want to live."

Colton and I could do nothing. It all depended on Wyatt.

44

Has pain ever overpowered you? I wanted it to end. I needed it to end. But no drugs could take it away. No TV show could distract me from it. The days and nights blurred together. The faceless hospital personnel walked in and out at all hours, wearing gowns, masks, and gloves.

I wondered if I dreamed her, the nurse who came that morning as the soft light filtered through the window shades. She carried a small, wrapped gift. “This came for you,” she said, sounding much too cheerful. She placed the gift on the table beside my bed. Then she noticed Elly sleeping in the chair beside me. “Sorry to disturb you.”

I blinked, trying to focus my vision on the gift. The wrapping paper looked homemade. Someone had written on the glossy white paper with an iridescent gold pen. I could make out a few words from where I lay in bed: *The very instant that I saw you.* The words sparked my desire. I wanted to read the rest of that line, but moving would hurt too much.

“Can you hand it to me?” I asked the nurse as she walked away.

“Oh, sure. Sorry!” She turned back and placed the gift in my bandaged hand. “Do you want me to unwrap it for you?” she whispered.

“No, thank you.”

My swollen hands couldn’t grip the gold satin ribbon, and I couldn’t bend one elbow, but I managed to push the ribbon off the box. I searched the wrapping paper to reveal the entire sentence: *The very instant that I saw you, did my heart fly to your service.* Beneath that was Shakespeare’s sonnet comparing his love to a summer’s day.

This had to be from Wyatt. I looked for a tag and found one attached to the ribbon. It said simply, *To Maren, with love.* He didn’t have to sign his name. I knew he had sent the gift.

I had to wake Elly. "Look what Wyatt sent me." I knew once Wyatt found out about the accident, he'd come back to me.

Elly's eyes fluttered open. "What?" Wincing against the pain of movement, I held the package out to her. She read the tag. "To Maren, with love."

"Can you please open it for me? Be careful not to tear the paper. It has poems on it."

Elly slipped her gloved fingers beneath the wrapping paper. Everybody had to wear gloves around me. I understood the reasons behind it, but I still felt like a leper. MRSA wasn't that different from leprosy after all. It was a skin disease that could kill you. An ugly skin disease.

Elly unfolded the wrapping paper and opened the box to reveal dangling earrings made of freshwater pearls. Looking at them shimmering against the black velvet, I felt fully awake for the first time since the accident.

"They have to be from Wyatt. He likes the way white earrings stand out against my hair." Our relationship would be different now. We might even have to go to counseling, but at least he still felt something for me.

Elly examined the tag and wrapping paper. "How did it get here?"

"A nurse brought it," I said.

She turned the box over, searching for clues. "Huh."

"Will you help me put them on?"

Elly pushed back my hair to insert an earring. "They're pretty. You think Wyatt sent them?"

"Who else could it be? Do you think he delivered them himself?"

Elly scrunched her face as she put in my other earring. "Maybe."

"Will you ask them for me?" I begged. "Please?" If Wyatt was back in town, I needed to know.

Elly stood. "I'll see what I can find out." Approaching the door, she hung her hospital gown on a hook and deposited her gloves in the trash.

After Elly left, I rolled my head from side to side, feeling the cool pearls brush against my feverish skin. It didn't hurt so much to move my head anymore. The bump had grown smaller. When Elly got back, I'd have her bring me a mirror, but only after she put makeup on my face and did something with my hair. I could only guess how atrocious my hair looked after four days of nothing but dry shampoo. Dr. Jenner would have never let me lie here so long without makeup.

I must have fallen asleep while I waited for Elly because the next time

I opened my eyes, she sat in her chair, wearing the hospital gown and gloves.

"It came from a gift shop in town," she said. "A messenger delivered the package this morning. That's all they know."

"That doesn't make sense. Someone wrote on the wrapping paper. It's hand-lettered."

Elly shrugged. "All they said was it came from a gift shop."

I wished I knew more, but at least I knew Wyatt still cared. "Can you please see if there are any messages on my phone?" I asked. If only I could talk to him.

Elly reached across my bed to get my phone. "A text from Colton."

Colton? I hadn't seen him since he'd given me that blessing. "What does it say?"

"He wants to come watch a movie with you this afternoon."

Even if I did my makeup and hair, I couldn't allow just anyone to see me this way. It wasn't because of the bruises and bandages. I didn't like people watching while I slept or writhed in pain. "Does he know about the MRSA?"

Elly nodded. "He knows."

My eyelids drooped. "Okay."

"Okay, as in you want me to tell him to come?"

Sleep was about to take me again. "Sure." My hair and makeup would have to wait until I woke up.

I fought to come out of sleep, not only because I still felt tired, but also because I had no reason to be awake. Being awake meant being in torment. But I heard something. Music. Beautiful music. It seemed so long since I'd heard music.

Mom spoke. "I think she's waking up now. I'll call you back when she's ready for you."

"What is that music?" I asked, opening my eyes to see the sun streaming bright against the sheer curtains of the window.

"Vivaldi's *Four Seasons*. Colton thought you might like it. I can turn it off if it bothers you." Mom rose from her chair.

"It's gorgeous." Colton. I needed to remember something about Colton. "I never answered Colton's text."

"Yes, you did. He's waiting to visit you."

"Now?"

"He took Grace to lunch. When he gets back, he'll stay with you and Grace while I go to lunch."

"But the infection and my hair—"

Mom tipped her head to the side. "Yes. We'll have to fix your hair." Mom was never one for tact.

I clenched my teeth while she ran the brush through my hair. The left side went fine. My head felt only a little tender on that side, but when she got to the right side, I couldn't take the pain. "Please stop!" I shrieked.

Mom paused with the brush bristles halfway through a strand of my hair. "Sorry, *querida*." She extricated the brush as gently as possible. "Let me wash your face."

Mom found a washcloth in the bathroom and wiped it gently across my eyes and mouth. "The hospital staff will probably have to burn that cloth," I said.

Mom smiled. "Your first joke since the accident. Our prayers must be working."

"I wasn't trying to be funny."

She got my makeup bag from the drawer beside my bed. I didn't have the energy to tell her which colors I preferred. She swiped on the first color of lip gloss she found—a pearly mauve—and then brushed blush onto my cheeks. I never used blush. "That's much better," she said. "Are you ready for Colton?"

Why did I feel nervous? "I think so."

Mom kissed the air beside my face. "I'll go to lunch then."

Within seconds after Mom left, Grace pulled Colton into the room by his hand and started in on an explanation about the robes and gloves. He looked at me timidly. "I have to wear a gown?"

I nodded.

Grace donned her protective gear and approached me, looking closely at my face. "Your bruises are turning yellow and purple."

Colton came to stand behind Grace. "I think what Grace means is that you look better." Then I noticed Colton had picked a pink gown with flowers to wear over his jeans and T-shirt.

Even though it hurt, I laughed. "You could be wearing a blue gown with stripes. There's still one by the door."

Colton looked down at his robe. "I like this one." He pulled a chair over to sit beside my bed. "You do look better."

"Thank you."

"Wyatt sent her earrings," Grace said. "They're pretty." She sat on the edge of my bed, sending a shock of pain through my hips.

Colton took her hand and led her to the easy chair. "I'll have to check them out." He leaned over the bed, looking for my earrings.

I drew in my breath, trying to forget the pain. "You'll have to push back my hair to see them," I said. "It hurts me too much to do it." Colton started to take off his gloves. "Leave your gloves on," I added. "The MRSA is contagious. It's hospital regulations."

"I'm not going to touch you with gloves on," Colton said, reaching for my hair. "I can wash my hands." He pushed my hair back. "I can't say much for the earrings, but your ears look beautiful."

"Thank you." I don't know why it made me cry, having Colton touch me without gloves. I guess I'd cried so much over the last week that tears came too easily. "You can wash your hands now."

Colton obeyed me, washing his hands in the bathroom. When he came back to his chair, he brought his laptop case. "Are you ready for a movie? It's short."

"Okay."

The movie he brought was one he'd made himself, a slide show. He'd titled it *My Favorite Paintings* and set it to music by CAKE, which would have seemed odd if I hadn't liked CAKE so much.

The first painting was one I'd never seen, Rubens' *Daniel in the Lion's Den*. Each lion had his own personality. Next was a landscape by Constable with several cows grazing in the foreground. After that was a painting of a French lady on a swing by Fragonard.

"I'm not a fan of Fragonard," Colton admitted. "I threw that one in because I thought you'd like it." The screen faded to one of my paintings—the one of Mesa Verde. "I do like this one though."

I recognized the next few paintings by Caravaggio, Reynolds, and Rembrandt. Then we came to a painting of the woods with the sun shining through the branches. It looked so much like the woods in Maryland with green moss on the trees and the shine of the water in the creek.

"I can practically smell the mud," I said. "Who's the artist?"

"Allison Kimball. She used to be Allison Bradshaw."

By the time I processed that the artist was Colton's ex-wife, we looked at the next painting. "You mean your wife painted that?"

"My *ex*-wife." Colton rewound the movie to look at her painting again. "This is my favorite of hers. I paid way too much to keep it after the divorce."

I leaned forward, only to be stopped by the pain. "I didn't know your ex-wife was an artist."

"Wyatt didn't tell you? He and Allison were friends. She was a lot like you—she noticed everything." Colton bent to get a better look at the screen. "This painting used to remind me of her . . . Now it reminds me of the pioneer trek when you and I sat beside the creek."

It reminded me of the same thing, but I didn't say so. We watched the rest of the video in silence. Colton had a preference for landscapes, especially ones with cows grazing in the foreground. My mind wanted to float off like the clouds in those languid skies. The last few weeks had changed me. After all I'd suffered, I could forgive Colton for the Cow Festival fiasco. I could even see why Grandma thought he was handsome. In this harsh hospital light, he radiated a boyish energy. Maybe he wasn't right for me, but I could see him getting together with Elly. She needed someone reliable, someone emotionally open. Colton seemed like that guy.

For a moment, I wished Wyatt were more like Colton. If Wyatt cared, he'd do more than send me a pair of earrings. He would be sitting where Colton sat. A traitorous thought. I still thought it when the nurse carried in another present. It was wrapped in the same white paper, only this time the gold words formed song lyrics. Colton searched for them on his computer and played me Charles Bradley's "Victim of Love." It said exactly what I wanted to hear—*Let's tear down the walls between us and give love a chance.*

I closed my eyes, wondering how I should feel about that. "Are you going to open it?" Colton asked.

I kept my eyes closed. "Can you please open it for me?"

I listened to the paper rustling and then Colton setting something hard on my tray table. "It's a mug," he said. "Want to drink from it?"

I opened my eyes a slit, enough to see that the mug was handmade pottery. I longed to touch the ridges the potter's fingers left along the sides and feel the smooth brown glaze that reminded me of a tiger's eye gemstone. A dark red glaze ran around the rim, calling out for me to take a sip, but I wouldn't be able to tip my head enough for that. "Can you please ask the nurse for a straw?"

While Colton ran off to get juice and a straw, my eyelids drooped shut. As I drifted off to sleep, I remembered Wyatt didn't like soul music. He wouldn't have sent me the lyrics from a soul singer.

45

ELLY

NONE of us slept that night. Maren's condition got bad enough that we all stayed at the hospital. Though her sores looked better, her temperature continued to rise, making the doctors suspect the infection had moved inside to her abdominal cavity or to her lungs, causing pneumonia.

I knew from my Internet research that pneumonia was the worst thing that could happen to Maren. It would mean more pain and more infection that didn't respond to drugs. I didn't want to say it out loud, but I knew what everyone thought—this could be the end.

We prayed. In our exhausted states, Mom, Grandma, and I took turns either sitting beside Maren's bed or watching TV with Grace in the visitor's lounge. Colton stayed in the lounge with us, pretending to work on his laptop. He hadn't left since he visited the hospital that afternoon.

I'd reached the bargaining point with Heavenly Father. If He would let Maren live, I'd never complain again about money. I wouldn't worry about my job or Grandma's clutter. I wouldn't try to sue Jake. I just wanted my sister back. Maren had once said she felt like God had abandoned her. As I sat there, watching her struggle, I fought to believe our Heavenly Father still cared. After all we'd experienced, how could He let this happen too?

I listened to Maren's breathing as she slept, trying to convince myself that it didn't sound raspy. When she coughed, I asked myself whether it sounded dry or congested. I watched the nurse's expression when she took Maren's temperature and swapped out her IV fluids. Did the nurse seem hopeful? Or was she waiting for Maren to die? I felt useless—I couldn't take away the fever or figure out what caused it. I couldn't even make Maren comfortable.

I thought of Ethan. Watching Colton that day had sent me on a guilt trip. The fact that Maren didn't love him back didn't change his feelings for her. He loved her as she was. Ethan deserved as much from me.

I called his phone at 2:00 a.m., 11:00 p.m. his time. It went straight to voice mail. I knew exactly what I would say. I would tell him about Maren and apologize for ignoring his phone calls. I would say "I love you." There was no use denying my feelings anymore.

But his mailbox was full. I couldn't leave a message. I could only send a text, asking him to call me.

I needed to talk. I couldn't hold it in anymore. "You are stressing me out," I told Maren while she lay asleep. "You're stressing all of us out. Grace keeps asking who's going to help her walk the dogs if you die. Mom's cried off all her mascara. Colton hasn't left the hospital since he came this afternoon. He loves you, you know. And Grandma is asking people to pray for you—it's two in the morning, and she's still calling her friends on the phone."

Maren showed no sign that she heard me.

I went on. "Just do me a favor and get better. We've already lost Dad. We can't lose you too." I sounded angry. And I was angry. This was her fault, after all. She was the one who rode a motorcycle without taking lessons.

Maren moaned. "It would be easier to get better if you stopped talking."

"Okay," I said. "Sorry."

After that, Maren's temperature went down a tenth of a point. Each time the nurse took her temperature, we stood around, waiting to hear the results. And each time, her temperature dropped a few more tenths. The nurse told us that was normal—temperatures tended to drop in the morning. It might not have been great news, but it wasn't bad news. My body relaxed.

Mom and Grandma agreed that Maren looked better. We all felt so relieved to see a slight improvement. But with that relief came exhaustion. I wanted to collapse to the floor and sleep for days.

"I'm going home," I told Mom. If I left right away, I could get two hours of sleep in my bed before I went to work.

Nothing could have prepared me for what I saw as I walked out through the hospital's security doors. There, standing at the welcome desk, was Wyatt, Maren's Wyatt.

"Elly!" he called, racing after me as I walked past him, his hair spiked in a new style.

I did not want to talk to him. "She's still alive. No thanks to you." I kept my eyes ahead of me as I exited the front doors.

"They won't let me in to see her."

"Good." I gripped my keys and imagined using them to gouge out Wyatt's eyes. Not that I would ever do that. All I wanted to do was walk across the parking lot to my car. Then I'd drive away, leaving Wyatt in the dust.

"I can understand why you'd be upset with me," Wyatt said. "Sometimes to get a job, you have to do things you don't want to do."

I sighed. "I'll never understand what you did."

"Jillayne and I are partners now—business partners. Money isn't going to rule my life anymore."

I'd arrived at my car, but I couldn't leave without speaking my mind. I turned on him. "Is that what Jillayne thinks—that you're business partners? Or does she think it's something more?" I already knew the answer to my question.

Wyatt tugged at his collar. "Whoa, Elly. Calm down. I did it for Maren."

"For Maren? You ignored her calls for a month. You stood by while she got arrested. You sent her a cruel note. You did all that for Maren?" My voice came out so loud, other people in the parking lot stopped to stare. I spoke more quietly. "Maren's not doing well, Wyatt."

Wyatt tipped his head to the side. "I thought you said—"

"I said she's alive. I didn't say she was doing well." I leaned against the Subaru.

"She'll make it. Maren's a fighter." He looked at his feet. "I was sorry to hear about your friends in California. You didn't need that on top of everything else."

I rubbed my eyes. I didn't want to deal with Wyatt's drama. "What are you talking about?"

"You didn't hear?" Wyatt glanced up at me as if it pained him to tell me. "That Lanita person was in an accident the day after Maren's." He swallowed. "I don't know much about it. She called yesterday and said she wouldn't be needing the invitations for her engagement party, that she'd be going to a funeral instead."

"A funeral? Who died?" I couldn't trust Wyatt. He didn't always tell the truth.

"The guy she was driving with—her passenger. Jillayne looked it up online."

The guy she was driving with? That had to be Ethan. But Ethan couldn't be dead. I would have heard. Someone would have told me. "I have to go," I told Wyatt. "Don't tell my family about the other accident, okay?"

I got in my car and drove to the other end of the parking lot. Why hadn't Ethan returned my call? I parked the car and dialed Ethan's number. Once again, it went straight to voice mail, and, once again, the mailbox was full. I dialed his roommate Dave. The message on Dave's voice mail explained that he'd be out of the office for the week, and I remembered he'd said something about taking his kids on a cruise. I called Jake. No answer. I called Candi. She answered.

"Hi, Elly." She sounded sad. Or maybe tired. It was 6:00 a.m. in California.

"I heard there was an accident."

Candi sniffled. "Yes. He passed away yesterday."

Who passed away yesterday? Did she mean Ethan?

"The funeral's Thursday."

What day was today? Monday? Or Tuesday?

"I know there have been hard feelings between us, but I know you loved him too." She *did* mean Ethan. "I want you to come."

I couldn't speak. How could this happen? How could all of this happen in one week?

Candi's words came out garbled because she cried while she spoke. "He wrote you a letter before it happened. We found it in his things. He was so sorry about everything." She broke down, sobbing. "I don't blame Lanita, but I can't help wishing things had been different. If Ethan had chosen you—"

I should have told her not to think that way. I should have asked whether Ethan had suffered, but I could barely breathe, let alone speak. I didn't hear anything else Candi said. I didn't notice she'd hung up until the recording spoke: "If you'd like to make a call, please hang up and try again."

I could never call Ethan again. I could never tell him that I loved him.

46

How could Wyatt look so different than I remembered? He stood at the foot of my bed, where Colton had stood a moment earlier. He looked pale in the blue gown—as pale as a marble statue.

"I know it's hard to understand, Maren, but I did it all for you. I did it so we could have the kind of life we've always dreamed of."

What he said didn't make any sense. Maybe the drugs in my IV clouded my understanding. "You did it . . . for me?"

He knelt beside my bed. "You know how it is. I needed a job, and I knew Jillayne wouldn't hire me if she knew about you, so I pretended to be unattached. It worked. I'm now part-owner of the new San Francisco store, and I can stop pretending."

I still didn't understand. "Pretending?"

He reached with his gloved hand to touch mine. "I love you, Maren."

Wyatt was back. This was what I wanted. Why did I feel so empty? I closed my eyes, trying to collect my thoughts. "Why did you send me that note then?"

"What note?" The fluorescent light cast an eerie blue glow upon him.

I shifted in the bed, trying to get more comfortable, but the movement sent pain through my body. "I'm talking about the note on the gardenias. It said, 'I'm sorry if I led you to believe I felt more for you than I did.' "

Wyatt rolled his eyes. "Jillayne sent the flowers. She must have sent the note too."

He had let Jillayne send me flowers? "You couldn't send flowers yourself?"

"Jillayne is a very controlling woman." He didn't seem sorry about it either.

"And you're still working for her?"

"Working *with* her. Now that we're partners, things will be different."

I tried to push the hurt from my mind—all those nights I waited for him to call and the way he ignored me at the store. That hurt still outweighed whatever joy I felt in seeing him again. If it weren't for the earrings and the mug, I wasn't sure I could forgive him.

"I'm wearing the earrings you sent." I hoped he'd touch my hair the way Colton had.

His eyebrows dropped. "Earrings?"

Grimacing, I pushed my hair back along the left side of my face. "Did Jillayne send these too? And the mug?"

Wyatt pulled his mouth into a pout. "Look, Maren, I can understand why you're upset. But you need to understand my point of view. I was in a bad place financially, and this was the only way out."

"Did you send me the earrings or not, Wyatt?" I had to know. I could forgive him for everything that happened if he had sent the earrings.

"No. Why does that matter? I came all the way across the country to see you."

Though my heart had once softened and expanded in Wyatt's presence, it now shriveled to a prune-like lump. "You couldn't have answered any of my calls? You couldn't have sent me a text?"

He bit the side of his lip. "I was wrong. Can you forgive me?" He reached to touch my face with his gloved hand. "Things will be different now. I promise."

"But you're still working for Jillayne. Is she the one who sent the earrings?"

"I don't think so."

"How about the mug?"

"Look, Maren, I don't know what you're talking about. I didn't send any gifts. I worked like crazy to get a couple days off, and I'd rather not spend them arguing with you."

He was only going to stay a couple of days? Perhaps that's what made the difference. Or maybe it was because he hadn't sent the earrings or mug. Or because he would only touch me with gloves on. I finally saw the real Wyatt.

The Wyatt I loved wasn't real. He was my mind's creation. The real

Wyatt did things for himself—not for me. This Wyatt could never fill the void left from Dad's death. He wasn't like Dad at all. Why hadn't I seen it before? I closed my eyes, hoping that sleep would come. I didn't want to say what I needed to say.

"Will you forgive me, Maren?" Wyatt repeated.

I opened my eyes to see him still kneeling beside the hospital bed. "I'm sorry, Wyatt. It isn't enough."

He flinched. "What isn't enough?"

I turned away from him. "It's not that I don't love you. I do love you. But it takes two people to love, and you're not capable of loving me the way I need to be loved."

Wyatt stood and folded his arms across his chest. "Have you been talking to Colton about me?"

"No." Why hadn't I asked Colton about him?

"Colton's still angry because I told his wife to leave him."

"You told Colton's wife to leave him? Why?"

Wyatt crossed to the other side of my bed to sit in the royal-blue easy chair. "Because he was a terrible husband. He treated the cows better than he treated his wife."

"Are you saying Colton abused his wife?" I didn't believe it.

Wyatt popped up the footrest on the chair. "I'm saying he ignored her. I was the one who fixed things around the store for her. I was the one she came to when she had a problem."

Was that how Wyatt knew his way around the store so well? He'd spent time there with Colton's wife?

I remembered when Colton told me about his divorce. I'd seen how much it still hurt him. "Colton didn't deserve for you to do that to him."

Wyatt cradled his head in his hands. He looked as relaxed as a Saturday morning. How could he be so calm about this? "She's better off without him," he said. "Believe me."

"It's time for you to leave, Wyatt." Talking to him took too much energy. I closed my eyes. But, for the first time since the accident, I couldn't fall asleep. Anger rose inside me as I thought of what Wyatt had done to Colton. Why had Wyatt spent so much time with a married woman anyway? Was he trying to steal her away for himself?

It didn't help that Wyatt kept talking. "If you want me to quit working with Jillayne, I will. You make my life richer than any amount of money could, Maren. I see the world differently when I'm beside you."

I breathed deeply, mimicking sleep. In a way, the last few weeks of my relationship with Wyatt reminded me of the months when Dad was sick. We spent so much time hoping Dad would live while we worried he would die. When he finally died, it was almost a relief. We could finally make peace with our grief.

I couldn't keep living halfway between hope and grief with Wyatt. My hope had run out. Breaking up was the only choice. We'd reached our end, and I could make my peace with grief.

47

ELLY

I STUDIED my reflection in the bathroom mirror at the dairy store. It wasn't pretty. Dark circles under my eyes attested to almost a week of sleepless nights. No wonder three different customers had asked if something was wrong.

I'd learned when Dad passed away that it was no use second-guessing my decisions. Time travel wasn't an option. I couldn't go back to last Friday and return Ethan's phone call. I couldn't tell him not to drive with Lanita. I couldn't go back to Muir Woods and run away with him. Looking back, I felt sure we could've escaped . . . if I hadn't been so proud.

If I went back, I would be more like Maren. For once, I didn't regret that kiss I'd given him in the driveway the day we moved.

My worries about money seemed pointless now. Would it be such a big deal if I had to live in Grandma's house for the next few years? There were worse things than living with people who loved me. And there were definitely worse things than scooping ice cream cones for little kids. Maybe my job didn't pay as well as the head programmer job Dave offered me, but where else could I find a boss who let me tap-dance during work hours? Not that I felt like tap dancing.

Ethan's funeral was two days away. In between customers, I looked up the price of airline tickets. But even if I'd had the money, I couldn't have gone. Going would mean telling Mom and Maren. They'd had so much bad news. It would be too much to tell them about Ethan too. I needed to keep Ethan's death a secret until they recovered.

I was scribbling a note to Candi about why I couldn't come to the funeral when Colton walked in holding a spoonful of ice cream.

"I'm trying to replicate Maren's recipe for Lemon Chiffon. Do you think she'll like this?"

I tasted it, letting the sour taste roll around on my tongue until I had to spit it out in the sink. "She'll love it."

Colton raised an eyebrow. "But you spit it out?"

Remembering the health codes, I grabbed a bottle of disinfectant and sprayed the sink. "Maren likes her lemon extra lemony. I promise she'll love it."

Colton walked toward the ice cream case. "I thought I'd take a few different flavors when I visit this afternoon—see what tempts her. Which ones do you think she likes best?"

I felt too brain dead to answer. Colton picked Cherry Chocolate Cheesecake and Raspberry Rush on his own, proving he knew Maren's tastes as well as I did.

I couldn't stop thinking of Ethan. I'd been so sure things would work out between us. There were times in my life when it seemed easy to believe Heavenly Father cared. Watching Maren recover from her fever was one of those times. Finding Maren after her accident was another. I knew He answered our prayers. But then there were times when I prayed with no obvious result. It was like that with Ethan. Why had I felt so hopeful if it was going to end this way?

"You okay?" Colton asked.

"Don't tell anyone—I got more bad news this morning." I held my breath, trying to steady my emotions. "My friend died."

Colton stepped toward me and before I knew what was happening, took me in a bear hug. "I'm sorry, Elly. You didn't need that."

That did it. Something broke loose inside me. For the first time, I could cry about Ethan. I stepped back from his embrace as my tears fell. "Sometimes there's just no logic to life. It's like some heartless software application, running us through random trials and killing off people we care about too much."

Colton handed me a napkin to dry my eyes. "About a month after my wife left, I felt like you do now. I was at the lowest point of my life. I spent my days at work or in front of the TV. I ate nothing but ramen and peanut butter sandwiches. One day, I had to mend the fence. It was wintertime—probably the coldest winter we've ever had on the dairy. My hands felt so cold that I couldn't grip my hammer. I'd had so many disappointments, I'd almost stopped believing God knew who I was. I'd stopped feeling worthy of His love. But I thought I'd give Him one more chance—one more time I'd ask if he knew me and knew how cold I felt. Not one minute after I said that prayer, your grandma's car stopped beside me. She asked me if I'd like to come to dinner. It might not seem like a big deal, hearing me tell the story, but it was a big deal to me. It meant that despite everything that happened, God still watched my back. Even in our darkest times, God hasn't abandoned us."

After crying and praying with my grandma for the past four days, I would never again see her as my crazy hoarder grandma. "You're right." I sighed. "Heavenly Father hasn't abandoned us. For one thing, He sent you and Grandma to take care of us this summer. I just have to believe He'll help me through my next trial too."

"He will," Colton said. Then he chuckled. "You know what your grandma fed me that night she found me out in the cold? Vegan lasagna."

As funny as that was, I couldn't laugh. Not so soon after finding out about Ethan. I returned to scrubbing the sink. "Is Wyatt still at the hospital?"

Colton put lids on his Styrofoam containers. "He was when I left."

Yet Colton still wanted to bring Maren ice cream. Good for him. "You should tell Maren how you feel. Before it's too late." If Maren died, I didn't want him to feel how I felt about Ethan.

Colton slid the cups of ice cream into the freezer behind the counter. He didn't say anything.

"Maren's different now," I said. "Since she got the earrings and the mug." I suspected Colton had sent them, but he didn't give me any hint that I was right. No blush. No shy smile.

He turned to look out the window, his hands in his pockets. "After I got divorced, I thought I'd spend the rest of my life alone. Maren's the only woman who's made me wonder about that decision. Then Wyatt came along, and I stopped wondering." His shoulders drooped. Maren hadn't ever given him reason to hope. She'd rejected the idea of dating Colton from the start.

"Maren would be better off with you than with Wyatt," I offered.

He drew in a breath. "Before this week, I never thought she could be happy with me. My ex-wife left because I was boring. Also because I worked too hard, but mostly because I was boring."

I thought of Colton's James Brown imitation, his cowbells tuned to the key of F, and the whimsical home he'd designed for himself. "You're anything but boring, Colton. Even if you were, Maren has enough creativity for both of you."

"Before the accident, I would've never considered it," he said, still looking out the window. "Now I can see it's not a question of what I need. It's what she needs."

Colton was the man Maren needed. He just had to convince Maren of that fact.

48

Why was Colton sitting beside my bed? I shut my eyes and opened them again. He still sat there, posing like Rodin's *Thinker* sculpture with a pencil in his hand.

"Your mom took Grace to an appointment at her new school. I told her I'd sit with you." He tipped his head to get a better view of my face. "Unless that makes you uncomfortable."

The sadness I'd once seen behind his smile had disappeared. When had it left?

I eyed the sketch pad he held on his lap. "What are you doing?" I asked.

He closed the pad. "Sketching." His pencil looked like an artist's 4B.

"Can I see your sketch?"

"You'll have to wait until I finish." He slid the pad into his bag. "I'm supposed to tell you Wyatt wants to visit again."

It came thundering back to me—Wyatt hadn't sent the earrings or the mug or the flowers. "I don't want to see him."

Colton stifled a smile. "Would you rather watch a movie? I brought my download of *Cyrano de Bergerac*. It's the only chick-flick I own."

It was as if Colton had come out from the shadows. Everything about him seemed brighter and more animated. A mosaic of emotion danced in his eyes—joy, empathy, and humor blended together.

"*Cyrano de Bergerac*? That's not in English, is it?"

"It's in French. It has subtitles."

"I'm sorry, Colton. I don't have the energy to read subtitles."

"I'll read them. I can do the voices and everything." He paused, trying to gauge my reaction. "You seem skeptical."

I *was* skeptical. I couldn't imagine him doing voices. "I brought your favorite ice cream to go with it." He pulled a Styrofoam cup from his bag.

"Lemon Fluff?"

"Lemon Chiffon," he corrected. We'd disagreed over the name before. "But you can call it Lemon Fluff today if you want."

His smile brought me back to the dairy—the rolling green fields, the sound of the cowbells, and the sugary smell of the dairy store. I took a bite of the Lemon Fluff he held out to me, letting it melt on my tongue. The lemon flavor gave a kick, the way I liked. After I swallowed, I said, "I'm going to change your name today too. You seem more like a Colt than a Colton."

He grinned. "My dad used to call me that."

We started the movie. Colt turned down the volume and began his one-man reader's theater, trying his best to speak as the actors' lips moved. It wasn't the shy, introverted reading I'd expected. He gave Cyrano a deep voice with a French accent that transported me to the world of the movie. I couldn't help laughing at Cyrano's antics.

"Could you please stop being so funny?" I pleaded. "It hurts to laugh."

Colt paused the movie. "Would you rather watch something else?"

I rested my head against my pillow. "No. I like the costumes."

Colt read Roxane's voice in a gentle pitch that matched the pastel tones in her gowns. He saved the shrill tones for the more humorous characters. Though I'd never seen the movie before, the story seemed familiar. Cyrano loved Roxane, but was too scared to confess his passion for her. Instead, he helped a better-looking but less intelligent man, Christian, to win Roxane for himself. Colt's voice held the right combination of devotion and frustration as he read Cyrano's words. Almost as if he felt them himself.

After an hour of reading, Colt paused the movie. "I need an ice cream break."

"You never told me you were an actor," I said.

"I'm not." Colt held a spoonful of Cherry Chocolate Cheesecake for me. "Maybe if you eat more, they'll let you get rid of that feeding tube."

I took the spoon from him. Pushing against the pain in my shoulder, I fed the ice cream to myself. It was like I'd tasted chocolate for the first time. I took another bite and then another, letting the flavors burst on my parched tongue. With Colt's help, I ate the entire six-ounce cup. While I was at it, I swallowed the pills my nurse left for me to take.

"Is Cyrano ever going to tell Roxane how he feels?" I asked.

"You'll have to wait and see."

I closed my eyes. "But it has a happy ending, doesn't it?"

Colt chuckled. "You haven't seen many French movies, have you?"

When I woke, a paper lay on the tray table in front of me. It was an intricately sketched picture of a tree, much better than anything I'd seen Wyatt draw. Beside the tree was J. R. R. Tolkien's poem from *The Hobbit* that began "All that is gold does not glitter."

It was one of my favorite poems. Was this Colt's sketch? I looked for a signature, but found only the words "To Maren, with love" written in the bottom right corner.

49

ELLY

IF I'd known Maren would be improving by now, I would have bought the airplane ticket. People always said funerals brought closure. I wasn't sure that was true, though. A funeral was simply a time to express sympathy for the family.

"Elly, did you hear anything I said?" Maren asked. What *had* she said?

I swallowed. "No. Sorry."

Maren rolled her eyes. "I was talking about *Cyrano de Bergerac*. It's made me rethink all my opinions about love."

I yawned. "Oh yeah?"

"Someone who can love despite rejection makes a better hero than anyone whose love is accepted from the beginning. I need a man whose love refuses to die."

Death. Why did the men I loved have to die? First Dad and now Ethan. Maybe if I flew on standby, I could still make it to the funeral. Even if I only made it to the burial. I needed to make it real somehow. It didn't seem real.

"What's wrong, Elly?" Maren asked.

"Nothing." I rubbed my eyes. I couldn't keep thinking about Ethan. I had to stay cheerful until Maren had her next operation. There would be time to read his obituary and visit his grave after she recovered.

Maren fingered her latest secret-admirer gift, a pearl pendant. "Does it bother you that Colt's spending so much time with me?"

Evidence of Colton's love surrounded us. He'd decorated the room's walls with pictures of trees, streams, cows, and birds. His portable stereo played her favorite music. And beside me, a mini-fridge held Maren's favorite flavors of ice cream. By now, she had to suspect Colton was the one who'd sent the gifts.

I faked a smile. "The only thing that bothers me is that you've named him after a horse."

"I like the name Colt."

"As long as he doesn't start calling you Mare."

Maren laughed and then grimaced from the pain. "I didn't think about that." She shifted in the bed, trying to make herself comfortable. "Colt's a better man than I realized. I'd like to have him for a brother-in-law."

I arched my eyebrows. "Maren, I don't think Colton is interested in me."

"Maybe once you get over Ethan." The day before, she'd launched into a comparison between Ethan and Wyatt.

I jumped in before she had a chance to renew the topic. "I don't think I'm going to get over Ethan."

Maren didn't seem to notice the sorrow in my voice. "But Colt would make a better husband than Ethan."

I looked at my copy of *Wired* magazine, trying to compose myself. "You sound like Grandma. Now you can tell me how hard he works and how much I'd love to live in his house."

Maren leaned forward. "Have you seen his house? Grandma told me he has an art studio on the third story."

I told Maren what I remembered about Colton's house—the stained glass on the door, the arched entryway, and the way it looked like a tree house. "I'll take a picture of it if you want."

She looked tempted. "No, thank you."

"It's no big deal. I'll drive by after work tomorrow." I turned back to my copy of *Wired*, but I couldn't stop thinking about the comparison Maren drew between Ethan and Wyatt. If Ethan was like anyone, he was like Colton. They both kept secrets for the benefit of other people, secrets that harmed their own interests. "Did Colton ever tell you why he had to leave on the day of the Cow Festival?"

"No. That's the one thing that still irritates me."

"He wasn't sure I should tell you—Wyatt was the reason he had to leave." I filled her in on the story of how Wyatt stole from his aunt. Then

I told her how Colton had hesitated to call Wyatt's cousin because he felt it might hurt Maren.

Maren's eyes grew wide as I explained how Colton felt partially responsible for the accident. "But Colt saved me. If it weren't for him, I might still be with Wyatt. That would be worse than the accident."

50

Could the day before my second operation be a new beginning? I hoped so. After recovering from my staph infection, I didn't need another ending. Now I lay in a different hospital bed in a different hospital. The next day, a surgeon would repair my broken pelvis.

Colt helped me paint a still life of the organic fruit lying on my tray table as I thought through the events of the last month. For me, every still life was like a therapy session. I always came away with a new perspective. "I think I need to start over," I said.

Colt tipped his head to the side. "You want another piece of paper?" Colt knew me well enough that he'd brought my favorite watercolors and a brush for each color. Since I couldn't sit up all the way, he'd taped the paper to a board and held it at an angle while I sketched the scene.

I dropped the pencil. "I meant I need to start my life over. Look at me. I should be working at the dairy store right now. Instead, I stopped taking my medicine, fell in love with a selfish jerk, and almost killed myself. Who knows what would've happened if you and Elly hadn't found me."

"We found you. That's what matters." Colt touched my forearm. "Everybody makes mistakes, Maren."

"I need to be more like Elly."

The corners of his lips rose. "Some of us would miss you if you changed too much."

I rolled my eyes. "I doubt that."

Colt leaned in closer. "After all I've done for you, Maren, you should at least tell me what you're going to change before you change it. Like if you said you were going to change the way you laugh, I'd have to object. There's music in the way you laugh. And if you decided to stop bugging me about next year's Cow Festival, I'd have to object to that too. I like to hear your ideas—as impossible as most of them seem."

He smelled fresh and outdoorsy—a nice contrast to the plastic smells of the hospital. I'd begun to suspect Colt was the one who sent the gifts with the handmade wrapping paper. It wasn't too surprising. Grandma always said he liked me. What surprised me was that *I* hoped he'd sent them.

Colt went on. "It goes without saying that I wouldn't want you to change your hair or the expression you make when your grandma's parakeet lands on your head. Let's see . . . another thing I wouldn't want you to change would be the way you comport yourself as my employee. You should feel free to laugh loudly and kiss passionately while you're on the job."

I giggled. "And you don't mind who kisses me?"

Crimson tinged the skin above his collar. "That's the one thing I'd like you to change."

I found my pencil where I'd dropped it on my lap. "I'm taking applications for the position. All you have to do is write *To Maren, with love* on a piece of paper."

I handed him the pencil. He looked at me as if this might be my way of rejecting him. "I don't think—"

"Don't turn our lives into some French drama, Colt. I already know you're the one." I'd uncovered more than the mystery of my secret admirer. I'd found the creative soul Colt kept hidden away. "And if it's not you, I'll be very disappointed."

He scrawled out the words on the edge of my watercolor paper. It was the same script I'd learned to recognize—fluid yet angular.

"Do I pass?" he asked. The dark centers of his eyes grew large as they took me in. Watching him, I felt something I'd never expected to feel in his presence—joy.

I closed my eyes and tipped back my head. His kiss was like a whisper. He barely pressed his lips to mine. It was a kiss as gentle as his love for me had always been. Though small, it started something inside me. Like pulling at a bit of yarn in a sweater, all my illusions about love began to unravel. I couldn't pull them back. They simply left, rushing out like so many stitches slipping. Until I had no illusions at all. I had only a beginning. An untainted beginning for Colt and me.

51

ELLY

OUTSIDE Maren's hospital window, rain fell in sheets onto the wet pavement of the parking lot. It didn't seem like 8:00 a.m. on an August morning. In a few minutes I'd be driving down Route 70 on tires that were balder than ever.

Maren's doctor had declared the second operation a success. Now all that was left was healing—for her and for me. Hers would take physical therapy. Mine would take time. Over the next few months, my brain would stop expecting his phone calls. I would learn to make new plans.

I recognized our van pulling into a parking space below. Grace popped out in Maren's red trench coat, twirling Mom's black umbrella above her head. For her, rain still called for a celebration. She hopped over puddles as Mom hurried to keep up.

Soon they met me in the hospital room. Grace squeaked her boots on purpose as she walked across the linoleum floor. "You got mail yesterday," she said, handing me a damp white envelope, its ink smeared from raindrops. It was Candi's writing. Was this the letter Ethan wrote me? With shaking hands, I slit the envelope open and pulled out a folded piece of paper.

The letter was printed, not handwritten as I'd expected. And it was short. As I unfolded it, a check fell out—a check for five thousand dollars signed by Candi. This wasn't a letter from Ethan. It was from Jake:

Dear Elly,

I sincerely regret anything I have done to bring hardship upon your family. Though my lawyer assures me I am in no way liable, I see now that I have not been completely ethical in my business practices. Please accept this payment as a token of my apology.

Sincerely,

Jacob Cannon

At the bottom, Candi had written: *In the future, I hope to compensate your family more fully for their losses.*

Two weeks earlier, I would have faxed the letter to my lawyer and tapped an angry dance over the phrase "I am in no way liable." Today, it seemed enough. In all the time I'd known Jake, I'd never heard him apologize. This was progress. And, as long as I didn't consider how much we'd lost, the check was more than I expected.

I showed the check to Mom before I kissed her good-bye. "I'll deposit it on the way home," I said, looking at my watch. Since Maren was now in a different hospital, I had an hour-long drive ahead of me. "I'd better get going."

Even though Maren no longer showed signs of MRSA, the hospital still required us to wear gloves and a gown in her room. Once I took them off, I hurried through the hospital hallways and out to the parking lot, which seemed one big puddle. Holding my purse over my head, I splashed through the shallow areas, remembering a rainy day at the bishops' storehouse. Ethan wore a green T-shirt that day and his old Levi's jeans. I could see him walking hand in hand with Grace through the puddles, both of them smiling as they approached my car. Back then I told myself I wasn't someone Candi's brother would date. I was wrong—wrong about a lot of things.

Driving home, I sorted through my personal database of memories: Ethan joking about a prosthetic nose, Maren testing Ethan's knowledge of Impressionist artists, Mom scrubbing tile with a toothbrush, Grandma driving Colton's tractor, and Ethan rubbing cream onto my hands at the Kennedy Center. I felt so much more for Ethan than I ever had for Jake. It had been a good year—the tragedies couldn't erase the good parts.

I rewound and replayed my memories from the past—sometimes praying to thank Heavenly Father for the good things—until I pulled into the parking lot at the dairy store. I'd forgotten to stop at the bank.

Parked to the side of the store was a white sedan. Through the rain, I could see the outline of someone inside—probably one of our senior citizen customers. Who else, other than a senior citizen, would arrive fifteen minutes before the store opened?

I hurried into the store and raced to put on my apron and hairnet. I counted the money in the cash drawer and then uncovered the ice cream buckets in the glass case. I barely got that done before I had to flip the open sign and unlock the front door.

Grandma's Cadillac pulled into the parking lot about two seconds after I returned to my place behind the cash register. She carried her cane in one hand and a bowl of oat bran cereal in the other. "I brought you breakfast."

I hurried to take the bowl from her, almost dropping it when I discovered how hot it was. "Thanks, Grandma." I ran to place the bowl on the metal counter.

Grandma turned to look out the window. "Who owns that sedan? I don't recognize it." Grandma seemed to know everyone within a fifteen-mile radius of her home.

I blew on a spoonful of oat bran. "I don't know. He or she hasn't come in the store."

She walked closer to the window. "Do you think it's stolen?"

"Someone's sitting inside, so probably not."

"It could be a body." Grandma watched a lot of detective shows at the hospital with Maren. "Look, the seat's reclined."

I laughed. "Maybe he's asleep."

Grandma reached for her phone. "Or it could be a drug dealer. I'll call it in to the police. Better to be safe than sorry."

"It's probably some poor guy who pulled off the highway to take a nap. I'll go look." I grabbed one of the quilts. "I'll let you know if we should call the police."

"Don't get too close," Grandma warned.

I held the quilt over my head as I walked through the rain to the white sedan. Raindrops obscured the windows. I could make out the shadow of a reclined driver's seat and some of the driver's dark clothing, but that was all. Whoever sat inside didn't move as I approached. Grandma, watching from inside the store, opened the door to warn me. "Don't get any closer."

That gave me just the incentive I needed. I walked to the driver's side door and wiped off the window with the edge of the quilt. I wasn't prepared for what I saw. There, lying inside the car was a sleeping man who looked exactly like Ethan. I jumped back, stumbling over the cracked edge of the asphalt parking lot.

"What's the matter?" Grandma yelled.

I stared at the man. His arms were folded across a blue T-shirt like Ethan would wear. And he wore jeans like Ethan's. I watched his chest rise and fall. Could Ethan be alive? Why would Candi tell me he was dead, then?

Could I be hallucinating? I tested the door. Unlocked. I swung it open. Ethan sat bolt upright. "Elly."

I bent to get a better look. "You're alive?" Could I trust myself to be happy about this?

He reached for my hand. "I came to apologize. Again."

I looked at his hand on mine. I could feel it. How was this happening?

Grandma still stood at the front door of the store. "Are you okay?"

Without taking my eyes off of Ethan, I yelled back. "I'm great." In a quieter voice, I said, "Candi told me you were dead." I sat on the edge of his seat and hugged him. He pulled me in, breathing warmth over my hair. His chest rose and fell as if I'd startled him. This had to be real. It was better than any dream.

His lips touched my temple. "You must have misunderstood. It wasn't me. It was Jake."

I tipped my head to look into his face. "Jake?"

He held me tight, tighter than he'd ever held me before. "After you left, Candi invited Lanita to stay at her house. The next day, when Jake had to drop his car off to get the stereo fixed, Lanita volunteered to drive him home." His voice broke. "After they left the car dealership, Lanita saw something that scared her and ran a red light to get away." He held his lips closed tight, trembling.

A strange mix of relief and sorrow filled me. I had a second chance to make things right with Ethan. But Jake was gone. I could erase all the mourning and regret of the last week. But Candi had lost her husband. Our plans could fall back in place. But Jake wouldn't hold his newborn baby. I didn't want to trade Ethan's death for Jake's. I wanted them both alive.

"I'm so sorry," I said.

As much as Jake had hurt me and my family, he didn't deserve to die. He loved Candi and cared about his employees. And Candi was pregnant. She'd have to deliver her baby alone. "Poor Candi!" I cried. No wonder she'd been too upset to talk clearly on the phone. I wished I'd talked to Ethan instead. "Why didn't you call me?"

"You didn't answer my calls for three weeks, Elly. I thought it was enough that you talked to Candi."

I traced my fingers over the hairs on his arms. "But I texted you."

Ethan frowned. "I lost my phone on the day of the accident. With the funeral and everything, I was too busy to get a new one."

"I thought you were dead. I'm so sorry about Jake, but I'm not sorry you're alive."

He looked as if he expected me to be angry. "I'm sorry too, Elly. For all of it."

I hugged him again, burying my face in his chest, feeling his warmth and strength. If he only knew how much I'd missed him. "I'm sorry I never told you I loved you."

I could have stayed there for the rest of the day sharing that driver's seat with him, but Grandma called me again. "You have a customer, Elly, and I don't know how to run the cash register."

Ethan kissed the top of my head. "I love you too."

I reached to touch his face, feeling the stubble from his whiskers. "This is real, right? You're alive?"

"This is real." He placed his hands on mine. "You'd better go before you lose your job."

Holding his hands, I stood up. "The only way I'm going back in that store is if you come with me. My boss won't care. Maren brought Wyatt all the time." I tried to pull him from his seat.

He resisted. "I know how you felt about Maren bringing Wyatt to work." He winked. "I'll be there in a minute."

When I got back in the store, I realized the whole right side of my body and the quilt I'd worn were sopping wet from rain. As I rang up a couple of customers, I wondered if I'd dreamed the whole experience. Could stress and lack of sleep make dreams that real? Then the door jingled open and Ethan entered holding a box. I hadn't imagined it.

As soon as I finished with the customers, I came from around the counter to hold his hand. I had to touch him, to feel he was real. "What's in the box?" I asked.

He pulled out a book, handing it to me. I read the title: *The Language of Flowers*. Ethan then plopped down a paper bag on the counter in front of me. Inside nestled three flower bulbs. "They're hyacinths," he explained. "Go ahead and look them up."

I was about to open the book when one of my customers returned. I'd given him the wrong change. While I sorted that out, Grandma flipped through the pages of the book. " 'Hyacinth,' " she read. " 'I am sorry. Please forgive me.' "

Ethan looked at me nervously as I finished with the customer.

"I forgive you." I hugged him, holding my rain-soaked body against his. It felt so real. "Please tell me you and Lanita are—"

"I took her back to the hospital yesterday. She knows I won't be calling her anymore. And she won't have the number to my new phone."

The news didn't make me as happy as I'd thought. I knew how hard it would be for Lanita to lose Ethan, especially after the accident. "Are you ready for the next flower?" he asked, pulling out a white pitcher full of artfully arranged silk flowers.

"Don't tell me you couldn't find any real flowers at this time of year," Grandma said.

I set the pitcher beside the napkin dispenser. "I think they're beautiful."

Ethan took a paper from his pocket and read from it. "These are forget-me-nots, camellias, and lilacs. I wanted to give them to you before you left California, but . . ." He sighed. "You know how Lanita got toward the end."

I looked them all up in the book. Red camellias: *You're my heart's desire.* White camellias: *You're adorable.* Forget-me-not: *Memories of true love.* And lilac: *Do you still love me?*

I couldn't help it. Though three customers stood watching, I stepped from behind the counter and threw myself at Ethan, kissing him more intensely than I'd ever seen Maren kiss Wyatt. This time, he didn't hesitate. He took the lead, wrapping me in his arms and taking my whole mouth. His kiss soothed the ache I'd felt. It made up for all my wounds.

We only stepped apart when we heard an old woman remark that "there is such a thing as too much public display of affection." She'd probably seen Maren and Wyatt together a few too many times.

Ethan kept his eyes on mine. "Excuse us, ma'am." He didn't look at all repentant.

Grandma pounded her cane down onto the floor. "I'd rather they display their affection where I can see than in private where who knows what will happen." If I hadn't blushed before, that did it for sure.

I stepped back behind the counter to ring up the woman's half-gallon of skim milk. While I helped the next customer, Ethan pulled a scraggly little vine from his box and set it in a tin can of water on top of the curved glass ice cream case. I suspected putting a plant there was against the health code, but I overlooked it. After I'd helped everyone, I asked Ethan about the vine.

"It's honeysuckle. It symbolizes the bond of love."

Grandma pulled a stamen from a tiny yellow honeysuckle flower and sucked the nectar dripping from its end. "Try it," she challenged me. I plucked off a flower and pulled the stamen to bring out a drop of nectar. It tasted like sweet perfume.

In between the customers, Ethan, Grandma, and I sucked the nectar from every single honeysuckle flower. Grandma told Ethan about Maren's accident. He hadn't heard anything about it, which was probably a good thing, considering how much he'd had to worry about Candi and Lanita. "I hope she'll be okay," he said.

"Oh, she will be," Grandma said. "She's gotten through the worst of it. After two operations and a staph infection, physical therapy will be a piece of cake."

Grandma rambled on, telling Ethan about how she'd met Grandpa at a college dance and how he'd given her daisies on every anniversary of the day they met. "Even after getting them every year for fifty-two years, I still love daisies." Grandma looked at Ethan's empty box, now pushed against the store's back wall. She picked up my forgotten bowl of oat bran cereal. "I guess I've seen all there is to see. I'll be heading home."

Ethan walked her to her car while I mixed the batter for waffle cones. When he came back through the door, he carried a vase filled with a dozen pink long stem roses. No one had ever given me those kinds of roses. Sure, I'd gotten grocery store roses in cellophane cones. But not long stem roses in a vase. And, coming from Ethan, a guy who wore his clothes until they fell apart, long stem roses meant commitment.

"They're beautiful," I said. "But you didn't have to—"

"Yes, I did."

I let the batter run over the edge of the waffle iron while I considered my feelings. With Jake dead and Lanita in the hospital, I couldn't be completely happy.

Ethan waited while I rang up a few customers. After they left, he stepped behind the counter. "You okay?"

I swabbed up the spilled batter with a rag. "I feel so bad for Candi and the baby."

Ethan set the roses beside the sink. "I do too. I promised Candi I'll do everything I can to help her." He grabbed a paper towel and knelt to wipe up batter that had dripped onto the floor. "We can talk about that later. While it's just the two of us, I want to tell you something."

I looked out into the parking lot to make sure there weren't any more customers coming. "I think there's time."

He held my hands in his. "When I first saw you, I had to look away. You were so beautiful—unlike any woman I'd ever expected to see in the bishops' storehouse. I had to remind myself I wasn't there to meet women. But I liked you. The way you handled your sister, I remember thinking you were the one who should be named Grace. Then when you came to work for our team, I felt like we could be friends. The fact that I'd made a commitment to Lanita didn't enter my mind. We were coworkers, and I'd never been in love. I didn't expect it to be so easy. You made it too easy."

He dipped his head to kiss me, a slow tender kiss that left me barely able to stand. I clung to him afterward, feeling him breathe in and out. It still seemed a miracle to hold him.

He whispered into my hair. "I wanted to get you every color of rose they had in the shop, but the florist said you'd like it better if I stuck to one color."

I lifted my head to look at the bouquet of roses. "I like the pink. They remind me of those tulips we saw on our first date with Grace."

Ethan kissed my forehead. "I've been praying for a miracle—that you'd take me back despite everything that's happened."

I breathed in the subtle scent of sunblock. "You only had to break up with Lanita. That's what took the miracle."

Ethan stepped back to look me in the eyes. "I was hoping to convince you to come back to California with me, but now that I know about Maren, it doesn't seem as easy."

"Maren will be fine," I said. "Mom, Grandma, and Colton will take care of her. If anyone moves, it should be me. You need to be there for Candi."

Ethan drew in his breath and looked off to the side. "I was hoping—I don't know if I should ask."

I tipped my head until I established eye contact with him again. "What?"

"Remember how I told you LibraryStar had some financial struggles, and you had ideas for solving the problems?"

The timer on the waffle iron went off. "Yeah." I let go of his hands to get back to my work.

"You know how to run a software company as well as Jake did, if not better."

I shook my head as I removed the waffle. "I don't know if I'd say that. I was kind of angry when I went off about the finances."

"Candi wants to offer you the job as Chief Executive Officer. She needs someone she can trust."

I curled the waffle into a cone shape and stacked it with the other cones. "But—"

"She wants to help your family, and she wants to help her employees. She doesn't need the company. Jake's life insurance policy will support her for the next twenty years."

"But she fired me." I would beg on a street corner to be close to Ethan again. But work for Candi? As much as she needed me, I didn't think the two of us could ever get along.

Ethan hugged me. "Maybe you could try it on a temporary basis."

52

ELLY

IT was Ethan's idea that I should be Candi's Lamaze partner. It made sense. After working together for three months, she and I trusted each other. Plus she felt comfortable yelling at me. And yell she did. For twelve hours, she squeezed my fists, shrieked that she didn't want an epidural, and exhaled into my face. I told myself that being a dutiful Lamaze partner was one more thing I could add to my skill set. I fed her ice chips, played her favorite music, massaged her back, reminded her to breathe, answered her phone, showed her pictures of her nursery, and whispered positive affirmations.

When the little girl finally emerged, screaming and pink, I felt that somehow, through those long hours of labor, Candi and I had become sisters. We could never be friends, but sisters we could handle. And with her makeup worn off, she looked more like me than ever.

"Thank you, Elly," she whispered as she held the baby to her breast. "I'm sorry I yelled at you."

The doctor and nurses left one by one until all fell silent. Love charged the air. I imagined Jake there, looking on his wife and child. If he ever got a chance to visit them, he would surely be with them now. Feeling like I didn't belong, I left Candi with her little family to find Ethan.

He stood outside the cafeteria, talking on his phone. He put the phone to his chest as I approached. "Did she have the baby?"

I nodded, showing him the pictures on my phone. "She's here, and she's beautiful."

"Can I see her?"

As anxious as Ethan was to visit his new niece, I couldn't let him. "Let's give Candi a little more time alone. I think she's enjoying the quiet." I inhaled the French-fry-scented air. "I'm starving."

"Me too," Ethan said. "But before we eat, Maren's on the phone. She and Colton want to stop and see us on the way back from their honeymoon. She wants to know what's a good time for you. They'll be here around New Year's."

That meant I'd get to see Maren twice in the next month—once when we flew out for the wedding and again when she came through California. "Whatever they plan will be fine. I can make room in my schedule."

Maren and Colton had started planning a humanitarian trip at the end of last summer during her long recovery. Gradually, as their relationship progressed, their mission to help build a school in the Philippines turned into a humanitarian honeymoon. Now, instead of planning next year's Cow Festival while she worked at the dairy store, Maren sketched designs for school murals.

Ethan finished his phone call with Maren while I wandered into the cafeteria. After twelve hours without food, everything looked good, including the shriveled up hotdogs revolving on the roller grill. I had the tongs in hand, ready to grab one, when Ethan came up behind me.

"I still have that reservation at the Jade Palace. Do you think Candi will be okay for a couple hours?"

I thought of the sacred feeling that enveloped her hospital room. "Candi will be fine, but I'm not in the mood for Chinese. Much less *fancy* Chinese. Can we go somewhere else?"

Ethan's eyes crinkled at the corners as he smiled. "You're the one who always wanted to go there."

His smile still had the power to make me forget what I wanted to say. I had to stare at the wrapped sandwiches to compose my thoughts. "I still want to go to the Jade Palace, but not today. Today I'm all about protein."

He stepped into my line of sight. "That little Cuban place is close."

"*Our* little Cuban place? Perfect."

As we walked toward the parking lot, I texted Candi about our plans.

She replied, *Have fun. It's nap time for Jacqueline and me.*

When I got in Ethan's car, I noticed two potted orchids on the floor in front of the backseat. "The purple one's for you. The pink's for Candi,"

Ethan said, passing me *The Language of Flowers* book before he turned the key in the ignition. Under *orchid,* it read, *You are a rare beauty, possessing both wisdom and strength.* Below that, Ethan had written in pen: *Purple orchid: I love you more than I can ever express.*

On our way, I related the high points of Candi's birth story. She'd ordered me around and groaned with pain, but never once had she felt sorry for herself. As difficult as it was, she wanted the experience. That baby was everything to her now.

Ethan told me about his day helping the other employees move LibraryStar to a less expensive office space. "There wasn't room for all the managers to have their own office," he told me. "So I figured you and I could share." Ethan had taken over Candi's job.

I laughed. "It'll be like old times with our double cubicle."

"Only now we have a door and a view of the pizza place across the street."

I worried that our employees and customers would notice that the new office was a step down. "Has anyone complained?"

"They're okay with it. They know it's about helping the company succeed." He stole a glance my way. "And I gave Stan an office."

"Why? He never had one before."

Ethan popped his eyebrows up and down. "So there wouldn't be enough room for everyone to have their own office." He pulled the car to a stop in front of the restaurant, rummaging around for some files on the backseat before he came around to get my door. It wasn't like him to bring his work home.

"What are those?" I asked, pointing to the files as we walked up to the restaurant.

He opened the door for me. "A contract and a proposal I wanted to show you."

Hadn't he noticed how tired I felt? "They can't wait until tomorrow?"

He fought back a smile. "I think you'll want to see them."

The maître d' sat us at a booth near the back. I ordered a mango shake before I opened the menu. Then I slipped off my shoes and rested my feet on the bench beside Ethan. He stroked the top of my foot as he read his menu. I leaned back and closed my eyes. "I'll take whatever has the most calories."

"Hmm. That would probably be the roast suckling pig."

"I'm not eating suckling anything."

He chuckled. "Okay, then, how about Cuban-style pot roast?"

"Sounds good."

I relaxed into the vinyl seat, enjoying the feel of Ethan's hand on my ankle while I listened to the sultry Cuban music. I still enjoyed that about Ethan—we could sit in silence without either one of us trying to fill it in. Maybe that was why we could talk about things we didn't want to tell other people. I remembered how we'd sat there six months earlier while he revealed his dreams to serve his country. It seemed odd then that a guy like Ethan could have such an interest in war. Now I saw him better—as a man who couldn't allow others to suffer, whatever the reason.

The server, a teenage boy, brought our shakes. I drank mine while Ethan ordered our food. "Do you need a refill?" the server asked, eyeing my empty glass as I set it back on the table.

"Yes," Ethan said, exchanging his full shake for mine and handing the empty glass to the server. The server's eyes traveled up and down my body as if judging whether I could handle another large shake. "Thank you," Ethan said, a little too loudly.

As the server scurried back to the kitchen, Ethan pushed the manila folder across the table toward me. His eyes still held the amusement he'd tried to hide earlier. Was he playing a trick on me? I opened the folder to see a legal contract with my mother's name at the top. "What is this?"

"Candi and I have been working on a settlement."

"For my mother?"

"It's not much, but it's all the company can afford now. We'll pay her on a monthly basis."

In an instant, I moved to Ethan's side of the booth and threw my arms around him. "Thank you."

He reached behind me to pick up the papers. "You haven't looked at the numbers."

I slid around to face the documents, skimming through the numbers. As best as I could tell, the settlement provided a monthly installment for my mother and sister with the amount increasing as LibraryStar profits increased. The installments, even at their lowest, would be enough to cover our monthly debt payments. "How did you get the lawyer to agree to this?"

"Candi did it. There's nothing more persuasive than a pregnant woman with a temper." Ethan shook his head. "If she ever remarries and has another baby, we might want to move closer to your family." I kissed him on the cheek. I loved that he and I had become *we*. "So you approve?" he asked.

I got up to move back to my side of the table. "I approve."

Ethan held onto my hand. "Why don't you stay here?" He scooted over, making more room for me on his side of the booth. "Now for the proposal." He slid the other folder toward me.

I opened the folder and read the line at the top: *Proposal for Merger*. "Proposal for a merger? What merger?"

Ethan wrapped his arm around me. "Keep reading."

I read: *Situation: Two individuals live in separate apartments but spend almost all their waking time together. One of the individuals would like to spend more time together. Every minute they're apart, he misses her.*

My heart beat faster as I read the next paragraph: *Proposed Solution: A merger would allow both individuals to share housing, transportation, and affection.*

Feeling like my heart might pop out of my chest, I looked at Ethan. "Is this a proposal?"

He pulled me toward him with his right arm and pointed with his shaking left hand to the top of the paper. "That's what it says, doesn't it?"

I grabbed onto his hand as I read more: *Steps Involved: 1. Please say yes. 2. Wear my ring. 3. Marry me in the temple. 4. Listen to me tell you I love you every day.*

Ethan brought my hand to his lips. "Will you marry me, Elly?" He looked as uncomfortable as he did on the day of Lanita's surprise arrival.

Although I'd waited for this moment, it stunned me that Ethan wanted me to be his wife. He'd met me at my worst—when I barely had the patience to deal with a broken-down car and office politics, not to mention the bishops' storehouse. "Of course I'll marry you."

He brought a tiny, orange, silk bag from his pocket and, without showing me what was inside, emptied the contents into his palm. "I know you'd probably rather have a paint job for your Subaru, but I had to get you this." He slipped a ring onto my finger. "Maren and Colton made it. Do you like it?"

I stared at the gold ring on my finger. It held a square-shaped diamond in a low setting—so much simpler than the multi-colored starburst shape Maren designed for her own ring. "I love it."

Ethan looked at his hand holding mine. "You'll have to deal with my family and my imperfections."

"And you'll have to deal with mine." I swiveled so that my bent legs bridged across him and my feet rested on the opposite end of the bench. My arms looped around the back of his neck. "Grace might come live with us someday."

Ethan smiled like a kid on spring break. "You know I love Grace, Elly." That was the first thing that had attracted me to him—the way he treated Grace.

Could I say it? "And I love Candi."

"I can believe it." He pulled me in for a mind-numbing kiss. "But I'm still amazed you love me."

Not everything in my life was exactly the way I wanted it. My family's trials weren't over. But in Ethan's arms, I felt secure. I knew he would stand by me through everything.

ACKNOWLEDGMENTS

SO many people helped bring this book to life. I obviously owe a debt of gratitude to Jane Austen, my writing role model. I'd also like to thank authors Jennifer Griffith, Jennifer K. Clark, Monique Bucheger, Michael Young, Marcia Mickelson, Susan Dayley, and Michelle Jefferies, who helped me find ways to improve this story.

A big thank you to the employees at Cedar Fort. My acquisitions editor, Alissa Voss, showed enthusiasm for this story from the start, which really helped me get it finished. Once I turned it in, Deb Spencer, Katie Parker, and Melissa Caldwell helped me polish up the details. Thanks also go to Kristen Reeves for the fun cover design and to Kelly Martinez for his marketing smarts.

My family has been so patient with my little trips to the *Sense and Sensibility* world. My husband, Eric, helped me brainstorm ideas and research military details. Meanwhile, my children only complained a little about the time I spent writing. Thanks also go to my sister-in-law, Dr. Tina Latimer, who advised me about medical details. And I'm always grateful to my parents and in-laws, who help spread the word about my books.

My sister, Caroline, served as the model for Grace. For me, autism is a normal part of family life. I will always be grateful to Caroline for all she's taught me.

Above all, I want to thank my Heavenly Father, who sends me my best ideas.

Discussion Questions

1. WHY DOES MAREN feel that God has abandoned her? Have you ever felt that way? How can we feel the love of God when life is hard?

2. IS IT POSSIBLE to sacrifice too much for the good of others? How can you tell if you're going overboard in your service?

3. COMPARE THIS BOOK with Jane Austen's *Sense and Sensibility.* How are the modern characters similar to their Regency counterparts? How are they different?

4. SOMETIMES, IN THE world of business, it's hard to know right from wrong. How do the characters in the book act ethically in their business decisions? Which business decisions would you make differently?

5. WHAT DOES THIS book teach us about helping those with depression? What can we do to help our friends and loved ones who suffer from depression and other mental illnesses? What kinds of help are not as helpful?

6. HOW DOES ELLY'S past color her present relationships? How is this an advantage? How is it a disadvantage?

About the Author

Photo by Rachael Nelson

Rebecca H. Jamison has lived on a live volcano, excavated the bones of a prehistoric mammal, and won first prize at a rigged chili cook-off. She wrote novels just for fun until she made a New Year's resolution in 2011 to submit a manuscript to publishers. Her first two published works are *Persuasion: A Latter-day Tale* and *Emma: A Latter-day Tale.*

Rebecca grew up in Virginia. She attended Brigham Young University, where she earned a BA and MA in English. In between college and graduate school, she served a mission to Portugal and the Cape Verde islands. Her job titles have included special education teacher's aide, technical writer, English teacher, and stay-at-home mom.

Rebecca enjoys running, dancing, reading, and watching detective shows. She lives with her husband and children in Utah. You can learn more about her at www.rebeccahjamison.com.